Tainted

Other books by Morgan L. Busse

TAINTED

THE SOUL CHRONICLES SERIES

BOOK ONE

MORGAN L. BUSSE

ENCLAVE

PUBLISHING

TAINTED by Morgan L. Busse
Published by Enclave Publishing
24 W. Camelback Rd. A-635
Phoenix, AZ 85013
www.enclavepublishing.com

ISBN (paper) 978-1-62184067-1

Tainted
Copyright © 2016 by Morgan L. Busse
All rights reserved

Published in the United States by Enclave Publishing, an imprint of Gilead Publishing, Wheaton, Illinois.

This is a work of fiction. Names, characters, places, and incidents are products of the author's imagination or are used fictitiously. Any similarity to actual people, organizations, and/or events is purely coincidental.

Cover Designer: Kirk DouPonce, DogEared Design

Printed in the United States of America

*To my sisters Jenny and Dani,
I love you both dearly!* *

1

Today I make history.

Kat ran trembling fingers across the top of the cream-colored letter and took a deep breath, savoring the moment, calming the quiver in her stomach. The margins of the parchment were smudged from frequent perusal, though the letter itself contained very few words, and she had each one memorized.

> *To Miss Kathryn Bloodmayne:*
> *We are pleased to inform you that you have been accepted to the Tower Academy of Science. Please report for classes on the first of September at eight o'clock in the morning.*
> *Sincerely,*
> *The Tower Academy*

Not only accepted, but one of the first women chosen to attend the Tower Academy, *the* most prestigious school in all of World City.

Warmth filled her entire being, and a smile spread across her face. In a nearby corner, Cricket let out a mechanical chirp. She glanced at the gilded cage where the clockwork bird preened its metallic feathers, pausing to bob its head in her direction, emerald eyes twinkling.

Kat smiled and brushed the letter again. Never before the arrival of this letter had her future felt so full of possibility. She could pursue physics—develop the next great airship or locomotive. Or perhaps she would excel in biology. She did find the way life worked fascinating. Mechanical in some ways, and yet so much more. Or it could be research or chemistry. Maybe she would become an inventor, like her mother, and conceive and build whimsical devices like Cricket.

She tapped her finger along the linen tablecloth and sighed. If only Mother were here to see this day. She would be proud of her daughter. Unlike . . .

The chime of the clock in the hall broke Kat's reverie. A matronly woman in a dark, conservative dress bustled into the formal dining room, carrying a plate of steaming sausages and one of sliced fresh bread. She set them down next to a small metal contraption with gears along the side, then took a slice of bread and popped it in the metal box, twisted the gears, and the box began to hum.

Smoothing her pristine skirt, Ms. Stuart frowned at Kat. "Kathryn, have you eaten anything?"

Kat glanced away from the box—another invention of her mother's— and down at her empty plate. "I'm not sure I can. My middle feels like a thousand butterflies are dancing around inside."

Ms. Stuart snorted. "And won't the naysayers dance when you faint on your first day." She straightened the bright yellow chrysanthemums in the vase that stood in the middle of the table. "They already insist we women are too weak for such study."

She had a point. Kat set her letter aside.

Ms. Stuart picked up the teapot on the other side of the vase. Unlike the other tableware, it was a simple white ceramic pot Kat had given Ms. Stuart for her birthday when Kat was seven. "Tea?"

"Yes, please."

Ms. Stuart poured the tea, its earthy aroma filling the air. Then she moved around the table to the place opposite Kat's, where another setting of white china cast a sterile gleam in the morning sunshine. She held the teapot over the cup, paused, and then set it back on the table, unpoured.

Kathryn glanced at the plate across from her, and the elation from minutes ago evaporated. Her shoulders drooped. Empty. Always empty. She couldn't remember the last time Father had joined her for breakfast, or for any meal. Today she had hoped that it would be different. That he would be here to share one last meal with her before she left for the academy. She swallowed and looked away. Apparently not.

Ms. Stuart stared at the empty seat, then at Kat. "Would you like me to join you this morning?"

Kat gave herself a shake. No. She would not let Father ruin today. Today was hers, and hers alone, and if that meant enjoying her breakfast with the housekeeper, so be it. She smiled. "Yes, please do."

Ms. Stuart sat down in the other chair and placed her napkin on her lap. The gears stopped on the metal box, signaling the bread was done. Kat pulled the golden toast out with her fork.

"Would you like butter or jam?"

Kat shook her head and held the toast up, still impaled on the fork, contemplating it. With the way she was feeling, she would be lucky to eat the toast dry. Still, she had no intention of fainting on her first day of school. She nibbled on the edge.

As Kat took a sip of her tea, letting the hot liquid force the small bite of toast down to her tumbling stomach, Ms. Stuart placed two sausages on her own plate and picked up her knife. "You will do well, Kathryn. You are intelligent, resourceful, and accomplished. I can think of few others who are as suited to the task before you."

Ms. Stuart's words warmed her, soothing the butterflies in her middle. "At least I won't be the only young lady." Kat picked up the toast and took another bite along the edge. Marianne would be there. And a handful of other young women, but she didn't know them yet. She took another bite, then decided that was enough. Tea would just have to do.

"Still, you will need to be careful. You are entering a world known only to men until now. And there are people who are not happy about that."

Kat frowned. "You think there will be opposition at the school?"

"I don't know. What I do know is that people hate change. And letting women attend the academy is a big change."

Kat tapped her finger along the white tablecloth, her mind wandering to visions of the academy. Would there be a crowd this morning in front of the school? Probably. If nothing else, reporters from the *Herald* would be there.

"It's hard to believe how fast time has flown." Ms. Stuart placed her teacup down on her saucer and looked at Kat. "You're a full-grown woman now."

Kat glanced down. A corset squeezed her small figure into a more curved one. She wore a blouse beneath and a long dark skirt, complete with button up boots. Her rich, dark hair was pulled back in a simple chignon.

Ms. Stuart sighed. "It is sad to think you won't be here anymore."

Kat looked up sharply. "I'll come back and visit."

"Yes, but it won't be the same."

Her mouth grew dry and she placed her silverware down. "You don't think Father will let you go, do you?"

Ms. Stuart smiled and shook her head. "No, I will still be here. But it will be quiet with you gone."

Kat looked away. Outside the dining room window hundreds of smokestacks filled the horizon, washing the blue sky away in a haze of gray. Faintly, she could hear the early morning bustle of World City. Carts rolling along the streets, bakers calling out their goods, horns blasting as factories opened their doors. "You can't leave. If you're not here, then there will be no one left for me to return to."

"That's not true, Kathryn."

"Yes, it is. Who will greet me at the door? Father? Father is never home. He hasn't been home in years." The words left a bitter taste in her mouth. Dr. Alexander Bloodmayne, recently dubbed the 'greatest scientist of this age' by the *Herald*, never had time for familial relationships. At least not with his only child.

"Perhaps that will change now."

"Why?" Kat turned and leaned forward, her tea forgotten. "Because I'm finally following in his footsteps?" A cold lump formed in her chest, beating with hard, heavy beats. Her breath came faster, and her fingers tensed across the table. Blood rushed through her head like the whooshing of water through narrow pipes. "I'm not doing this for him!"

Ms. Stuart's gaze darted from her face to her hands. "Kathryn," she said in a warning tone.

Kat barely heard her over the blood coursing through her body. The cold lump beat faster. "I'm doing this for myself. And someday I'll—"

"Kathryn!"

Ms. Stuart's sharp voice snapped the coldness inside her. Kat sat up and gasped. She stared down at her fingers. She had almost lost control.

"It's happening again, isn't it?" Ms. Stuart said quietly.

Kat swallowed. "I don't know why." Tears prickled her eyes. "Nothing has happened in years. I haven't lost control since . . . And then suddenly . . ." She made a fist and pressed it against the top edge of her corset, right above her heart. "I feel like it's taking over."

"How long ago did it start?"

Kat shook her head. "A couple of weeks. Nothing happened, but I felt it there again, inside of me, waiting."

Ms. Stuart pulled her lips into a grim line. "And you never told me?"

"I hoped it was nothing. But now . . ."

"Kathryn, you can't let it out."

"I know. But I don't want to live like this. I can't live like this! Always wondering when I'm going to snap and do something awful!"

Her breath came fast again, and along with it came the cold lump. She closed her eyes and concentrated on her breathing, slowing it with each breath. She then moved to her body, visualizing her heart, her lungs, her fingers, willing each part to calm down.

A hand covered hers.

Kat took a deep breath.

"You will find an answer, Kathryn. But until then, no one must know what you can do. And you need to keep it under control."

"I know." She shivered and pulled her hand out from beneath Ms. Stuart's. After each incident, it felt like something had died in her, like a piece of her soul had been ripped out. Even now she could feel another part of herself shrivel up and die, and she hadn't even fully triggered the power. What happened when every part of her died? Would she even be human?

Ms. Stuart let out a long breath. "I know you don't like this, but maybe there is a chance your father could help you."

Kat looked up, horrified. "No! Never! Please, you can't tell him. Father would only make me a guinea pig in his research." She rubbed her arms and trembled. "You know he would. He only cares about his discoveries and doesn't care about who or what he hurts." She had seen his laboratory and the experiments he conducted there. "No, I will figure this out on my own."

"But what if it gets worse, Kathryn? What if someone is injured?"

"I will leave." She had decided that a couple of weeks ago and had already hidden away a small cache of bills.

"Promise me you will see me first."

Kat glanced up.

There was a serious look on the other woman's face. "You are like a daughter to me, Kathryn. I would do anything to help you. "

"You would help me leave?"

Ms. Stuart nodded. "If it were best for you and for everyone else, then yes."

"And you wouldn't tell my father?"

Ms. Stuart's face paled. "Yes. But let's not dwell on that choice right now. Instead, let us focus on your first day at the academy. That is your future."

Ms. Stuart was right. Focus on today, not on tomorrow. Today she started her career as a scientist. Maybe she would find an answer to who she was, *what* she was.

Kat pushed her chair back and stood. "You're right." She glanced at the clock. A quarter till seven. "And I don't want to be late."

"One thing, Kathryn, before you leave."

Kat looked back.

"Be careful. Guard your emotions. Do not let them rule you. The moment you let them rule you, they will destroy you, along with everyone else."

Ms. Stuart's words sent a chill through her heart.

"I won't. I promise."

"You are strong, Kathryn. Just like your mother. And you're not alone, remember that."

Kat grabbed her letter and nodded. But as she dashed past her mother's mechanical bird and out into the hall, she felt alone. Very alone.

2

Kat's carriage rolled up in front of the Tower Academy and came to a halt just behind one of the new phaetons. Wisps of steam fluttered above the horseless carriage from the engine in front of the vehicle. Kat leaned over the side of her open carriage, craning her neck to see past the horses, hoping to catch a glimpse of the owner. Mother would have loved the phaetons with their glossy metal bodies and steam powered engines. Maybe that's why Father had not invested in one.

The phaeton shuddered, and the last of the steam disappeared into the pale blue sky above. A young man climbed out: tall, with ash blond hair and high cheekbones. New student, perhaps? Round goggles covered his eyes, and he wore leather gloves over his hands. He went around the phaeton and disappeared.

Kat sat back and turned her attention to the academy itself while she waited for Reginald to come around the carriage and open the door.

Three stories of brick and paned windows loomed over the street. Tall, iron gates completed the square enclosing the academy grounds. On either side of the courtyard were more brick buildings, each one housing laboratories, libraries, dormitories, and offices for the scientists who worked for the Tower.

Behind the academy, the Tower's namesake jabbed the sky a good fifty feet above an eight-story laboratory building. The Tower could be seen from almost every part of the city and stood as a monument to the scientific pursuits of World City.

Reginald opened the door and stepped to the side. "Miss?"

"Thank you, Reginald." Kat emerged from the carriage and looked up toward the top of the Tower. Somewhere amongst those windows was her father's office. Home, more like it. He lived at the Tower night and day, working for the World City council, creating new weapons for the war with Austrium or finding ways to expand the scientific horizon.

A band began to play just beyond the gates, drawing her attention. The academy had hired a band? For the first day of school?

Kat approached the open gates, her book bag secure across her body. A few young ladies stood just inside the gates, dressed as she was, book satchels clutched in white-knuckled hands. Probably her new classmates. But why weren't they going inside?

She reached the gates and stopped a couple of feet away from the cluster of girls. Now she knew why.

Fifty feet beyond the gates, a crowd gathered in front of the wide staircase that led up to the front doors of the academy. Green banners hung above the double doors at the top of the stairs like bright colored ribbons waving in the wind.

Kat held onto the shoulder strap of her bag and stared at the people gathered. There had to be at least a hundred, certainly more than the handful of reporters she had expected from the *Herald*. And no clear path to the doors ahead.

"Do you need anything else, miss?"

Kat looked back. Reginald stood behind her, stiff, his features carefully neutral. Unlike Ms. Stuart, Reginald believed in utmost propriety in station, even in unconventional households like the Bloodmaynes'.

"No, Reginald. Please take my chest up to my room."

He gave her a small bow. "Yes, miss."

"And let Ms. Stuart know I will be fine."

Reginald straightened. "I will."

Another carriage came rumbling up behind as Reginald headed back to his own transport. He paused to soothe the horses as the phaeton took off in a cloud of steam and sound, soon disappearing around the corner at the end of the block.

Kat turned and watched the crowd, taking note of the knot of young men standing near the fence, dressed in dark blue shirts and trousers with book bags slung over their shoulders and hands in their pockets. They appeared as uneasy as the women students and made no move to blaze a path.

Where were the professors? Or academy staff? Wasn't there someone here to greet them? Two uniformed men stood to the left of the crowd and another near the stairs. Perhaps they would help. At any rate, none of the other ladies seemed to know what to do. Maybe if she started across, the crowd would let her through.

"Kat!"

Kat looked over to find a young woman hurrying her direction from down the street. Her carrot-colored hair appeared bright orange in the sunlight, and her mauve skirt whipped around her ankles. She waved and grinned.

Kat laughed. "Marianne!"

Marianne closed the distance between them and grabbed her in a tight hug. "You're here!" She let go of Kat and turned toward the crowd, her hands clasped together. "Can you believe it? All these people are gathered here for the opening."

"But in support or protest?" Kat turned her attention back toward the crowd. Ms. Stuart's words from that morning fluttered through her mind. How many were happy with women attending the academy, and how many were not? Her gaze found the policemen again, their telltale olive green uniforms standing out amongst the colorful gowns of the women and darks suits of the men. For the first time, it struck her how incongruent their presence was.

Ms. Stuart had been right. Kat drew back and held her book bag in front of her. "Does the administration expect a riot? And why isn't there someone here to greet us?"

"No, not necessarily." Marianne stared at the crowd, her face beaming. Marianne always did enjoy a crowd. "Papa says the World City council ordered a police patrol to keep the crowd in check, just in case they get rowdy. And I think I see one of the professors over there." She pointed toward a group of men, all huddled together, talking. One wore a long white lab coat.

A church in the distance chimed the hour. Half past seven.

Kat eyed the professor again, but he seemed too intent on his conversation to lead the students inside. It seemed they were on their own. She straightened and held her chin high. Riot or no riot, classes would be starting and she did not want to be late. "Well, let's go, Marianne. They aren't going to bring the classes to us." She started across the courtyard. Marianne caught up to her, and together they approached the crowd. A couple of the young ladies and the young men by the fence followed them.

The band started another song, some sort of upbeat tune. The buzz from the mass grew louder. A couple of people turned. Kat took a deep breath, her heart thumping inside her chest. One of the women at the edge of the crowd, dressed in a gaudy violet dress with an oversized hat, pointed at Kat. "Look, here they come."

More people turned around and started walking toward Kat and Marianne.

"Are you ladies new students at the academy?" a high-pitched voice shouted.

"How were you chosen for the academy?" the lady in the violet dress asked.

"Women do not belong in the academic world." The man who spoke glared at her and Marianne. The other men around him nodded.

Kat bit her lip and came to a stop, a shiver running down her back. She attempted to ignore the men while twisting her head back and forth, looking for a way through the throng of people. There was none. And the men were drawing closer.

Marianne seemed to be enjoying the attention. "Yes, we are students here."

"What do you plan on doing with an education like this?" another man shouted.

A large baroness of a woman sniffed and held a handkerchief to her nose. "The delicate psyche of a woman cannot handle such knowledge. What was the city council thinking?"

Marianne lifted her chin. "We want to work at the Tower, contribute to science and society, just like men do."

A couple of people laughed and one man snorted. "You really think they will let you work at the Tower?"

By now the crowd had surrounded them. Questions flew from every direction. Kat could hardly breath. An elbow caught her in the ribs and a hand brushed her backside. She jerked away from the touch and twisted around. She couldn't see over the crowd and the heady smell of perfume and body odor was making her lightheaded.

Marianne bumped into her and fumbled with her bag. "We, uh, need to go now."

No one seemed to hear her.

"Why do you think the academy is finally allowing women students?"

"Do you really think you can compete with men?"

Enough! Kat straightened to her full height and brought her gaze on those in front of her. "Please excuse us."

No one listened.

Kat raised her voice. "Make way, we need to get to class."

Hands shoved her from behind and something wet and foul hit her across the cheek. Kat stumbled forward and fell against the woman in front of her.

The woman pushed her away with a shriek. "Ugh, what is that on your face?"

Kat reached for her cheek and tried to straighten.

Another push. Kat threw out her arms and tried to catch herself, but her skirt twisted around her ankles, trapping her legs. She hit the cobblestones hard. Pain shot across her kneecaps. The crowd moved and someone stepped on her hand. As she yanked it free, the foul stuff across her cheek dripped onto the pavement, brown and runny.

Kat grit her teeth. A red haze filled her vision. Her heart beat faster and her fingers began to tingle. The cold lump returned. She would make them move!

She arched her fingers and bared her teeth.

She would make them all move!

The cobblestone cracked beneath her palm. Tiny flames appeared along the crack, rising as if she were pulling fiery weeds from the ground.

Out of the corner of her eye, she saw the crowd move away from her as someone dressed in green came near.

Kat blinked. *Oh no!* She stared at the flames spreading beneath her hands. *No, no, no!* She struggled to breathe as she swatted at the fire. *I can't do this. I can't*—she gasped—*I can't lose control.* She brought her palms down across the flames and crushed them beneath her hands. She curled forward, a cold sweat spreading across her body. Her skin burned where the flame had been moments before. *Can't lose control!*

"Back away. Now!" A masculine voice rang out across the crowd. The people responded and moved back even more.

Kat checked the ground one more time. No flames, but she couldn't close the crack in the pavement, couldn't erase the telltale char marring the stone.

How could I have done that? Right in front of the Tower! What if Father had seen it?

The faint smell of hot stone hung in the air, fueling her panic. Black spots appeared before her eyes. The cold lump began to beat again in her chest and her fingers tingled. Kat closed her eyes. *Calm down.* She took a deep breath through her nose and let it out her mouth. *Just*—she trembled—*just calm down.*

"Are you all right, miss?"

Her eyes flew open. A man crouched before her, dressed in olive green. One of the policemen. He tugged at his breast pocket and pulled out a white handkerchief. Kat looked up into hazel-green eyes beneath an olive-colored cap.

"Here." He held out the handkerchief. "For your face."

Kat touched her cheek and flushed. "Thank you," she said with a mumble and took the cloth. Her face burned more as she wiped away the foul brown refuse. Why would someone throw such rank sludge at her? What had she done? Tears prickled her eyes, but she held them back and took a deep breath. She didn't want to lose control again.

She finished and looked at the cloth. "I'm sorry. I don't have a way to clean your handkerchief."

The policeman took the cloth and wrapped it up in another one. "Don't worry about it. Now let me help you up." He held out his hand.

Kat hesitated, then took it, wincing as her burned skin touched his.

With one strong pull, he helped her to her feet. Once she was steady, she dropped his hand, wanting nothing more than to hide. Instead, she worked on making herself presentable.

The policeman bent down to retrieve her book bag—was it her imagination, or did his fingertips linger on the charred cobblestone?—as Marianne came rushing to her side. "Kat, are you all right? What happened? Did someone push you?"

"Yes." Flustered, she brushed her skirt, her face still hot.

"Your bag, miss." The officer handed her the book bag with a grim countenance. Though young, he already bore the inspector medal on his chest, and there were traces of maturity beneath his carefully trimmed blond mustache. A patch of hair grew beneath his lips, now slightly open. His olive green uniform and coat emphasized his lanky, muscular build. "I'm sorry. I should have reached you sooner when I realized what the men were about to do."

She pressed a hand to her cheek. "I'm fine now." Perhaps she'd been mistaken. He'd seen nothing.

He nodded, then turned his attention to one of the other officers, who approached and saluted. "You caught those men, Patrick?"

"Yes, sir."

A man yelled from the crowd and something flew into the air.

Both officers looked back. "Very well," said Inspector Grey. "Grab Reid and Stanson and get this crowd out of here. They have no business harassing the students. I'll see to the ladies."

"Yes, Inspector."

Inspector Grey turned back toward Kat. He studied her, his gaze steady and penetrating.

Had he seen the fire? Kat looked away and brushed back a wisp of hair. "Thank you, again, for your help."

Inspector Grey gave her a curt nod. "'My pleasure, Miss . . .?"

"Bloodmayne."

His eyes narrowed, but he didn't remark on her name. Instead, he motioned toward the stairs. "We should get you and the others inside before anything else happens."

Three officers were already herding the crowd toward the gate behind them. Only a few reporters remained, their notebooks out as they scribbled away.

Inspector Grey extended his arm toward her.

Kat looked at it and blinked. No man had ever offered her his arm before. She tentatively took it, the heat rising again across her cheeks.

He pulled her close, but not too close, and started across the courtyard. "I am sorry you had to experience that."

Kat set her jaw and kept stride with Inspector Grey. Marianne conversed with the students behind them. "If we are to enter a man's world, then we better be able to take care of ourselves."

Inspector Grey lifted one eyebrow, but said nothing more. When they reached the bottom of the stairs, he released her arm, giving her a slight bow as if in dismissal.

Before Kat could say anything, Marianne had her hand and was pulling her up the stairs, chatting in her ear. Kat didn't hear a word. At the top, she paused and looked back. Inspector Grey stood at the bottom of the stairs where he had left her, talking to two other police officers.

"So that's Inspector Grey!"

Kat turned around. "Who's Inspector Grey?"

Marianne giggled and reached for the door. "He's the youngest inspector ever to be named on the World City Police Force. Papa says Stephen Grey is slated to become one of the district superintendents."

"Really?" Kat glanced back. Inspector Grey stood alone now, like a sentry at the bottom of the steps. The other ladies walked past him, but he didn't watch them, his eyes on the crowd leaving through the gates. There was an aura of authority around him. Yet at the same time, he didn't seem to be much older than some of the apprentices Father worked with. "He does seem young."

"He's brilliant, too. On his tests, he scored higher than any other cadet ever." Marianne held the door open.

"And how do you know this—wait, I know." Kat held up her hand. "Your father."

"Papa." Marianne giggled again.

Kat's chest tightened as the other students—men and women—bypassed them and entered the academy. She glanced up at the Tower. Was her own father watching her now?

She felt someone else watching her from behind. Kat stopped inside the doorway and looked back.

Stephen Grey had turned around, his gaze on her. Their eyes met and her throat seized up. He *had* seen the fire. There could be no doubt. What other reason would there be for him to watch her? The look in his eyes . . . like a cat contemplating a cornered snake—wary and aloof.

"Pity he's engaged to Vanessa Wutherington."

"What?" Kat turned back toward Marianne, thankful for the distraction. "The shipping magnate Wutherington?"

"Yes." Marianne let out a small sigh as they entered the building. "Grey is one of the more handsome men I've met. But my father would never let me have a policeman for a beau."

Kat raced to catch up to the conversation. "No, nor mine. Not that I'm really interested in courtship right now."

They followed the other men and women down a long corridor with rows of doors on either side.

"And I will never have a chance. I do not possess your beauty." Marianne gave her a small pout. "What man would want a plain, intelligent woman? And one with this color of hair?" She pointed to her carrot-colored top.

Kat shook her head, her chest loosening the farther she drew away from Stephen Grey. "Better to have an education than a husband. At least you know what you're getting with the education."

Marianne laughed, the sound ringing through the hallway.

A smile sprang across her own face. But she could not completely erase Stephen Grey from her mind. Even if he did see the fire, how would he explain it? If he were a sensible man, he would dismiss it as a figment of his imagination. Right?

Kat let out her breath. In the end, it didn't really matter. She lifted her chin and set her mind on her first class. She would probably never see him again.

3

Kat stepped into the first-floor classroom and stopped. She placed a hand across her chest and let out a long breath, setting aside everything that had happened thus far. Those problems would keep. For now, she was here, really here, a student at the Tower Academy.

The room was bigger than the parlor and dining room back home combined. Large, narrow windows lined one wall, letting in natural light. The rest of the walls were lined with shelves laden with books, jars of herbs, mechanical contraptions, and even an armillary globe, similar to the one in Father's study back home.

Rows of desks occupied the majority of the room. Students started filling the desks, the men on one side, the women on the other, a boundary drawn without comment. A couple of the young men sent scowls across the invisible line.

Kat's smile ebbed, then she straightened her back and headed for the desk closest to the front and adjacent to the men. As Ms. Stuart had said, she was entering a man's world now. Best show that she was not afraid.

She sat down and placed her bag beside her feet, sensing eyes on her. Minutes ticked by and the feeling persisted. Finally, she looked over her shoulder.

A young man sat in the desk next to hers, one row behind. She furrowed her brows. He looked familiar. Wait. He was the young man who arrived in the phaeton this morning. Ash blond hair, high cheekbones, and now she could see his eyes. Light blue. Judging from the phaeton and the fine cut of his clothes, he definitely belonged to one of the high-class families of World City.

He shot her a grin. "I wasn't sure about women being allowed entrance to the academy, but if I have the pleasure of looking at you all day, I won't complain."

Kat turned back and stared at the front of the classroom, her hands curled in her lap. What a crass, rude, *arrogant*—No. She relaxed her fingers and focused on the map that hung behind the instructor's desk. She couldn't afford any more episodes. No more feeling. No more emotions. She needed to become cold and calloused if she was going to make it through the academy—and life.

"Did I say something wrong?"

She took a deep breath before looking in the young man's direction. "On the contrary. I am the one who is wrong. I was expecting a more mature selection of students at the Tower Academy."

His face blanched, then his eyebrows dipped down and his lips curved into a snarl. "I don't think you know who I am."

"I don't." *And I don't care.*

"Blaylock Sterling, *at your service.*"

Sterling? She was right. He was from one of the top families, and his father was on the city council.

"And your name?"

Kat licked her lips. Of the students here, only Marianne knew who she was. Once the others found out, she would probably be held to a higher standard and watched closely. But she couldn't hide her surname forever. Might as well get it over with. "Kathryn Bloodmayne."

There was a gasp and flutter of whispers around her.

Out of the corner of her eye, she saw Blaylock start and his eyes widen. "You're Dr. Bloodmayne's daughter?"

"Yes."

The impish look came back. "That should make classes interesting."

She frowned. What did he mean by that? Before she could ask, the instructor walked in and silence filled the classroom. He was an older gentleman, with long white hair pulled back in leather strap, a generous matching mustache, and tiny spectacles across his large nose. He wore a white lab coat over a dress shirt and trousers.

He stopped behind the desk and looked out over the students. He didn't seem fazed by women in his classroom. A good sign.

Kat slowly relaxed in her seat and brought her hands out and across her desk. Her burned palms no longer smarted, but she didn't dare look at them just in case they were red.

"I am Professor Flintlocke. Welcome to General Science 101."

Without moving her head, Kat glanced around. Where was Marianne? She caught sight of her friend at the other end of her row. Marianne winked at her and grinned.

A fluttery feeling filled her middle as she focused back on Professor Flintlocke. She wanted to give into the excitement, but held back. If she was going to make it the next two years here at the academy, she had to start controlling her emotions, now. The good ones *and* the bad ones.

"We will start with the three main branches of science." Professor Flintlocke looked over the class. "Who can tell me what they are?"

Almost every woman's hand went up into the air. Kat kept hers down. Best keep a low profile as well. She would study hard, but she would stay in the background, the best place to be if she wished to remain unnoticed.

"Are you going to the library again? You've been there every night since we arrived!"

Kat slung her book bag over her shoulder. The drawing room was empty save for Marianne, who sat in one of the green floral-patterned high-back chairs, a book in her hands. A small fire crackled in the nearby fireplace and a gas lamp hummed on the wall nearby. The rest of the girls were in their dorms, studying or talking quietly.

So Marianne had noticed? Of course she had noticed. Kat smoothed her skirt. "I'm working on an extra project."

"For one of the professors?"

"For myself."

Marianne cocked her head to the side. "A private project? I'm intrigued."

Kat's stomach tightened, but she tried to answer lightly. "It's nothing."

"So you won't tell me about it?"

"I want to keep it a secret, for now."

Marianne shifted in her chair as if to stand. "Maybe I could hel—"

"No!" Kat held up her hand.

Her friend's pale eyebrows shot up. "Are you sure?"

Kat scrambled mentally for a way out of this conversation. "Yes. You have your own studies. But thank you."

Marianne eyed her for a moment longer, then settled back again.

Before Marianne could say any more, Kat spun and headed out the door. She would need to rethink her research. If Marianne had noticed her absence every night, others might too. And that would lead to questions.

Kat hurried down the hall to the main door. Outside, night was falling across World City. Far away horns blasted, signaling a shift change at the factories. Across the courtyard stood the Tower. She angled to the left and headed toward the side where the main library was located.

The last of the horns melted away into the night, leaving the courtyard quiet. No one else was about.

She reached the library and opened the door, breathing in the rush of warm air that greeted her face. The library smelled like hundreds of years of knowledge: wood with a hint of vanilla over underlying mustiness.

Tall bookshelves stood in long rows down either side of the narrow hall. Gas lamps were mounted on the wall between the bookshelves and gave the library a homey feel. There was a flutter of paper and the whisper of a pen.

Kat proceeded down the middle of the bookshelves. She passed the main desk where the librarian stood, bent over a large tome. The next aisle over was a table with one of the female students sitting next to a pile of books.

Kat recognized the girl and hurried to pass, but then she looked up at that moment.

"Well, well. Kathryn Bloodmayne."

Kat slowly turned around. "Nicola."

Taller than Kat, with thick auburn curls piled around her aristocratic face, Nicola had already proved herself to be one of the smartest students at the academy.

She smirked at Kathryn. "Here to study, I presume. I hear you're here quite a lot, but then, every little bit helps."

Kat inwardly rolled her eyes. From day one, for some reason Nicola had decided that Kat would be her rival. At least, that's how she felt with their every conversation. Maybe it was the fact that Dr. Bloodmayne was her father and Nicola had made it quite clear she would do everything she could to become one of his apprentices. Including putting Kat down at every opportunity.

Kat grabbed the strap of her book bag. "A brilliant deduction. Now if you'll excuse me . . ." She scurried away before Nicola could send more barbs her direction. She found a table in the back corner of the library and sat down with a long exhale. Yes, she would need to rethink the time she spent researching her condition in the library. Between Marianne's questions and her run-in with Nicola, it was clear she was drawing attention. Besides, she hadn't had an episode in a week, not since that first morning.

Maybe it's working. I can control myself, as long as I stay away from people when possible. It would be a long two years here at the academy, but it was doable. And she would keep searching for any links to her condition, but maybe she could slow down and actually enjoy school and her studies. She didn't want to fall behind.

Kat reached inside her book bag and pulled out her pen case and her inkwell. Then she pulled out a couple of pieces of paper and placed them down before her. A few notes were scribbled on the top of the first page.

Since she was here, though, she might as well do what she came to do. Tomorrow she would slow down, but she would never give up. If there were any recorded cases of people like her, she would find them. And if she were the only one, she would search out why, and how she came to be this way.

And maybe, just maybe, she would find a cure.

4

"So how did it go the other day at the academy?"

Stephen glanced at his partner as they turned and headed down one of the dark alleys in the Greensborough district. Smoke hung in the air, discharged into the sky by the factories nearby. Even at night, the factories still chugged away, churning out metal parts for the new horseless carriages or textiles for clothing. Tonight the smoke masked the stars overhead and the moon looked hazy in the smog.

Harrison was a couple of inches taller than him, with dark brown hair and a clean-shaven face, unlike the most of the men on the force, including himself. Harrison held his truncheon loosely, his gaze darting along the alley looking for trouble.

Stephen shrugged. He held his own truncheon in his right hand, a recent invention by the Tower. Pale blue light emitted from the intertwined circles that surrounded the smooth baton. Two gears were located near the handle, allowing him to adjust the shock settings. The truncheon would let off a charge on contact, shocking the assailant, assuming one could get close enough to use the weapon. He didn't put much stock in the light stick, hence the revolver that sat holstered along his left hip. "It was interesting."

"Explain."

"We had a group of men not happy about the academy letting in women students."

Harrison grinned. "I knew there would be a riot. Wish I had been there."

Stephen shook his head. "Just a small demonstration."

"Anyone hurt?"

"No. Although there was some excrement thrown and one of the women fell." His thoughts rushed back to that morning, the moment he had knelt down to help her up. He had seen fire, a couple of flames bursting up from the pavement near her hands. At least, he thought he had, and there had been char. But where in the world would fire have come from? Still, he couldn't shake it from his mind that he had seen something. Miss Bloodmayne had appeared frazzled, but who wouldn't be after being hit with something foul and pushed to the ground?

Wait. His brows furrowed. His Aunt Milly worked for the Bloodmaynes. So that was the young woman Aunt Milly used to write to him about during his school days? Funny, she didn't strike him as the curious little thing Aunt Milly had painted in her letters.

Harrison switched the truncheon to his other hand. They emerged onto the main street and headed west. "Not sure what I think about women learning science. But throwing excrement? That's not right."

Stephen scanned the street. A dim light appeared at the end of the next alley. "I agree. Allowing women into the academy was a bold step for the Tower, and you know how people can be with change. Something like that was bound to happen. But that was going too far. No matter the disagreement, men should still act civil."

Harrison nodded. "True. What do *you* think of women being admitted to the academy?"

Stephen shrugged. "If they can keep up with the men, why not?" If his younger days on the streets had taught him one thing, it was women were as tough and smart as men. Maybe more so.

"Not everyone thinks that way. What would you think if Vanessa joined the academy?"

An image of his fiancée filled his mind. Beautiful, vivacious Vanessa. No, he couldn't picture Vanessa attending the Tower Academy. She was intelligent, but she was also a socialite through and through. And she had no interest in higher learning. But if she had been interested?

"I would let her," Stephen said a moment later. He would let her do anything she wanted. He couldn't say no to Vanessa.

Harrison's eyebrows shot up. "You would?"

They drew near the next alley. Looked like there was a fire somewhere down the narrow street.

"I would. If Vanessa wanted to improve herself through education, then I would let her. Not that I could stop her if she put her mind to it anyway."

Harrison let out a loud guffaw that echoed between the buildings. "Yes, she is a bit stubborn, isn't she?"

Stephen frowned. "Yes, she can be." How did Harrison know that? He barely knew Vanessa.

Harrison pointed down the alley. "Looks like we have some vagabonds loitering down here."

The three ragged men looked up from their fire as the two officers approached. One was young, almost Stephen's age. The other two were much older. All three sported unkempt beards, dirt-scuffed faces, and haunted eyes.

"Stephen Grey?" one of the older men croaked.

Stephen furrowed his brows. "Mr. Hensley?"

"Yes, yes!" The older man tried to stand, but his whole body trembled and he fell back to the ground.

Stephen knelt down and grabbed the man's hand. "What are you doing here? What happened?"

Mr. Hensley coughed, his body shaking from the action. A bit of bloody spittle escaped his lips. "Evicted. All of us."

"From Pernrith?"

"Yes. Every building along the Meandre in the Pernrith district."

Stephen sat back, stunned. He hadn't been back to Pernrith in years, not since his parents had died and his aunt paid for him to attend the police institute. "When did this happen?"

"A couple of months ago, after the textile factory closed and everyone lost their job. Most of the families left, either finding homes in Greensborough, or . . ."

Stephen swallowed. "Or the workhouses."

Mr. Hensley's eyes watered and the older man next to him grunted in disapproval.

"Me and Ben here, and Little Moe, have been making our way through World City south to Covenshire. Maybe find a ship to the mainland. But now with this cough and this infernal feve—" He broke into another fit of coughing.

Stephen squeezed his hand. "We need to get you to a doctor."

Mr. Hensley shook his head and wiped his mouth. "Can't afford a doc. And between you and me, I'm nearly done for. I keep telling Ben and Little Moe to go one without me, but they're afraid the reapers will get me."

"Reapers?"

Suddenly Mr. Hensley's eyes sharpened. "People are disappearing, Grey. Poor people, sick people. People like me, on the verge of, well, you know. One day they're there and then the next, gone. No trace."

Stephen sat back on his heels. "Maybe they ended up in a workhouse or died."

The young man—Little Moe—growled, but Mr. Hensley waved him off. "No, they've been seen being taken by men in black with black hoods. Little Moe watched his sister taken away."

Little Moe gave Stephen a quick jerk of his head.

Stephen looked up at Harrison, who had been watching the proceedings silently. "Have you heard of these incidents? These reapers?"

"No, I haven't."

"Police don't listen. Say we're drunk or worse." Mr. Hensley squeaked out another cough.

Stephen made a note to check in at the precinct and see if there were any more stories. "Here." He dug into his pocket and pulled out a couple of bills. "There's a doctor in Southbrook. You need to go see him."

Mr. Hensley pushed back the money. "I couldn't take your money."

"You helped me when I was a kid. I'm paying you back now. Take it." He wished he could take Hensley to the doctor himself, but he still had a couple of hours on patrol.

"You've grown into a good man, Stephen. Your parents would be proud." Mr. Hensley placed the cash inside the front pocket of his dirty overcoat. "We'll start for Southbrook in the morning."

Stephen stood up. "Be careful. Other officers might take you to a workhouse."

Mr. Hensley laughed. "We know. We've been careful."

"I'll check in at the doctor's and see how you are sometime tomorrow or next."

Mr. Hensley smiled and bobbed his head. The other two men watched stoically.

Stephen and Harrison started back down the alley.

"You know that's what we should be doing now," Harrison said.

"What? Taking them to the workhouses?" Stephen's nostrils flared. "I wouldn't take a sick dog to the workhouses. Better a chance at life on the streets than certain death in one of those places."

"Still, if the captain found out you let vagabonds wander the streets . . ."

"Then I'll have a talk with Captain Algar. Hensley needs medical attention. And they're leaving World City. What harm is there in letting them go?"

Harrison snorted. "You're usually a stickler for the rules, Grey."

Stephen shrugged. "Yes, I am. But in this case, I think mercy is a better option."

5

Their patrol ended when the first rays of morning pierced through the foggy streets of World City. Stephen rubbed the back of his neck and yawned. His eyes felt like each lid was holding up a ten-pound lead.

Harrison yawned beside him. "I'm going to head to my flat and sleep the whole day."

"Don't forget you need to get me the new schedule to turn in to the captain."

Harrison nodded. "I won't forget. I'll have it to you tomorrow."

Stephen held up a finger. "Early morning."

"I know, I know. Later, Grey."

"Later, Harrison."

Stephen watched Harrison walk down the street and turn. Seconds later, a phaeton came flying down the street and passed him, purring like one of those big cats from the mainland, with puffs of steam emitting from the engine. It disappeared around the same corner.

What he wouldn't give to have one of those. Or even a bicycle. Instead, his paychecks were going toward a bigger flat for Vanessa and himself after the wedding. It was a good thing

Vanessa's family was paying for the wedding, or else she would be having a much smaller ceremony than she desired.

Stephen put his hands in his pockets and started for the precinct on foot. He wanted to check on those reapers Mr. Hensley had talked about before heading toward his own flat.

"Check out today's *Herald*!" a newsie yelled on the street corner. The young man held up a newspaper. "Reapers strike again! More people gone missing and the city council is doing nothing about it!" A case of papers sat beside his feet.

Stephen walked over.

The newsie looked up. "Paper, mister?"

"Yes, thank you." He handed the newsie a coin and took the paper. Sure enough, on the front page in large bold letters was the word *reapers*. He opened the paper and scanned the article. Unlike some of the smaller newspapers, the *Herald* prided itself in its reliability, which meant that there had to be some truth to these rumors about reapers. He read further and came across the paragraph about the city council. He snorted. Someone was in hot water over at the Capitol building.

Stephen folded the paper and placed it under his arm. A couple of minutes later he stepped into the large two-story police station at the end of the street. A few other officers were coming off the night shift while more were heading out for the day. Across the room, a bounty hunter with a waxed blond mustache and twin pistols on his hips stood with the morning desk clerk, no doubt collecting the bounty on some hapless criminal. The absence of said criminal seemed to indicate he'd been captured dead rather than alive.

"Mornin' Grey," Patrick called out as he headed for the doors.

"Good morning, Patrick."

"Any plans today? A bunch of us are heading to the Boar's Head tonight for drinks. Want to join?"

"I can't. I'm surprising Vanessa and taking her to the new restaurant up in Parkway."

Patrick whistled. "High class."

Stephen pulled on the collar of his shirt. It was a bit expensive, but it was where she wanted to go. He hadn't seen her in over a week with the double shifts he had been pulling. It was worth it.

"Well, have fun. The wedding is what, a couple of weeks away?"

Stephen nodded.

"Getting nervous?"

He paused. "No, not really. I'm ready to settle down." More than ready. He and Vanessa would marry in two weeks, he would become superintendent of the lower district next spring, and maybe they would start a family in a year. He wanted to give his children what he had missed out on after his own parents passed away.

Patrick laughed. "Better you than me. Later, Grey."

Stephen entered the lobby and headed for the offices to the right. He found Captain Algar just sitting down with a stack of reports inside his office. At his knock, the older man looked up and blinked. His eyes were a watery gray and his peppered mustache quivered above his lip. "Inspector Grey. What can I do for you?"

Stephen placed the newspaper down in front of the captain. "I wanted to ask about these reapers."

The captain glanced at the paper, then back at Stephen. "You know you can't believe everything you read."

"True, but we also know the *Herald* will only print a story if there are at least two sources. And I met a couple of men on my shift last night who also spoke of these reapers. Something's going on, Captain, and people are scared."

Captain Algar brushed the newspaper to the side. "Stories, Inspector. Just stories."

"Sir, I met someone who has seen them: men dressed in black, with black hoods. They said the reapers are preying on the very sick."

"I haven't had any reports of such things."

Stephen paused. Hensley had said they'd reported the incidents. Had the desk officers not filed the reports? Or was there something darker going on? "Maybe because the people being preyed upon are the low class. The homeless."

Captain Algar harrumphed and shifted his reports around on his desk. "You know how dangerous the streets of World City are. You walk them every night. I would wager that is the cause of the disappearances. Old-fashioned criminal activity."

"But Captain—"

"Enough!" The captain slammed his fist on the desk, a vein throbbing in his forehead. "We have real work to do, not chasing after ghost stories. There will be no investigations into this matter. Do I make myself clear, Inspector?"

Stephen pressed his lips into a grim line. "Yes."

"Then you are dismissed." With a flick of his hand, Captain Algar went back to his reports.

Stephen twisted around and headed for the doors. Why was the captain so adamant about the falseness of the article, or the stories? Something didn't add up, and he suspected it was going to keep him up most of the day. At least when he met with Vanessa that evening, he could count on her to carry the conversation.

The interior of *Charles's* was nothing like Stephen had experienced before. Crystal chandeliers hung from the high ceilings, casting soft light across the expansive room. Small mahogany tables filled the hall, topped with white linen cloth and delicate china. Most of them were filled tonight with other couples. The air smelled of roasted beef, poultry, herbs, and fresh bread, all tinted with the aroma of the extravagant flower arrangements strategically placed to supply privacy to certain tables.

Vanessa took a sip of her wine and placed the goblet down while looking around the room. She barely touched her quail, which sat centered on her plate with a light sauce around it.

Stephen studied her. The dim light of the restaurant made her dark eyes appear even darker, matching her hair. She wore her curls piled up in the latest fashion and her blue gown cut low. A single golden chain hung around her neck with a sapphire at the end. Exquisite is the word he would use for her. And maybe cool. At least, that was how she seemed tonight.

"Are you not hungry?" Stephen asked, cutting into his own quail.

Vanessa glanced her meal. She picked up her fork and knife and cut into the bird, taking a small bite of the flesh. Then she went back to her wine.

His hands began to sweat as he chewed on the meat. This was not how he had envisioned their evening together. He swallowed and looked up. "How is your family?"

She glanced at him. "They are well, thank you. Father has been asked to join the World City council."

His eyebrows climbed. "That is quite an honor."

She went back to looking around the room. "Yes, it is."

Of its own volition, his right knee bounced beneath the table as he sliced another bite from the quail. The bird was good, but the strained silence between him and Vanessa ruined the flavor.

He placed his silverware down and frowned. "Vanessa, is something wrong?"

She held the goblet between her fingers and stared into the dark liquid. "I'm afraid I'm not feeling well this evening."

Disappointment swelled in his chest, but he pressed it down. No matter. There would be other dinners. He wiped his lips with the linen napkin and placed it beside his plate. "Then let me take you home."

She gave him a small smile. "Yes, please."

Stephen stood and came around the table. He pulled out her chair and waited as she stood. She was tall, her eyes level with his. But tonight, she seemed more interested in looking at everything but him.

Maybe she was mad at all the shifts he had been pulling this week. Or maybe she was growing nervous about the upcoming wedding.

He held out his arm and she took it without a word. The other couples in the room looked their way. Vanessa turned heads wherever she went. Usually he enjoyed the attention, but tonight he just wanted to disappear inside his flat.

After paying the tab, he led her outside the restaurant and hailed a carriage.

"Stephen?"

Stephen turned back to Vanessa, his heart lifting. Maybe he would finally find out what was bothering her. "Yes?"

"You don't need to accompany me home. I know you've been busy the last few nights."

His mouth flew open and he blinked at her. "You know that I could never let you ride alone at night. It's not fitting for a woman of your standing. And what would your father say?

"But—"

"No!" What the blazes was Vanessa thinking? Stephen turned toward the carriage that just arrived and yanked the door open. If anything happened to her, he would never forgive himself. Neither would her father.

Vanessa stepped into the carriage without waiting for him. He shut the door and gave the driver her address, then climbed in on the other side.

If the atmosphere in the restaurant had been cool, the tension inside the carriage was downright icy. Vanessa sat facing away from him, her arms crossed, a scowl across her face.

Stephen faced the other way. What happened to them?

The carriage lurched forward and started down the dark street. He rubbed his face. He didn't want to end the evening this way.

He stared out the window and watched the buildings and gas lamps pass by. He didn't remember much of his parents. Both of them worked long days in the textile factory. But one thing he did remember is they always said sorry to each other after a fight, usually long after he had gone to bed. He would hear them on the other side of the wall, their voices low.

That's what he wanted for his marriage as well.

He took a deep breath and turned around. "Vanessa, I'm sorry. I should not have been curt with you."

She didn't answer.

"I don't know what's going on, but if I can help, let me know."

Silence.

He waited. Seconds later his fingers began to shake. He pulled them into a fist and turned back toward his own window. She just needed time. He nodded to himself. He would give it to her.

They pulled up to the Wutherington house, a three-story mansion on the far side of Parkway. Stephen climbed out and went around and opened the door for Vanessa.

He held out his hand and she took it with cold fingers. "Good night, Stephen," she said in a dead voice.

Stephen took a deep breath. "Good night, Vanessa."

She dropped his hand and proceeded to the front door. He had half a mind to follow her, but the family butler met her at the door and ushered her in. She never looked back.

Stephen paid the driver and took off south. He would walk home. He needed the time and physical activity to cool his head. And he had his revolver. He never went anywhere without it. If trouble showed up, he was more than capable of taking care of himself.

He stuffed his hands into his pocket and started off. There were no stars tonight. The dense fog from the Meandre River and the smoke from the factories and smokestacks merged to create what many called "pea soup."

At least it wasn't cold, not like his time with Vanessa.

He passed by the opulent homes of the elite of World City, with their ivy-covered wrought-iron fences, carefully manicured lawns, and brightly lit windows.

Why had Vanessa accepted his proposal? It wasn't the first time he'd wondered. She was from one of the wealthiest families. Beautiful, too. The only reason he had even met her was because he had been invited by his superintendent to the World City Gala over a year ago.

It had been love at first sight followed by a whirlwind courtship. The *Herald* had been full of their activities. He didn't care. He had Vanessa, and that was all he needed.

But now, after tonight . . .

He shook his head. No, there could be no doubts. Every marriage had its ups and downs. As long as they had a marriage built on love and trust, they could weather anything.

He passed the district of Parkway and kept south through the heart of World City. To the far left stood the Tower, the tallest building in World City and the pride of the scientific community. Past the Tower was the marketplace. Then Southbrook, and then Greensborough.

A couple of hours later Stephen began to wonder about his judgment on walking home. His feet ached from the dress shoes and his fingers were numb from the chill that had settled across the city. Unfortunately, there were no more carriages this evening. He was on his own.

He crossed the river at one of the bridges and spotted a fire along the bank. More beggars. Maybe they would let him warm himself before he continued. As he approached, he recognized the two men. Ben and Little Moe.

The two men looked over and flattened themselves against the dirt bank.

Stephen held up his hands. "Don't worry, I'm not here to make you leave. I just want to warm myself by your fire."

Little Moe pointed at him and whispered to Ben. They both nodded and waved him over.

Stephen glanced around. Mr. Hensley was not with them. Good. That meant his old friend had gone to the doctor.

He stopped a foot away from the fire and spread out his hands. A sigh escaped his lips and he closed his eyes.

"The reapers, they took him."

Stephen's eyes shot open.

Little Moe looked at him with bulging eyes.

He dropped his hands. "What did you say?"

"The boy said the reapers took your friend."

Stephen jerked his head. "You saw them?"

Ben and Little Moe glanced at each other. "Yes," Ben said. "Last night, after you left."

He stared at the two men, dazed. "And you didn't do anything about it?"

Ben pulled his overcoat and dirty shirt away from his body. A large bruise covered the right side of his neck. "We tried." He let his coat fall back into place. "And we failed."

Little Moe nodded.

"We're done with World City. Tonight's our last night. Tomorrow we head south and never come back."

"I can understand that." Stephen took a step back and placed two fingers along his forehead. First Vanessa, now this.

Captain Algar's words rushed through his mind.

You know how dangerous the streets of World City are. You walk them every night.

Stephen grit his teeth. Who better than the World City police to counter these reapers? Ghost stories, his eye! Captain Algar was wrong. The reapers were real and needed to be dealt with!

"Leave at dawn." Stephen pulled two bills out of his pocket. "Use this and get out of here. In the meantime, I plan on talking to my captain again. This needs to stop."

Ben took the bills. "Thank you, mister. Mr. Hensley had a lot of nice things to say about you. We will miss him."

"He was a good man," Stephen said softly. "I need to get going. Do as I said. Get out of World City."

"Yes, mister."

Stephen turned around and started south, his blood hot. If the captain told him no again, he would find another way to investigate these disappearances.

He owed it to Mr. Hensley and the people of World City.

6

It took every ounce of strength Stephen had left not to slam the door behind him as he left Captain Algar's office. Instead, he closed the door deliberately and stood to the side, clenching and unclenching his hands. Every time he thought of their conversation, his vision went red. What the *blazes* was the captain thinking? Even if he didn't think the reapers were real, they should still look into it, or at least into the disappearances.

Something was going on in World City.

Stephen clenched his hand.

He could feel it.

He unclenched his hand.

But there was nothing he could do about it. And the captain forbade him to get involved.

He slumped against the wall and closed his eyes. *God, I don't know what to do. I know I should obey earthly authorities, but this . . . This isn't right!*

It felt like the weight of World City sat on his shoulders. He pinched his nose and straightened up. He was tired. Dead tired. There was nothing more he could do here. Maybe a bit of sleep would help him think properly and figure out what to do next.

His eyes shot open.

Blazes! He still needed to get the schedule from Harrison.

"Blast it!" Stephen moaned and rubbed his face. Best get it done now. Then he could head home and finally sleep.

He stumbled away from the wall and past the other offices toward the front doors. His head pounded from the rush of emotions and lack of sleep.

Dark clouds rolled over World City as he walked to Harrison's flat, enveloping the sun in its gloomy embrace. A raindrop hit his nose and he groaned. An airship rumbled overhead as it maneuvered toward the nearby sky tower. Another drop fell.

After ten minutes, he reached Greensborough, which may have been green hundreds of years ago, before World City swallowed up this section of town, but now hunched beneath the black veneer of decades of smog and dirt. Women tugged on laundry that hung along ropes strung between the multistoried flats as the rain started in earnest. Children dashed through the gutter, squealing in the downpour.

Stephen ran across the street and took cover under an awning with two other men, one of whom held a damp copy of that morning's *Herald*. Nothing about reapers or disappearances. Instead, the headline announced that World City had captured a key point along Austrium's coast in the latest war campaign. He wondered how much of it was true and how much of it was propaganda spun by the city council. Maybe it was the *Herald's* way of retracting yesterday's story about the council's failure.

Far off, a church intoned the hour. Nine o'clock. He looked down the street. Just one more block. If he hurried, he could take care of the schedule and be in bed by ten.

Stephen took a deep breath, then ran out into the rain. Harrison's flat was just around the next corner, couched in one of the narrow two story buildings.

He glanced both ways and raced across the street. At the top of the stairs, he used the metal knocker. He rubbed his arms and counted to ten, then lifted the knocker again. Nothing.

Stephen looked up at the second-floor windows, the rain pounding down across his face. *Harrison, where are you?* He squinted at the door. There was no way he was going back without that schedule. Harrison had better have left it somewhere inside.

Stephen squatted and pulled back the woven mat, revealing a small key beneath the corner. Predictable.

He unlocked the door and poked his head in. "Harrison?" When no answer came, he stepped inside.

Harrison's flat looked like any other flat: long narrow rooms and hallways, faded wallpaper, the hum of gas through the walls. And a musty smell overlaid with smoke.

So Harrison smoked. No matter. It wasn't his business what his partner did during his off hours.

After mopping his face and hair, he made his way through the living room, past the spindly chairs and table topped with a garish lamp, and down the hallway. A staircase stood at the end of the hall, next to the doorway that led into the kitchen. He chose the kitchen first.

Nothing but a small black stove, a table, and a cupboard shoved up next to a dingy window. Looked like Harrison got his meals the same way he did: at a local tavern or inn. He checked the door in back. It led to the alley.

Stephen glanced back at the hallway. Perhaps the study was upstairs.

He'd just started up the stairs when laughter drifted down. He froze, his hand along the railing. The laughter came again, a man and a woman.

Blast it! Harrison had a lady friend over. Just another thing he hadn't known about his partner. Stephen turned to go, but the woman's voice brought him up short.

He stared at the wall. It couldn't be . . .

He looked back up the stairs. He should leave, now. Pretend he didn't hear anything and go home.

Before the thought was complete he recognized its impossibility. *No, I have to know.*

The knot forming inside his gut grew thicker and heavier with each step. Low laughter trickled down the stairway. His heart sped up and a cold sweat broke out across his body. He reached the second floor. Two doors stood along the right side of the hallway, both closed. A third door stood ajar at the end of the hall, and the woman's voice drifted out.

Stephen made his way down the hall, his boots silent on the threadbare runner. His hand stole to the gun at his side. *God, what do I do if . . .*

He licked his lips and reached for the door, then paused. If he looked inside, his life might change forever.

But he couldn't go back now. He would forever wonder, and a marriage could not be built on distrust.

He pushed the door open another two inches.

Harrison sat in bed, bare-chested, his back against the dark wood frame. A woman lay beside him, her dark curly hair spread across the pillow. They laughed again, then Harrison leaned down and kissed her.

Black spots appeared before Stephen's eyes, and his fingers tightened around his gun. This—this couldn't be happening.

The woman sat up, the cover falling from her body as she brought her hand up to caress Harrison's neck.

Stephen looked away, his teeth clenched, his heart beating again.

Vanessa.

He worked his mouth, his body ready to burst into action. Steady. He took a deep breath and stepped into the room. "So when were you going to tell me?"

There was a gasp and a curse.

"Stephen, what the *blazes* are you doing in my flat?"

He jerked his gaze back to the scene. At least Vanessa had pulled the blanket up across her chest. He looked from her back to Harrison. His nostrils flared. "Really? That's all you can say?"

Harrison glared back. "I could charge you with breaking and entering."

Stephen stepped into the room. "And drag both your names through the dirt? I came to get the schedule for next week's patrol. Apparently you never heard me knocking or when I called out." *Of course. How could they?*

The black spots appeared again, along with a wave of nausea.

Harrison pointed at him. "That doesn't give you the right to enter my home."

"We're partners, Harrison. I dropped by, as a partner. As a friend." The word hung in the air between them.

Stephen glanced at Vanessa. At least she had the decency to blush. She pulled the cover higher up and his blood boiled over. "Why, Vanessa? *Why?*"

She sucked in her lips and looked down. "Listen, Stephen. I should have been honest with you. It wasn't going to work between us."

"And when were you going to tell me? At the altar? During the honeymoon?"

Vanessa looked away, her body rigid.

Sweat poured down his back, and his body tingled from all the adrenaline. "You know, you're right." His hand shook as he slowly raised his gun. One shot, right in the heart. In his mind he pictured blood spreading across her chest, smearing across the cover she held. "It wouldn't have worked between us. I detest liars."

Harrison raised his hands. "Stephen, put the gun down."

Stephen swung the gun toward Harrison. "Don't you dare speak to me!"

"You're not a murderer!"

"I'm not a lot of things!" he shouted. His finger inched toward the trigger.

Control.

Stephen took one long, even breath. They weren't worth it. Harrison and Vanessa weren't worth prison time. And Harrison was right. He wasn't a murderer. But he was going to shoot one or both of them if he stayed much longer.

With inarticulate shout, Stephen spun around and left the room. He hardly noticed the hallway or stairs as he flew down them two at a time. Each time he thought of Vanessa and Harrison, his body exploded forward. How could she? *How could they?*

He reached the door and wrenched it open. The streets were empty. Thank heaven for that. Stephen didn't bother shutting the door behind him. He needed to leave now or he would do something he would regret.

Would he really regret it?

God, help me!

Stephen slammed his gun back into his holster and headed north at a run, rain pouring down across his head.

Had he been blind this entire time? How long had Vanessa and Harrison been having an affair under his very nose?

What a fool he had been!

He passed a man scurrying across the street with a newspaper over his head. A dog barked from a nearby corner. Things he saw and dismissed, his mind twisting and turning over the scene in the bedroom.

Stephen turned into an alley a couple of blocks away. He stopped and panted, sweat and rain running down his face. With a yell, he hit the building with the side of his fist. The bricks tore his skin and his hand burst into agony. He hit the wall again and again, then kicked it.

His hand throbbed as blood rushed to the injury. Stephen tucked it next to his body, sagging against the wall and letting the water drip off the end of his nose and chin. Each wave of pain cleansed the memory of Vanessa and Harrison in bed together.

He scrunched up his face and looked up at the sliver of sky between the buildings. "Why, Vanessa?" he whispered. "Why?" Every dream he had held dear for his future burned up inside his mind. There would be no wedding. No honeymoon. No children.

And Harrison . . . His own partner!

Stephen pushed away from the wall and stumbled back out onto the street. The doc's office was about a dozen blocks away in Southbrook. He would walk. He needed to walk. If he didn't keep going, he might stop and never move again.

He turned left and headed down the street. An omnibus came rumbling by, water streaming down the horses' flanks and back. He curled in on himself and stumbled on, his head bent, his injured hand tucked safely next to his chest.

This changed everything. There was no way he could walk back into the district office, not with Harrison there. And not after his confrontation with Captain Algar. Not after today. Could he even go back to the force?

No.

Stephen clenched his teeth. He was done with both.

He would move as well. His flat held too many memories, memories of Vanessa and his hopes for the future, their future. He would destroy every single thing that linked him with Vanessa. He would reforge his life and create something new, something hard, something that could not be broken.

And he would never trust another woman again.

7

It had been months since Kat's last visit to the library. Even longer since her last episode on that first day of school. She tapped the pen against her lip and stared out the library window, her brow furrowed. In fact, it had been over a year.

Has it really been that long?

Absently, she watched the snow fall outside the frosted glass panes as she mentally ticked off every class she had attended, every experiment she had performed. She had been so busy with schoolwork that her real problem had been eclipsed by her education. But, dormant though it may be, the monster was still there, deep inside of her, waiting to be let loose. It was time she began her research again. Especially now that she had only a few months left before she was done with school.

Kat pushed her homework away and stood, looking around the library at the rows and rows of leather-bound books and faded journals. Study tables dotted the space between the rows. A clock ticked quietly on the other side of the hall.

She turned and moved along the shelves to retrieve another armful of journals.

Returning to her table, she scanned the title of the first article—"Steam Engineering and Its Applications for World

City"—and turned the page. A couple more articles, but nothing even remotely related to her condition.

Kat shut the journal and placed it to her left before reaching for another.

At least she hadn't experienced another episode. Of course, avoiding almost every person at school and keeping her emotions to a minimum helped. But how long could she live like that? Her life stretched out before her, an old maid, buried in books and articles, never straying from her house or lab. A caged animal for the rest of her life.

Kat stared ahead, her fingers curled. *I don't want that. I want a real life, and I want to spend it with people.*

After an hour, she pushed another journal aside and leaned forward, placing her head in her hands. All the fear and discouragement she had hidden beneath her schoolwork over the last few months came rushing back.

I can't be the only one like this.

Can I?

She clutched at the scarf around her neck, holding it like a noose. *But what if I am? What if there is no cure? Maybe I really am destined to live out my life as an old maid. Or risk losing control and . . .*

And what? What was the worst that could happen?

Memories long buried rushed through her mind. Six years old and angry with Ms. Stuart. The cold lump swelling inside her chest. Waving her hands. Flames popping up across the nursery like tiny red flowers blooming. And the smoke . . .

Ms. Stuart had hidden the real reason for the nursery fire from her father, stating that a spark had flown from the fireplace.

But they both knew it had been something quite different. It had come from her.

She had set the nursery on fire.

And not just fire. Another time she had pulled everything in the room to herself like a magnet, creating a barrier between her and Ms. Stuart.

Both times she had been lucky not to hurt Ms. Stuart. And the other times she had been able to stop herself before the monster inside her unleashed. But the next time she might hurt someone, or worse.

Kat grabbed another journal, her fingers trembling across the pages. *There has to be something—or someone—who can help me! I just need to keep looking.*

Muffled laugher broke out behind her, pulling her back to the library. She turned and looked behind her.

A group of young men entered the back of the library. One of them caught her eye and said something indistinguishable to the others, sparking a rash of wicked grins.

Blaylock Sterling.

Kat twisted back around and fumbled with the journal in front of her. Since that first day, she had more or less successfully avoided Blaylock, sitting on the opposite side of the classroom when they shared a class, pairing up with Marianne for dissections, or studying in her dorm.

Why did he have to come in here just now?

Boots clapped across the wooden floor behind her. Heat crept up her neck and along her ears. She closed her eyes. *Don't let them come over here, don't let them come over here . . .*

She reached for another journal when a hand came to rest on the table to her right.

"Well, well, well. What do we have here? Miss Bloodmayne has come out of her hidey hole."

Kat gritted her teeth and looked up at Blaylock. His ash-blond hair fell across his forehead, covering the left side of his face. He brushed his hair aside, smiled at her, and winked.

She folded her arms and sat back. "What do you want?"

He took a seat on the table next to her journals and fingered the closest one. "I just wanted to say hello. It's generally nice manners to do so."

His friends gathered behind him, three in all.

Kat turned the page of the journal. "Then you have done just that. Now, I am busy and—"

"But you haven't said hello."

Kat flushed and curled her fingers over the edge of the journal. "Greetings, Mr. Sterling."

"Please call me Blaylock. Funny, I haven't seen you lately in class. I've missed seeing your pretty face." His gaze traveled across her face, then dipped down.

Kat narrowed her eyes. "Considering many of our classes are separate, not to mention our dorms, and our lives, it is not surprising. Now, Mr. Sterling, I am busy at the moment and have no time for your flirtations."

His gaze jerked back up and his lips tightened. "You do realize that by attending this academy, *Miss Bloodmayne*, you have limited your choices. Most men do not want an educated woman for a wife. Men want other things. I would suggest not ostracizing the only males who might take an interest in you."

Kat cocked her head to the side. "Are you saying you're interested in courtship, Mr. Sterling?"

He snorted. "I'm saying you could use a few lessons in things other than school."

Kat stood and gathered up the journals. "And you would teach me those things?"

Blaylock straightened and gave her a lazy grin. "I would be willing to give you a few lessons."

Was he serious? Kat sniffed. "I'm afraid I'll have to pass. If you'll excuse me . . ." She made her way between the young men and scurried down the aisle toward the main library desk, her heart thumping madly inside. Blaylock gave her the chills. No wonder the other women students avoided him and his entourage, despite the young men's attractive appearances.

She placed the journals down on the desk in front of a long, lean woman dressed in a dark brown suit with a set of tiny spectacles perched across her narrow nose. "May I check this out over the weekend?"

The librarian glanced down at the journals and wrote the titles across a long piece of paper. "Return them Monday morning promptly."

"Yes, ma'am."

Kat grabbed the journals and cast a glance over her shoulder. Blaylock stood by the table she had been sitting at, his arms crossed, a scowl across his handsome face. Something told her this was not over. Blaylock seemed to be in pursuit of something more than just an exchange of coy comments.

Another chill went down her spine.

Kat clutched the journals to her chest and hurried to the front door.

The winter air hit her with a blast of ice and wind. She sucked in her breath and ran across the courtyard toward the dormitories ahead. Tiny flakes clung to her face and eyelashes. She wiped them away and reached for the thick wooden door.

With a hard tug, she yanked the door open and scurried inside, pausing in the foyer to catch her breath.

Nicola entered the room from the right, caught sight of Kat, and stopped.

Kat sighed. Just what she needed. Another overprivileged heir of World City.

Nicola crossed her arms, her rich auburn hair down for the night. Even in her robe, she cast an imposing figure. Inches taller than Kat and with a tongue that could skewer the heart of anyone who crossed her path. Which seemed to be Kat all the time.

Nicola's gaze moved to the journals Kat clutched, then back to Kat. "Studying some more, Kathryn?" She smirked and shook her head. "It won't help you. You know you'll never catch up to me."

I don't care. "I'm not in competition with you, Nicola."

"You're right. You wouldn't even qualify." With a flounce of her auburn curls, Nicola turned and headed down the hall.

Kat drew her lips into a thin line. Nicola was right in one regard: she should be studying if she wanted a chance to be one of Father's apprentices. On the other hand, if she didn't find a cure, an apprenticeship would be out of the question anyway. One episode in front of her father and *she* would be the one the Tower would be studying.

She pushed away from the door and headed into the drawing room to the left. A fire burned in the marble fireplace, filling the room with a warm, orange light. Two high back chairs, upholstered in a floral green brocade, sat before the fire. An Austrium rug lay on the floor, filled with intricate designs of flowers and leaves.

Kat went to the chair on the left and sat down with a long sigh. She had the room to herself.

She placed the journals on the small side table and lifted the most promising one from the stack, a staid collection of medical articles. "Germ Theory of Disease." Interesting, but no. "Chloroform and Its Uses in the Surgical Theatre." Professor Flintlocke said something the other day about chloroform and ether being used in surgery. Still, not what she was looking for today.

The last article in the journal caught her eye. "The Connection Between the Spirit and the Body" by Dr. Joshua Latimer. She skimmed the article, then went back and read it more fully.

In our pursuit of science, we are forgetting the soul, yet there is no disconnect between the physical and the spiritual. One affects the other. To only focus on one is to overlook what ails the other. Some physical symptoms are caused by maladies of the soul; when the soul is wounded, the body will give evidence.

Father never put much stock into religion or anything remotely related to the spiritual. The little she knew about the soul came from Ms. Stuart, who believed everyone had a soul inside his or her body. She used to tell Kat stories about God until Father found out. Kat had heard his livid rant all the way up in the nursery, and Ms. Stuart had never mentioned the subject again.

Could Ms. Stuart have been right?

Kat brushed the area above her heart. Did a part of her exist somewhere inside here? Was she more than a merely physical collection of chemicals and impulses?

She held out her hand and flexed her fingers. But then why didn't anyone else possess this problem? Why was it when she lost control, she moved things or lit things on fire? And she always felt cold and hard inside afterward.

Was that her soul she was feeling? That cold, hard thing?

A sudden sadness gripped her as she thought through the possibilities. Perhaps she had a soul and there was something terribly wrong with it. With her.

One way to find out . . .

Kat put the journal away and stood. She would find this Dr. Latimer and ask him.

Professor Flintlocke paused, his fingers spread along the spine of the book he was in the midst of pulling out from the bookcase. "Why do you want to know about Dr. Latimer?"

Kat sat in the chair beside his desk. "I read an article of his last night."

"An article?" Professor Flintlocke pulled the book out and turned around.

"In one of the journals I checked out from the library."

Professor Flintlocke frowned and took a seat behind his desk. His long white hair was pulled back and wrinkles lined his face. His fingers shook slightly as he opened the book. "And what did Dr. Latimer write that has you so interested?"

"Something about the body and the soul being connected."

His frown deepened. "I see." He paused, considering her. "Dr. Latimer was once a member of the Tower. But he and Dr. Bloodmayne—your father—disagreed on something. They had a falling out and Dr. Latimer left. No one has heard from him since."

Kat leaned forward, her hands clasped together. "So you don't know where this Dr. Latimer is?"

Professor Flintlocke shook his head. "I'm afraid not. A year later he was removed from the archives and from the Tower's list of scientists."

Kat frowned. "That seems a bit harsh for a mere disagreement."

Professor Flintlocke smoothed the page across the book. "We have standards here at the Tower. If you cannot follow our creeds, then you do not belong here."

"So you're saying Dr. Latimer was removed because he didn't adhere to the Tower's beliefs?"

"Dr. Bloodmayne and the council believed that Dr. Latimer had proven himself incapable of being an unbiased scientist."

"I see. And does that bias have anything to do with the article I read?"

"Miss Bloodmayne, I have no idea how you got ahold of that article. All of Dr. Latimer's research was purged shortly after he left. If I were you, I would not search for a man whom both the Tower and the World City council barred from practice. Now, I have a lot of work to do before class. So if you will excuse me . . ." The professor looked down at his book and grew silent.

Kat waited a moment, then stood and grabbed her book bag. "Thank you for your time, professor."

He waved her off without glancing up.

Kat sighed and turned around and headed out the door, the questions she hadn't asked rushing through her mind. Why had the Tower barred Dr. Latimer? What had he said or done that had warranted such severe treatment? And where was he now?"

She stepped into the hallway, where students were already mingling and preparing for their next classes. She headed toward the end of the hallway. One thing was for sure, instead of deterring her, Professor Flintlocke had only increased her curiosity about this Dr. Latimer.

8

Stephen sat in a booth in the farthest corner of the Brass Griffin, nursing a cup of bitter tea. The pub itself was long and narrow, with a dark wooden counter along one side and booths with deep blue cushions lining the other. Lamps hung above each booth, creating an intimate atmosphere in which business could be conducted over a pint.

Most of the booths were filled on this warm spring evening, and the low hum of voices echoed across the pub. Smoke hung in the air, turning the pub into a dark hazy den. Barney, the proprietor, stood behind the bar, serving drinks in small tin cups or mugs. A couple of men sat at the counter and talked with him, lifting their cups every now and then and downing the amber liquid.

Stephen turned his attention to the booths. From his spot here in the back corner of the bar, he could see the entire pub and its occupants.

In the nearest booth sat Antonio, head of the Greensborough faction, with a couple of his burly henchmen. Their heads were bent low over the table, their eyes darting around every few minutes.

They were planning something, Stephen could feel it, but criminals could not be arrested unless the deed was done, or

there was evidence of the upcoming crime. He had neither. pity, really. It would save everyone time and money if he could just take Antonio in now.

Antonio caught sight of Stephen and froze.

Stephen gave him a small salute and took another sip of his tea.

At least his presence kept the felons on their toes.

His gaze moved down the other booths. A couple of business men. Factory workers just coming off the second shift. And . . .

Bingo.

Victor walked in and glanced around the pub.

Stephen moved to the right so that he could not be spotted from the door.

The door shut behind Victor, and he took a seat in the booth closest to the pub entrance. His ghostly pale skin, black hair, and angular features made him look more like a vicar than a mob boss. And the high-necked black overcoat he wore only emphasized his peculiar looks. He mopped his forehead and looked around.

It appeared his informant was right. No sign of Victor's usual bodyguards.

Stephen smiled. That would make his job even easier.

Barney left the counter and approached Victor's booth. Barney was a smart man, and had been paid too much to let Victor know that he was here.

Stephen took another sip from his teacup and watched, careful to stay out of Victor's line of sight He couldn't hear what Victor said, but a minute later Barney brought him a glass of red wine.

Well, Victor certainly didn't drink like a mob boss.

Stephen tugged at the bit of hair that grew below his lip, his gaze focused on his mark. Victor's bounty would see him through this month. Good thing, too; Ms. O'Hearn had come knocking yesterday for his rent.

Well, there was no use waiting any longer. Victor would either come with him or run. Stephen pulled out each of his revolvers and checked the cartridges. A smart man would come quietly. But his bounties were rarely smart.

He closed the second revolver and holstered it. No need to spook Victor. Words first, then weapons.

Stephen stood and left the booth. Eyes followed him. He ignored them.

Victor looked up at his approach, and what little color he had in his face washed away, leaving him looking like a corpse.

"Victor Manson."

Victor's Adam's apple bobbed up and down and another bead of sweat trickled down the side of his face. "Stephen Grey."

"So you know who I am."

"Who in World City doesn't? But that doesn't explain why you're standing here at my table. I've done nothing wrong."

Stephen mentally rolled his eyes. They all said that. "That is for the judge to decide."

A bit of color came back into Victor's face, and his lips turned downward. "You don't know what you're getting into, bounty hunter."

Stephen ignored Victor's protest and drew out his handcuffs. "Victor, you are under arrest for crimes committed against the people of World City."

Like wheels slowly turning, Victor studied him, his hands tightening on the edge of the table. "Like I said, Grey, this is not your business. And I haven't done anything wrong."

"I don't think s—"

Victor tossed his wine in Stephen's direction and tore out of the booth.

"Blazes!" Stephen wiped his face with the back of his sleeve and rushed out the door behind him, shoving the handcuffs into his duster as he ran. Why couldn't his bounties ever come quietly?

Outside, he spotted Victor ducking into an alley and took off in pursuit, charging through puddles and splashing mud and water up across his trousers. Victor glanced back every few moments, his black overcoat flapping behind him. As they neared the Meandre, steam rising from the water mixed with the factory smoke, creating a fog between the buildings, and at times threatening to obscure Victor from view.

Oh, no you don't. With a burst of speed, Stephen drew near his quarry. One, two, three—he pushed off one foot and leaped forward, tackling the man to the ground.

In spite of having taken the brunt of both their weights, Victor immediately twisted beneath him, thrashing like a sea serpent. "You can't take me in! You don't know what's going on! You're just a pawn of the city council!"

Stephen struggled to pin the other man's flailing arms so he could retrieve his handcuffs. "Don't fight me, Victor. It will go better for both of us if—"

Wham.

Victor's fist caught him in the face.

Stars burst across Stephen's vision. He fell back, his nose throbbing. Something wet dripped into his mustache.

Victor shoved him away and struggled back to his feet.

Stephen blinked and shook his head. By the time he was up, Victor was halfway down the block.

Letting his breath out in an exasperated hiss, Stephen planted his feet and, with one motion, drew his gun. He swung his arm up and took a heartbeat to aim. Right there, behind Victor's knee.

He pulled the trigger.

A crack echoed between the buildings.

At the end of the block, Victor bounced off the side of a wall and fell to the ground, clutching his leg, his screams punctuated by a flurry of foul descriptions.

Stephen holstered his gun and picked up the handcuffs. He started down the street, his face grim. Just once he would like to not have to shoot a man.

"You don't know what you're doing, Grey!" Victor glared at him. "You're after the wrong people."

"I don't know what you're talking about."

"They put that bounty out on me because I know what they're doing."

"Who's 'they'?"

"The Tower. But I told them I wasn't a grave robber. I have standards."

Grave robber? Stephen reached down and pulled Victor's hands behind his back, eliciting another string of colorful words. "Shut your mouth, Victor, or I'll find something to shut it with." He slapped the cuffs across Victor's wrists and hauled him to his feet.

Victor looked back, his eyes wide. "Listen, Grey, I'll give you anything you want. Just don't take me in. They're monsters up there in the Tower. The things they're doing to people, it ain't righ—"

Stephen stuffed his handkerchief into Victor's mouth and tied it behind his head. "I told you to shut up."

Victor's eyes went even wider and sweated dripped from the end of his nose. He mumbled something unintelligible and shook his head.

Stephen paused. Victor was scared, really scared. His bounties usually cursed him and grew violent, but Victor was terrified, not of him, but of something else.

Could the man be right?

As if drawn to it, Stephen looked over his shoulder. High above the rundown flats and smoky pubs of World City stood the Tower.

Was it possible Victor knew something? Was something going on at the Tower? It had been more than a year since the rumors on the street about the reapers had dried up. Was it possible they were back? And somehow connected to the Tower?

Or—he scowled and turned back—maybe Victor was just saying that to get out of his arrest. After all, in the months he'd spent searching for Mr. Hensley and the others, Stephen had never found anything. Why would it be happening again now?

He grabbed Victor by the arm. "Let's go."

Victor mumbled some more and motioned down.

Oh yeah. He'd shot Victor's leg.

Stephen sighed. This was going to be a long walk.

"You know Stephen, I don't understand why you insist on bringing your bounties in alive." Roy jerked his head toward Victor, who sat still in the corner. "This one is going to die anyway."

"I won't be their executioner," Stephen said coldly.

Roy looked at him with a wicked twist to his lips. "Is it because you still believe in God?"

He shrugged. It was the same with Roy every time he dropped a fugitive off at the precinct. The man had a grudge against religion and baited him at every turn. What Roy didn't know is he had walked away from God a long time ago, on that day he had found Vanessa in Harrison's bed.

"Doesn't matter now." Stephen crossed his arms. "If there is one thing I've learned, it's that a man lives only once."

"Are you sure about that?"

Stephen cocked one eyebrow. "Yes. Ever seen a man come back to life?"

"Well . . ." Roy turned his gaze toward the window at the side of his desk. "There's word on the street that someone high up, someone in the Tower, is trying to do just that."

Victor straightened, his eyes so wide Stephen could see the whites. He glanced back at Roy. "Trying to do what?"

Roy leaned across his desk. "Trying to bring the dead back to life."

He snorted. "Ha! Now give me my money."

"No, seriously." Roy waved his hands. "My sources are good, and they're saying some of the Tower scientists are experimenting on dead bodies."

"There's no way. The council would never allow that." At least not publicly. Stephen held out his hand. "My bounty, Roy."

Roy rose from his chair and headed toward the safe on the right. "I know you've heard the rumors. Graves dug up, bodies stolen."

He glanced at Victor but didn't answer, just held out his hand. Maybe it was time he reopened his investigation into the reapers and missing people. And maybe extend his search to include corpses.

Roy turned the small knob once to the right, once to the left, then once to the right again. A soft click echoed from the safe. "Who knows"—he reached into the safe—"Maybe Victor here will become one of their test subjects."

Stephen frowned and looked back. Victor might be a criminal who deserved the full weight of the law, but the thought of some mad scientist using Victor's body after he was dead didn't sit well with him.

Roy turned around and handed him a fistful of bills. "Here you go."

Stephen closed his hand around the money and shoved the wad into his coat pocket.

"Good doing business with you, Stephen."

He snorted. "Same to you, Roy. Let me know when you have another warrant." He turned and headed toward the door.

"If you ever want to come back to the force, just let me know. I know Captain Algar would love to have you back."

Stephen grunted in reply and left the precinct.

9

Kat studied herself in the mirror, turning her head this way and that to admire the cameo brooch at her throat, a gift from Ms. Stuart for graduation day. Her reflection looked older now—more sophisticated, more elegant than the girl who had set the cobblestones on fire two years ago. In spite of the occasion, she had pulled her lush dark hair into a simple, functional bun, and she wore a modest blouse tucked neatly into her long skirt.

Her eyes came back to the brooch.

Graduation.

She smiled and sighed. She was finally done.

"Some of us need to use the mirror, you know!"

Kat laughed, pulled out of her reverie. "All right, all right." She glanced at Marianne's reflection and gave a little bow. "I'm done. It's all yours."

Marianne folded her arms and shot a critical look at Kat's hair. "If I had hair like yours, I wouldn't hide it in that drab little bun."

When Kat just laughed again, she pouted. "You don't know what you have, and I'm wildly jealous."

Kat stood and pulled the bench out for her friend. "Yes, I know. You've been saying that for as long as I've known you.

You know, with your knowledge of chemistry, maybe you'll find a way to dye hair."

Marianne rolled her eyes and sat down. "With my luck, I'd probably turn my hair green." She stuck her tongue out at the mirror.

Kat stepped back and rubbed her chin. "You know, it might be an improvement."

Marianne brandished a hairbrush at her, and Kat hurried out of the room, laughing. She flopped down on the couch in the sitting room and grabbed a cushion to hug to her chest. She needed that. Laughing was good for the body.

At that thought, the smile on her lips faded. How many times had she sat here, in the dorm, hoping to hear from her father? He never came for a visit, and he never wrote. She sat up on the settee and placed the cushions back in the corners. Even the mere thought of Father made her cringe inside and want to straighten everything in sight.

Two years, and not once had she seen him except in passing. And even then, they were brief, cordial meetings, his coolness a stark contrast to Ms. Stuart's cheerful Sunday visits.

Kat watched the fire burn in the nearby fireplace, frustration with herself welling in place of the former laughter. She was a fool to hope. He wouldn't show up today, not to see what she had accomplished, at any rate.

She smoothed her skirt, her fingers cold. What would she have done without Ms. Stuart? At least she could count on someone coming to watch her graduate today.

She looked up as Marianne emerged from their shared bedroom.

"Well, it's the best I could do."

Marianne wore a form-fitting green gown, not too extravagant, but certainly elegant. Her carrot-colored hair was twisted up in the latest fashion, with a curl falling on either side of her face.

Kat shook her head. "Marianne, I don't know why you don't think you're pretty. You look wonderful in that gown."

"You really think so?" Marianne looked down and brushed the skirt with her gloved hand. "Father had it made for today. I wasn't sure about the color."

"Green is perfect on you." Inside, Kat's stomach burned. What she wouldn't give to have a doting father like Marianne's. She glanced down at her own simple clothing. Father didn't believe in excessiveness. At least she had the brooch. She fingered the oval trinket.

"I'm sorry." Marianne came and sat on the couch beside her. "I shouldn't have mentioned . . ." She sighed and took Kat's hand. "I'm sorry, Kathryn. But if it's any consolation, you are the most beautiful woman I know. Both inside and out. Someday your father will see that." She gave Kat's hand a squeeze then dropped it. "Me, on the other hand, I'm just shallow." She let out a throaty laugh.

Kat wiped her eyes, surprised to find she had been crying. "It's all right. Ms. Stuart is coming this afternoon. She's almost like a mother to me."

"But it's not the same."

Kat took in a deep breath and looked out the window. "No, it's not."

The auditorium filled slowly as hundreds of people filed in, each one taking a seat in the plush red velvet chairs that lined the rows. A chandelier hung high above the orchestra seats, casting warm light on the crowd below. The more affluent patrons of the Tower sat in the boxes that lined either side of the auditorium, with their servants in attendance behind them.

Gaslights encased in glass and iron lined the front of the stage, the newest in lighting technology. The air hummed with low voices and the occasional squeal of a folding seat.

Kat sat onstage in the chair farthest to the right, facing the crowd. Her stomach did flip-flops and her hands grew moist. She straightened up and placed them on her lap, her chin high. A photographer stood in front of the students, a couple of feet from the stage lights, his head hidden behind a dark cloth, his hand adjusting one of the knobs.

Behind him, a broad woman made her way along the front row, her dress suit a dark blue with a matching floppy hat with a white feather on top. Her gray hair was tucked in a bun beneath the hat, each hair perfectly in place. She reached a seat almost across from Kat and sat down. Gray eyes peered up from beneath the hat and a hint of a smile graced her face.

Kat fingered the brooch at her neck and smiled back. She could always count on Ms. Stuart.

The photographer's fingers came up and Kat dropped her hand.

One finger. Two fingers. Three fingers.

There was a poof and a curl of smoke rose from the tripod. The photographer came out from beneath the cloth. He was an older gentleman, with a large mustache, thick eyebrows, and dark disheveled hair. "Very good, ladies and gentlemen. One more, and remember, don't move."

Kat sat still as he prepared the slides again. Marianne sat at her left, along with the twenty other ladies who had completed the Academy of Science two-year program. Behind them were the male students.

The photographer disappeared again behind the cloth. He held up his hand. One. Two. Three.

Another poof and smoke.

He came out, his hair on end from the static electricity. "Good. Very good. This will be in the *Herald* tomorrow."

Kat caught sight of a man near the edge of the stage. She gripped her skirt, her heart pounding inside her ears. She turned her head slightly and searched the shadows again out of the corner of her eye.

Yes, it was him.

Her father.

He wore his Tower uniform—a deep green overcoat embroidered in gold, deep green vest, and dark pants. His wavy silver hair was combed back, exposing his hawkish face. He stood beside two of her professors, talking.

She gripped her skirt tighter. Could he have come for her?

"Kat? Is everything all right?" Marianne whispered beside her.

"What?"

"You look like you've seen a ghost."

"I . . . uh . . ." She let go of her skirt and smoothed away the wrinkles. "Yes, everything is fine. It looks like Father came for my graduation after all."

She glanced at the front row. Had Ms. Stuart known her father would be coming today?

"Your father is here?" Marianne craned her neck and searched the crowd.

Kat nodded to her right. "Yes. Off stage. Talking to Professors Flintlocke and Margrave."

Marianne turned and stared. "Cogglesfoot, you're right! I can't believe he cam—"

"Shhhh." Kat's face grew hot. "Please, Marianne."

"Oh, yes, right." Marianne sat back in her chair, her head high. "Do you think he'll choose his apprentices today?"

Kat licked her lips. "I don't know. I don't know anything my father does." Was that why he was here? Not to see her, but to choose his apprentices? Her stomach hardened. What if he didn't choose her?

Professor Flintlocke left her father and walked across the stage, his black robes swishing with each step. He stopped before the podium and the auditorium grew quiet. "Welcome. Today is a special day, one that will go down in history. Behind me is the first women's class to graduate from the Tower Academy of Sciences, along with our men. And here to celebrate today's historic occasion is Dr. Alexander Bloodmayne, Head Scientist for the Tower. Please welcome Dr. Bloodmayne." He waved toward the right.

Her father walked past the curtains and made his way across the stage, his head high, his posture regal. The auditorium broke out in enthusiastic applause. The people of World City respected Dr. Alexander Bloodmayne. After all, his latest invention—a healing serum—saved many of the soldiers on the front lines of the war with Austrium. Who wouldn't revere a man like that? A hero of the people.

But Kat knew better.

He never glanced at her, never looked her way as he crossed the stage to the podium. He had to know she was here. After all, he had been the leading scientist to push for women's admittance into the academy, and he had paid her tuition. She swallowed the lump inside her throat, her eyes prickling with tears.

Dr. Bloodmayne stopped in front of the podium. "Thank you, Professor Flintlocke." A few seconds passed as the crowd quieted down. "Today is indeed an important day . . ."

Kat stared at her father's back. Why did he treat her so coldly? She twisted her skirt between her fingers. She did everything to please him. Everything! Even when he wasn't around.

The blood whooshed through her veins.

He never came to visit, not once, during the two years she was here at the academy. Yet he shows up today, the celebrity speaker for her graduation. He had no right to be here!

Her fingers began to tingle.

And yet she still wanted his approval. To have him just once look at her and smile and tell her, "Well done."

Her vision grew red.

A movement in the front row caught her eye: Ms. Stuart's white feather, waving back and forth in concert with her shaking head. The plump housekeeper stared up at her, her face tight and pale, as if she intended to calm Kat by force of will alone.

Kat's eyes went wide and she sucked in her breath. No one seemed to notice. She concentrated on her breathing and flexed her fingers. *Not now, I can't lose control right now . . .*

She took another deep breath and the iron band around her chest loosened. The tingling vanished from her fingers and her vision returned to normal.

She had almost lost it, right here in front of everyone.

A cold sweat broke out across her body.

Ms. Stuart continued to stare at her, but now her gaze held compassion and concern.

Kat looked away. She hadn't come that close to losing control since that first morning two years ago.

I can't do this anymore.

". . . Mr. Blaylock Sterling, Miss Nicola Tremaine, and Miss Marianne Fealy."

Marianne gave a small squeal next to her. "I made it! I can't believe I made it! I—" She looked over at Kat and her face fell. "Kat . . ." she whispered, her face going from elated to stricken.

Kat looked from her friend to her father still at the podium. Wait, had he just announced . . . his apprentices? The bottom of her world vanished, and she felt as if she were falling. The applause of the audience echoed inside her mind.

Father never called her name.

Kat worked her mouth, her cheeks hot while the rest of her body grew cold. The tingling came back along her fingertips, and for one crimson moment, she wanted to see the whole auditorium erupt in a blaze: see each and every red velvet chair catch fire and listen to the people scream. But most of all, she wanted to see her father turn and look at her, really look at her, for the first time in her life.

Then she sank back into her chair.

"Kat," Marianne whispered. "I'm so sorry. I don't know what to say."

Kat shook her head slightly and gave Marianne a rueful smile. She would not take away from her friend's moment. But inside, she felt as though she had been stabbed by a thousand knives.

Her father said some closing words and then the rest of the professors joined him at the podium. Each graduate's name was called and each one stood and accepted a rolled piece of parchment, tied up in a bright red ribbon.

When they called her name, Kat stood stiffly and took the piece of paper, a small smile plastered across her face. She barely heard the applause of the crowd. Instead, a steady hum filled her mind and only strength of will kept her standing.

Then they were dismissed.

Marianne turned toward her and grabbed her hand. "Kat, if I could do something, anything . . . It's not right. You should have been named, not me. You were one of the Tower's best students."

Kat gave her a weak smile. "It's all right, Marianne. I am very happy for you."

"But I know how much your father's approval means to you."

"And right now he believes I would be better suited for another position."

"That's not true. You were the top of the class in biology."

"And Father works a great deal with chemistry. There was no one better than you in chemistry. You'll make a great apprentice."

"But what will you do?"

Kat clasped her hands together. "I don't know. Perhaps one of the steam factories will have need of me. Or maybe the military."

"You don't really mean that, do you? You'd join the war?"

Kat shrugged. "I don't know. But what I do know is that there is a gala tonight and I'm not going to think about my future any more today."

"But—"

"Your father is coming."

A robust man approached the stage, his orange hair swept to the side, a large grin on his face.

The sharp pain came back, right there above her heart. If only she could see Father look at her that way.

"My girl!" Mr. Fealy opened his arms. Marianne gave Kat one last look, then joined him in a hug.

Kat turned away. Her father stood to the left of the stage, reporters and fans around him. He wore a regal smile and used his hands as he talked. Would anyone notice if she slipped away? Maybe she could leave and take a walk in the park before the gala tonight.

"I'm proud of you."

Kat turned.

Ms. Stuart stood on the top stair, her purse held between her gloved hands. "So proud of you."

Kat sucked in her lips and nodded. She didn't want to cry, not here, not in front of everyone. Ms. Stuart seemed to notice. She cast a look at the other side of the stage and her face tightened.

"Come, Kathryn. I need some fresh air."

She nodded and followed Ms. Stuart down the stairs and along the side aisle toward the door in the back. Outside, the sun shone brightly across World City.

But inside, she was cold as ice.

Ms. Stuart led the way to Centennial Park a block away. "Kathryn, it's time you made your own way in the world. You're a woman now, and an educated one."

Kat nodded. Ms. Stuart was right. World City had a lot to offer a young woman. Everywhere there was progress. It was time for her to step away from her father's shadow and become her own woman.

They passed the iron fence and entered the park, where couples were strolling along the gravel paths between the gardens and trees. Men in suits and dapper hats. Women in dress suits with wide brimmed hats and a feather on top. The flowers that lined the paths were just starting to bloom, and green leaves sprouted along naked branches. A cool breeze blew across the park and Kat shivered. If only she had her cloak with her.

"Perhaps you will also find what you are looking for."

Kat glanced at Ms. Stuart.

"It happened again. On stage. Am I right?"

Kat rubbed her arms. "Yes. But that's the first time since . . . Well, it never happened at school."

"I know. You would have told me if it had."

Would she have? Kat wasn't so sure.

"Did seeing your father trigger it?"

Kat let her breath out her nose as they passed beneath an oak tree. Ms. Stuart understood all too well. "Yes."

Ms. Stuart gave her a firm nod. "Another reason to move away. Women no longer stay home."

"But where would I go? What would I do?"

Ms. Stuart waited until they passed a young couple. Kat glanced back. The couple looked like they were courting. They held hands and the young man was leaning down toward the young woman with a smile on his face. The young woman beamed back.

What would it be like to be a normal young woman? Would she have a beau? Would she be walking in some park, her arm linked with a young man's?

She shook her head and turned back. The only young men she knew were the few she had met at the Tower Academy.

They were either smart and dull, or looking for trouble. She wasn't interested in either type.

What was her type?

Ms. Stuart clasped her handbag between both hands. "What about finding a cure for your condition?" She said the last few words quietly.

Her heart sank. She had secretly hoped whatever was wrong with her would finally vanish once she reached womanhood; just a lingering effect of her changing body. But today had put that hope to rest for good. She was still a danger, a ticking time bomb that might go off any moment. And more than Ms. Stuart might be there to witness it. "I studied some of the Tower's scientific journals during school. There wasn't much of use, but there might be a doctor who can help me."

Ms. Stuart glanced at her with one raised eyebrow. "Why didn't you tell me this before?"

"I had hoped . . ." Kat looked away. They walked past a small pond with koi and ducks and large lily pads bobbing along the rippling surface. "I had hoped it was all over."

"I understand. Do you know how to reach this doctor?"

"No, I only know his name. There was no contact information. I even asked around."

"Well, it sounds like a good first step. In the meantime, I'm sure your father will be fine with you coming back home. At least until you find a position. And I am looking forward to enjoying your company again."

The sharp pain came searing back inside her chest. Just another reminder that her father had not chosen her to be his apprentice. Kat bobbed her head, but going back was the last thing she wanted to do. If she went back, all her work, all her struggles at the academy would be as if they never happened. It would be as if she never left.

They reached the iron fence again. The Tower stood before them, the pinnacle of achievement for World City. Kat glanced at it half-heartedly.

"I'll send Reginald to pick up your things tomorrow." Ms. Stuart turned and faced her. "For now, put all of this out of your head. Have fun tonight, my dear. The World City Gala is an opportunity to be a young woman. It doesn't last long and before you know it, you're an old spinster like me." She gave Kat a wink. "So enjoy now."

Kat smiled, the first real one since that morning. "I will."

"Perhaps you'll even meet a young man."

She rolled her eyes. "I doubt it."

"Well, at least dance."

"I will dance once, just for you."

"Good." Ms. Stuart motioned to the black carriage waiting down the street. "I want to hear all about it tomorrow."

10

Kat ran a gloved hand along the deep blue folds of her gown. Silver thread laced her bodice and the edges of her sleeves. Her dark hair was pulled up and held back with a silver comb in a style so elegant even Marianne wouldn't complain. The blue from the dress accented her pale skin, and her eyes appeared dark and full in the candlelight.

Ms. Stuart had chosen well. If only she were here to see her tonight.

"Kat, are you read—?" Marianne gasped and her eyes widened as she stood in the doorway. "Kat, you look . . . you look . . ."

"Like a socialite?" Kat laughed and brushed her gown. Only a tinge of hurt hung across her heart from earlier. Tonight was her night, not her father's. In fact—she straightened up and lifted her chin—tonight marked the first day of the rest of her life. She would no longer live for her father.

She looked up and gave her friend a wide smile. "You look lovely. I told you that color suits you."

"You really think so?" Marianne lowered her fan. She wore a deep green gown with gold accents. Her thick red hair was piled high on her head and a diamond necklace sparkled around her neck. Probably another gift from her father. This time, however, Kat noticed with no tinge of jealousy.

Kat smiled even wider, her heart light. "Yes. Now come, let's head downstairs." She walked across the room and reached for Marianne's hand. Yes, Marianne would be one of her father's apprentices, but she still loved her friend. And she was free to pursue her own studies, namely, a cure for—

No, I'm not going to think about it tonight.

She gripped Marianne's hand and held her dress up with the other as they left their rooms and joined the other students waiting for the carriages that would whisk them away to the World City Gala.

Twenty minutes later, they arrived before a three-story alabaster structure adjacent to the Capitol building. Rows of windows glowed from the light within, and soft music trickled across the street.

Kat stepped out of the carriage, careful to keep her dress up, away from the pavement. Marianne joined her a few moments later, and the ladies merged into a small crowd of well-dressed people that made their way inside and down a long hall to a set of interior doors that opened up to the ballroom. The room was three times the size of any classroom at the Tower—larger, even, than the library. Crystal chandeliers hung along the ceiling, bathing the room in warm light. Rich white paneling lined the walls and thick, luxurious green velvet drapes hung across the windows.

Kat stood in the doorway, her hands clasped, her eyes wide. At least a hundred people were gathered in the room: men in dark suits, women in elaborate, colorful gowns. The air hummed with conversation and laughter, with the soft undertones of music streaming from the musicians on the far side of the room. The aroma of perfumes and colognes wafted through the air as people waltzed by.

Everyone who was anyone in World City was here tonight. Including her father.

He stood with a group of somber looking men to her left.

Kat looked away, her chin tilted upward, her fingers entwined. Time to make her own way in the world.

Marianne and a couple of the other academy ladies came to stand beside her.

Eleanor readjusted her thick wire-rimmed glasses across her nose. "So this is what we've been missing the last two years."

Nicola sniffed and fanned herself. "Personally, I would rather have attended the academy than have been presented to society."

Eleanor sighed. "Well, at least you'll be staying on at the Tower as one of Dr. Bloodmayne's personal apprentices. I don't know what I'm going to do." She sighed again, then gave herself a little shake. "Yes, I do. I'm going to dance." She headed right, following the wall toward another group of men and women. A couple of the other young women trailed behind her.

Across the room stood most of the male students, glancing around or straightening their neckties, except for Blaylock and his cronies, who had already found dancing partners and were twirling around the room with women in brightly colored gowns.

Kat started across the room, but Nicola put a hand on her arm. "Strange, isn't it, that you weren't chosen, Kathryn?"

Kat stopped and slowly turned back. "What do you mean?" From the corner of her eye, she saw Marianne give a small shake of her head.

Nicola's eyes lit up. "That you weren't chosen by your father to be a Tower apprentice."

Kat's cheeks grew hot. "I'm sure he had his reasons. After all, it would seem like favoritism if he chose his own daughter."

Nicola let out a polite laugh. "Or perhaps there is more. I noticed he never came to visit you at the academy over the last two years. Or even spoke to you today."

Had Nicola been watching her all this time? Of course she had. Kat's cheeks burned even brighter.

Nicola gave her a dismissive wave. "Perhaps he is ashamed of his dense daughter."

"Nicola, that's ridiculous! Everyone knows Kat was one of the best in class!" Marianne's eyes blazed.

"Then why did he pass over his own daughter?"

Kat clenched and unclenched her hands and her blood whooshed inside her veins. She had to get away before she lost control. "Please excuse me." She turned around and spotted a double set of glass doors at the far side of the room, opening up to a balcony.

Behind her, she heard Marianne speak. "Maybe he has other plans for his daughter . . ."

Kat pressed a hand to her cheek. It was getting worse. A month ago, she would have been able to ignore Nicola's barbs, but tonight she couldn't keep Nicola's words out of her head.

She made her way through the crowd, past the men and women, past the chairs where the older dignitaries sat. Couples spun along the dance floor like colorful human-sized tops.

She reached the glass doors and stepped out onto the balcony.

A man stood beside the stone railing, looking over the gardens beneath the moonlight.

Kat stopped and sucked in her breath. "Pardon, me. I didn't realize . . ."

He turned around.

She paused, her mouth open. She knew him from somewhere.

He was medium height, with a small mustache and a patch of hair below his lips. His blond hair was parted and brushed to the side. He wore a knee length leather duster that gathered across his midsection, then flowed out from his waist. But it was his eyes that caught her attention. They were a peculiar shade of hazel, with a deep green band ringing the pupil.

He stared at her with that same vague recognition on his face.

She tilted her head. "Do I know you?"

He didn't answer. Instead, he gave her a cold, but polite bow and then walked past her back into the ballroom, his overcoat brushing past her dress.

Kat turned and watched him disappear into a crowd of men. She held her hand in a fist against her heart. What in the world had she done to illicit such a chilly response from him? And how did she know him? He seemed so familiar.

She let out a long breath and approached the railing; at the exact spot the strange man had been standing moments ago.

A cool breeze brushed her heated face. She gripped the railing and looked over the garden. The moon was full tonight, casting its pale light across the manicured trees and rosebushes. Gravel paths weaved through the well-kept grass and led to a white terraced pavilion in the middle of the garden. The soft streams of music floated out from the doors behind her.

She leaned forward and placed her chin on her hand. She wanted to move on with her life, more than anything. But she couldn't move past the question of why her father had not chosen her. Why? What was wrong with her that her father would ignore her all these years, as long as she could remember?

Her brows furrowed. Was it possible he knew? Did he know about the monster that lurked inside her?

No, he couldn't possibly know. If he did, he would not have ignored her. He would have studied her, tested her, and experimented on her.

Kat straightened. Perhaps she should be thankful for his indifference. At least he hadn't discovered her secret. And she would keep it that way.

"Kathryn, are you all right?"

Kat turned and found Marianne standing in the doorway.

"You shouldn't listen to Nicola. You are one of the brightest people I know." Marianne looked down. "Even more so than me. I don't know why I was chosen to be an apprentice."

"Marianne, it's all right."

Marianne looked up

Kat smiled. "I can't think of another person who deserves it more."

"I can. *You* deserve it."

She shook her head. "I don't know how well I would have done working with my father."

Marianne tapped her chin with her closed fan. "I hadn't thought about that. Would you have liked to work alongside your father?"

More than anything. "I don't think it would have been good for either of us." *I wish he loved me, or at least thought kindly of me.* "Anyway"—Kat gathered up her dress and headed toward the ballroom—"we shouldn't miss out on this ball. Probably one of the only times we will be invited to the World City Gala."

Marianne's usual smile came back. "You're right. And I haven't danced yet."

"Then let's go."

11

Stephen stared down at the gardens below and clenched his fist. He shouldn't have come here tonight. This place only brought back painful memories.

His gaze lingered on the pavilion in the middle of the garden, and a bitter taste filled his mouth. It was there he first met Vanessa over three years ago, during another World City Gala. She had been so beautiful, so full of life. Everything he had wanted.

Stephen raked a hand through his hair. Except faithful, he reminded himself. He was lucky to have discovered her wandering heart rather than end up married to a cheating wife.

Someone gasped behind him. "Pardon, me. I didn't realize. . ."

Stephen turned.

A woman stood in the doorway, short, with thick dark hair and deep brown eyes. The dark blue gown she wore accented her young, curved body.

Wait. His gaze came back to her face. He knew her from somewhere . . .

She tilted her head. "Do I know you?"

A hundred flashbacks snatched at his attention: Vanessa curious, Vanessa pouting, Vanessa coy . . . always with that same tilt to of her head.

His insides clenched and he pressed his lips into a fine line. He bowed to the young woman without a word and walked by her, close enough to brush the folds of her gown. A whiff of her perfume drifted past his nose: something light and flowery. Not Vanessa at all. And he'd snubbed the poor girl mercilessly. Great.

Resisting the momentary urge to turn back, he walked into the ballroom and spotted Patrick making conversation with a couple of bigwigs and their sons near the entrance. Now that Patrick was superintendent of the lower district, he was high enough to warrant an invitation to the gala, but still low enough to have to kiss the boots of every man there. At least Harrison and Vanessa weren't here. Last he heard, they had eloped over a year ago, much to her father's chagrin, and had yet to be readmitted to polite society.

Patrick spied him and waved, his face an almost comical mixture of relief and desperation.

Several people stopped talking and watched him as he bypassed the couples lining up on the dance floor to begin another set, but he ignored them. When he reached his friend, Patrick clapped him across the shoulders. "Stephen, I didn't expect to see you here."

Stephen shrugged. His own invitation had come from the World City council as a thank-you for his capture of Victor Manson. And, he had no doubt, to keep him quiet about anything Manson might have told him.

The men with Patrick nodded in turn as Patrick introduced them, and a couple of the women giggled behind spread fans.

One of the young men—Henry Richards, Stephen thought—crossed his arms and studied Stephen with open skepticism on his aristocratic face. "So you're the famous

Stephen Grey. Is it true that you brought in the mob boss Victor Manson?"

"I did."

The young man's expression shifted. He uncrossed his arms. "Manson's evaded arrest for years. How did you manage it?"

Stephen glanced at Patrick and rubbed the back of his neck. He wasn't here to share bounty stories. He came tonight because he knew he needed to get out more. Sitting home, brooding every night was not good for him.

But now he was starting to think he had made a mistake.

Patrick waved at the young man. "Perhaps another time, Henry."

Henry's face fell.

Stephen turned around. "I'm going to go get a drink."

"I'll come with you. Gentlemen, ladies, please excuse us."

Patrick walked beside him as he crossed the room and headed for the refreshment table. "Thanks, friend. I thought I'd be stuck listening to old Councilman Richards all night. Henry's his son, you know, and he's all right. But once the old man gets started on Austrium and the war, there's no getting a word in."

They walked by a group of young women who giggled as Patrick turned a charming smile their way. Stephen fought the urge to roll his eyes. Patrick always did like social events like these.

The table was covered in white linen and held trays of biscuits, tarts, and small cakes. Cups of deep red punch sat to one side. Stephen picked up one of the cups and took a sip. Making a face, he placed the cup down and went for the tea set out at the end of the table. In the weeks after the event with Vanessa, he had been tempted to go to the tavern and obliterate every memory with strong drink, but he knew that if he started down that path, getting off it would be difficult. Since then, he'd chosen never to drink.

Stephen poured himself a cup of tea and placed the pot back on the tray.

Patrick stood beside him, sipping his cup of punch. "You should dance tonight."

Stephen tightened his grip on the handle. "I didn't come here for the company of women."

"They're not all bad, not like . . ." Patrick gave a small cough and took another sip.

Stephen cocked one eyebrow and blew across the teacup. "Like Vanessa?"

Patrick lowered his glass. "You need to move on."

"I have moved on." He took a sip and let the hot liquid flow down his throat.

"No you haven't. You work all the time, then hunker down in your flat. That's not life, Stephen. That's existing."

"I came tonight, didn't I?"

"Yes, and I'm glad you did. But you need to do more than show up. Enjoy this evening. There are many fine women here."

"I already said I'm not interested in finding a woman."

Patrick looked at him. "Just one dance."

Stephen worked his jaw, his gaze roving across the room. Most of the women present were only interested in fashion, titles, and money. He had thought Vanessa was different, but he had been proven wrong.

"There." Patrick pointed across the dance floor. "Ask her. She looks like a nice, sensible kind of girl."

Stephen looked in that direction and froze. It was the woman from the balcony. She stood beside another young woman with carrot-colored hair and a long green gown. A tall gentleman walked toward them and a moment later the carrot-topped woman left for the dance floor.

The young woman rubbed her arm and looked around the room.

Stephen narrowed his eyes. "Who is she?"

"I don't know. But I do know she is one of the ladies from the Tower Academy."

Smart, then. He liked that. It meant she wouldn't be giggly or boring. Hopefully. He finished half of his cup of tea, then turned back toward Patrick. "All right. I'll ask her. But then you need to get off my case."

Patrick's smile came back. "I won't say another word tonight."

Stephen tugged at the hair beneath his chin. "And you're sure you don't know her name? She looks familiar."

"No. But she is beautiful. Who would have thought a woman like her would have ended up at the academy instead of out in society."

Stephen dropped his hand and shrugged. "Times are changing."

Before Patrick could say anything else, Stephen placed his cup down and made his way around the dance floor.

As he approached, she looked up. Her cheeks turned bright pink and she looked away. Oh, that's right. He had been a bit abrupt on the balcony. He straightened his overcoat. He would just have to apologize. "Excuse me, miss."

She glanced back, her eyes dark, her cheeks still flushed.

"I am sorry about earlier this evening. You caught me off guard." And she was doing it again. She was similar to Vanessa, but younger, with an innocence to her countenance that he now realized Vanessa had never possessed. Stephen worked his dry mouth and gave her a short bow. "Please accept my apology."

She gave him a small nod. "I accept. I'm afraid I was out of sorts myself."

Stephen straightened. "And how are you now?"

"Much better, thank you."

He held out his hand. "Then perhaps you would join me for a dance."

She hesitated, her gloved hand hovering in the air. Then she took his hand with a firm grasp.

Stephen led her to the floor just as the waltz began. Her fingers were small and curled around his hand. He slid his other hand around her waist.

She stiffened and looked at him. Stephen led her along the floor. "Have you never waltzed before?"

She shook her head. "I'm afraid I spent the last two years studying rather than dancing."

"It is a fairly easy dance. I will lead and you follow."

She nodded and bit her lip.

Stephen guided her, moving slowly, placing a small amount of pressure on her waist to turn her.

After a minute, she was moving as if she had always known how to dance.

Stephen found himself relaxing. Patrick was right. It *had* been a while since he had danced with a woman. It felt . . . good. "You're a natural."

She laughed—a strong, throaty laugh. "And you are a good teacher."

They made another round before Stephen spoke again. "I feel like I know you from somewhere. What is your name?" Blast it, where were his manners? He should have asked her before they started dancing. Come to think of it, he should have told her *his* name.

Her smile dropped from her face and she glanced away. "Kathryn. Kathryn Bloodmayne."

Bloodmayne . . . Bloodmayne . . .

It all came back. That first day at the Tower Academy two years ago. He was still on the force, overseeing the crowd. She was the girl who had fallen during a demonstration that morning. And there had been something else, too. Fire. Some sort of blaze had started across the pavement, and she had put it out with her hands. What a strange thing to remember now.

Kathryn Bloodmayne.

She had filled out since then, no longer a schoolgirl, but now a young woman. And if he remembered correctly, she used to be the charge of his Aunt Milly. He realized he had been silent too long. "I believe we met, briefly, a couple of years ago."

Her gaze flickered to his, then away, her body stiff under his hand. "We did?"

"On your first day at the academy."

Her brows furrowed and he could almost see her thoughts racing through her mind. Then her eyes went wide and she looked up at him. "I thought you looked familiar. You were one of the policemen. Stephen . . ."

"Stephen Grey."

Kathryn didn't react to his name. She must not have read the *Herald* much during her school days, or else she would have. The *Herald* just loved it when he made a particularly difficult catch. Stephen Grey, famous World City bounty hunter. It was kind of refreshing not to be known.

Her eyes narrowed. "I remember you. I heard you were an inspector. Do you still serve on the force?"

It was his turn to look away uncomfortably. No, she didn't seem to know anything.

"I'm sorry, did I say something I shouldn't have?"

His hand tightened across her waist and he watched a couple swing by. "Just something from my past. No, I no longer serve on the force." Time to change the subject. He looked back. "You're Dr. Bloodmayne's daughter, correct?"

Her lips tightened. "Yes."

Strange. Perhaps things were tense between her and her father. "I've heard good things about Dr. Bloodmayne."

Her face blanched and her lips tightened even more.

Their dancing was smooth, but he felt like he was mentally stepping on her toes, and vice versa. Stephen let out his breath. "Perhaps we should just dance."

Kathryn nodded, the color seeping back into her cheeks. "Yes, that would be good."

As he led her around the room, his hand resting across the narrowest part of her waist, every few seconds he caught her flowery scent. Her hair was thick and dark and pulled back in a pile of curls. Her skin reminded him of a porcelain doll, her lips full and pink, chocolate colored eyes beneath full lashes.

For one heady moment he forgot everything but the feel of a woman in his arms.

Kathryn looked up at him and her eyes darkened. Her lips opened slightly. Color tinted her cheeks. Such a look of innocence. She probably had no idea the effect she had on him right now, the first time a woman had stirred him since Vaness—

Blazes!

Stephen stiffened and the moment vanished. Would Vanessa forever haunt him?

When the song wound down, Stephen led Kathryn to the side of the room and let go of her hand. He gave her a short bow. "Thank you for the dance, Miss Bloodmayne."

She frowned and clasped her hands in front of her chest. "Is something wrong?"

"I'm afraid one dance is all I am capable of this evening."

He turned before she could say anything more and headed for the exit. He had been wrong. He never should have come.

Patrick gave him a quizzical look as he walked by, but Stephen ignored him and passed the crowds of people lined around the edges of the ballroom. The music started up again behind him. He reached the doorway and slowed. Against his better judgment, he looked back.

Kathryn stood against the opposite wall, her eyes on him, her hands still clasped in front of her.

For one dance she had made him forget his past and remember what it was like to be a normal man.

But he wasn't a normal man.

Stephen stuffed his hands into his overcoat and hurried down the hall toward the door.

He was a broken man.

And what woman would want a man like that?

12

Kat watched Stephen leave the room, her mind in turmoil. Did he remember the fire from that first morning two years ago? No, he hadn't seen it. Had he?

Someone touched her arm. She jumped and looked over.

Marianne stood beside her, peering across the room. "What are you looking at?"

"Nothing."

Marianne glanced at her with one brow quirked. "I saw you dancing with Stephen Grey. *The* Stephen Grey. He hasn't been seen in society in over a year."

Kat looked over at her friend. "*The* Stephen Grey?"

"World City bounty hunter."

Her jaw dropped. "He's a bounty hunter now?"

"The best. He left the police force about two years ago and went into business for himself."

"How do you know all of this? Wait—your father."

Marianne giggled. "That, and I read about it in the *Herald*."

Kat shook her head. "So why did he leave the force?"

Marianne fanned her face and shrugged. "I don't know. But I did hear he broke off his engagement to Vanessa Wutherington shortly after."

Kat looked back at the door, thinking of how cold he'd become when she'd mentioned the force. She had a feeling there was a story there.

The rest of the night passed in a blur. More young men came to claim her hand, but Kat could only think about her first dance. She could not connect the brittle man from the balcony—then the attentive man on the dance floor—with her idea of a bounty hunter. In her mind, bounty hunters were cold and ruthless. Mr. Grey had been a bit abrupt on the balcony, true, but not like that.

By midnight, Kat was ready to leave. Her feet ached, and she longed to loosen the corset around her waist.

She sat down in one of the chairs lining the wall and let out her breath. Music played and people twirled around on the floor. Marianne went by with one of the young men from the Tower.

Kat frowned. Wait. Ash blond hair, straight, narrow nose, high cheekbones, and light blue eyes.

Blaylock Sterling.

Kat sat up and watched her friend. What was Marianne doing with Blaylock?

She did not seem happy. She pulled away from Blaylock and attempted to leave the floor, but Blaylock grabbed her hand and jerked her back, whispering something to her. She flushed and looked around.

Kat scooted to the edge of her seat. The more she watched them dance, the more she was convinced that Marianne was not a willing partner. She glanced around. No one seemed to notice, and it looked like Marianne's father had left.

For a moment she wished Stephen were here. Even bounty hunters helped people, right?

Marianne flew by with Blaylock, her face a mask of misery.

Kat clenched her teeth and her fingers began to tingle. She pulled back. *I can't lose it.*

But what about Marianne? *I have to help her.*

Kat stood just as the music ended.

Marianne tore away from Blaylock and walked stiffly across the floor toward the refreshment table. Laughing, Blaylock turned away and headed toward a group of young women on the other side.

Kat hurried toward her friend. She touched Marianne's arm, and Marianne flinched. "Are you all right?"

"Yes. No." Marianne looked away. Her face was even more pale than usual, save for two bright spots along her cheeks. "I . . . I just want to go." She glanced back at Kat. "Do you think we can leave? Father already left but sent the coachman back for me. He should be here by now. Will you leave with me?"

Kat nodded. "I was ready to leave a half hour ago. I would be more than happy to escort you down to the carriages."

Marianne nodded and Kat caught a glimpse of unshed tears in her friend's eyes. Kat's hands tightened into two fists. The monster inside her stirred. Marianne was rarely discomposed. What had Blaylock said to her?

Kat led the way across the room, her head high, her back stiff. She caught Blaylock looking in her direction, but she ignored him. Instead, she looped her arm through Marianne's and they walked out the door.

Down the hall they went, the perfume from the ballroom clinging to their gowns. The walls were covered in crimson wallpaper and the gaslights in the hallway were dim. Kat caught a glimpse of one of the portraits and stopped.

The man stood beside a white horse with a severe expression on his face. He held a long-barreled musket between both hands. But it was the bottom half of the picture that stopped her. He stood on a pile of dead bodies.

Kat took a step back and held a hand to her mouth. "Ugh, who would paint such a gruesome portrait?"

Marianne shook her head. "I don't know, but I want to get out of here."

They continued down the hall, passing more paintings, though none as gruesome as the first one. Finally Kat slowed and looked back. "I don't think this is the right way."

Marianne gave her a hurried nod. "I think you're right. I don't remember any of these pictures."

Kat looked down the hall, then back again. "Let's head back."

A small group appeared in the doorway to the ballroom. Kat stepped forward and opened her mouth to ask for directions.

Then her mouth snapped shut and her stomach plummeted.

Blaylock Sterling and his gang.

"Cogglesfoot," Marianne whispered.

Blaylock looked their way and smiled. Slowly the men started down the hallway while the last young man shut the door to the ballroom.

Marianne stepped closer to Kat and took her hand. Her palm was sweaty.

Kat lifted her chin, though inside her heart was hammering like the cogs inside a watch. "Mr. Sterling, would you be so kind as to direct us to the exit?"

Blaylock stopped a couple of feet away and smirked at her. "You know, I didn't get a chance to dance with you tonight."

Kat let out a small breath. "Yes, I'm afraid that's true. And seeing as how we are now leaving, I'm afraid it will have to remain that way. Now, could you point us to the correct door?"

His smile widened and his comrades drew closer, blocking any way back to the ballroom.

Marianne squeezed Kat's hand. Kat swallowed the lump in her throat.

"I don't think so, Miss *Bloodmayne*."

The blood drained from Kat's face.

Blaylock stepped closer. "I always wondered what it would be like to kiss a smart girl."

Kat pulled Marianne behind her and let go of her friend's hand. Her fingers began to tingle and the blood whooshed inside her veins. "I think you've had too much to drink, Mr. Sterling. There will be no kissing tonight."

He closed the space between them and leaned in. His breath held the sweet scent of wine. "And I think you're wrong. But"—he leaned back—"if you don't want to, then I'm sure Miss Fealy will oblige." Blaylock grabbed Marianne and pulled her away from Kat, shoving her against the wall and blocking her from Kat's sight.

Marianne let out a muffled scream, and the young men with Blaylock laughed.

Time went still. All Kat could see was Blaylock forcing Marianne against the wall in a haze of red, and hear her friend's cries.

Something snapped inside her.

A wind came rushing from deep within her chest, exploding along her spine and through her hands, whipping her curls around her face.

The young men looked at Kat and backed away. Their faces paled in the dim light, and their eyes widened.

"Blaylock . . . " one of them said.

Marianne yelled.

Kat thrust her hands out. She could feel every particle in the room. With a snap of her wrists, she shoved the invisible particles near Blaylock's cronies to the side. The young men went flying against the walls and hung there, pinned by an unseen force.

Blaylock straightened and looked around.

Kat's hair came completely loose from the comb and flew around her face in a dark cloud. Her gown whipped around her body. Every hair stood on end, every nerve attuned to the rush of her blood and the monster roaring inside her.

Blaylock stumbled away from Marianne, his hands up to shield his face. "What the *blazes?*"

Somewhere Kat heard herself laughing.

Yes. Blazes. Lots of them.

She imagined the particles around the hall combusting.

Tiny sparks appeared along the carpet and up the walls.

Kat laughed again and raised her hands. For too long she had been waiting to do this, to set the world on fire!

Every particle burst into flame.

The men screamed as they struggled against the wall where they were pinned. When the carpet caught on fire beneath them, they brought their legs up and cried out.

Blaylock backed away down the hall where the flames hadn't reached, his hands up, his eyes as wide as two coins. "What *are* you?" he shouted.

"Kat!"

Kat turned and saw Marianne cowering against the opposite wall.

"What—what are you doing?"

The fire dimmed beneath the men against the wall.

The cold lump beat inside her chest, the same place the wind had come from moments earlier. *No, I shouldn't be doing this.* She lowered her hands. *This isn't me.*

"You monster!"

Kat turned to find Blaylock rushing her. She raised her hands and the carpet between them caught on fire.

Blaylock stopped before the wall of flames. His face was livid as he pointed a finger at her. "I always knew there was something wrong with you. Too pretty for a smart girl. There will be nothing left of you once I tell the authorities. They will take you to the Tower and dissect you, you little monst—"

To Kat his rant seemed like the buzz of a fly: annoying and futile. She snapped her wrists and blasted Blaylock against the wall. His buddies cried and shouted behind her, but she ignored them. Marianne whimpered nearby.

She never wanted to see Blaylock's face again.

The fiery wall between them began to move toward Blaylock like red fingers reaching across the carpet.

Closer. Closer.

Black spots filled her vision. Kat slumped against the wall and her hands fell to her side. She couldn't ... breathe. The cold lump inside her expanded across her entire body, engulfing her in a deep chill.

A man screamed nearby.

Kat fell to the ground. The last thing she saw were the flames as the rest of the hallway caught on fire.

13

"Wake up, Kat."

Someone shook her shoulders.

"Wake up, now!"

Kat blinked her eyes.

Ms. Stuart's face appeared above her.

"Ms. Stuart? Where am I? What happened—oh!" She pressed her hand against her heart. Her chest felt like it had turned to lead and then someone had taken a hammer to it. She rubbed the area and breathed faster.

She couldn't feel her skin.

She sat up and rubbed some more. "I can't—I can't feel anything!" She reached inside her dress with shaky fingers and felt beneath her collarbone. Her skin was smooth beneath her fingertips, but the entire area around her heart was numb.

She looked up, her breath coming in short pants. "Ms. Stuart, something is wrong!" Had something happened to her heart? Or her soul? That's where her soul was located, right?

Ms. Stuart shook her head. "No time! We need to get you out of here. Can you stand?"

Kat scrunched up her face. "I think so . . ." She pushed against the bed and stood up. A tingling sensation rushed through her chest, like the way her fingers would prickle after being out in the cold.

She looked around. She was in her room back home. The same familiar canopy bed covered in an ivory coverlet, a dark wardrobe in the corner, and the painting of a woman by a lake beside the door.

"What happened? How did I get here?"

Ms. Stuart paused and looked at her. "You don't remember?"

"No." She brushed her temple with her fingers. "Just flashes. There was the gala . . . Marianne and I were trying to leave . . . but we couldn't—"

Blaylock pinning Marianne. Her friend screaming. Throwing the men against the wall. And then fire. Lots of fire.

Kat's eyes went wide and her stomach clenched so hard that she thought she was going to retch. "Did I . . ." She took a dizzy step back toward the bed. "Did I . . ." She held one hand to her mouth, the other to her stomach. "Did I lose control?"

Ms. Stuart said nothing, only pulled out an old carpetbag and hurried over to Kat's wardrobe.

Kat collapsed beside her bed and clutched the coverlet. The room spun around and around until she finally closed her eyes and laid her head on the side of the bed.

Fire. Everywhere.

Her mouth went dry and her stomach heaved again.

It had finally happened.

There was a bang and Kat looked up. Ms. Stuart stuffed clothes into the carpetbag. "We don't have much time, Kat. You need to get out of here."

"Did I hurt anybody?"

Ms. Stuart's lip straightened into a thin line.

"Did I—did I kill someone?" Her voice shrilled.

Ms. Stuart looked grave, but she shook her head. "Nobody died that I know of. Everyone was rescued from the fire, but a couple of people were burned. One young man in particular was burned severely."

Kat closed her eyes. "How can I live with myself? How can I stop this?" She turned away and stared across the bed, the coverlet clutched in two tight fists. "He's right. I am a monster! I am a horrifying, wicked, vile monster!"

She felt Ms. Stuart's arms come around her as the plump woman sank to the floor at her side. Tears filled the older woman's voice. "Oh, my sweet girl. You didn't mean to hurt anyone."

Kat shook her head. "It doesn't matter. It will happen again, and then someone *will* die." She covered her face, her voice thick, her face hot and wet. "I don't deserve to live anymore. I should go to the bridge and end it."

"No!" Ms. Stuart shook her so hard her teeth clacked together. "We will find a cure. We will find that doctor and you will be normal again."

"But how long will that take? And what if Dr. Latimer can't cure me? I don't think we can afford to take the risk."

"I won't lose you!" Pulling her around so they were face to face, Ms. Stuart squeezed her shoulders hard. "Do you hear me, Kathryn? I won't lose you. We knew something like this might happen, and we had a plan. We are now putting that plan into action. But you will live, and you will find that doctor. No more talk about ending your life, do you understand?"

Kat swallowed and nodded.

"Right now we need to get you out of here." Ms. Stuart hauled herself to her feet and went back to the carpetbag. "I'm going to send you to someone I know, someone who is good at finding people. If anyone can find Dr. Latimer, it's him."

Kat wiped her face. "Who?" She couldn't remember Ms. Stuart ever mentioning someone.

"My nephew."

Her nephew? Wait. She remembered Ms. Stuart mentioning him a couple of times over the years. His parents died when he was sixteen and she paid for him to go to school somewhere.

Someone pounded on the front door downstairs.

Ms. Stuart looked up, her eyes wide. She thrust the carpetbag into Kat's arms. "Take this and go, now!"

Kat stood on shaky legs. "Are you expecting someone?"

"The police, the military. Perhaps your father."

"My father?"

Ms. Stuart's nostrils flared as someone continued to pound on the door. "Of course your father. Once he finds out what you did, he will want to know why and how. And you know what that would mean."

Kat nodded and backed away. He would do everything in his power to find out how she had set the hall on fire. Including—she clutched her neck—dissection.

"I will detain whoever is here, if they are here for you."

"But where am I going?"

"Fifty-Seven Samford Street."

"And his name?"

"Stephen Grey."

"Stephen Grey? Wait, I know h—"

Ms. Stuart pushed her out into the hallway. "You can trust my nephew. He is a good man and will help you."

Kat looked back. "Should I tell him?"

Ms. Stuart shook her head. "No. Tell no one what you can do until you find Dr. Latimer. Especially your father. Your father must never know. Now go!"

There was a loud crack and men's voices in the hall downstairs. Ms. Stuart turned. She straightened her gown and headed down the hallway toward the front door.

"Ms. Stuart!"

Ms. Stuart ignored her and disappeared down the stairs.

Kat watched her go, her throat tight. Would she ever see Ms. Stuart again? Would life ever be normal?

Loud voices below brought her back to the moment. Kat clutched the carpetbag to her chest and hurried down the dark hall to the back of the house. Stephen Grey. The man she had danced with last night. The bounty hunter. He was Ms. Stuart's nephew? Had Ms. Stuart mentioned his name before? She shook her head. She couldn't remember.

Ms. Stuart had left the gaslights off in the hallway, but Kat knew these halls well enough in the dark. She flew by paintings of previous Bloodmaynes: her grandfather, her great-grandfather. Men of scientific renown. Even the women in her family had contributed to science, paving the way until the Tower finally opened its doors to women.

Then there was her mother.

Kat rushed past that last picture, but she knew it by heart. Her mother leaning on a deep red settee with Cricket, the mechanical songbird she had created, perched on her shoulder. Her rich, dark hair pulled back, her skin perfect. A soft smile on her face, like she was content with the world.

Shouts erupted behind her and Kat glanced back and slowed to a stop. Her heart pounded inside her ribcage. Should she go back? If something happened to Ms. Stuart—

If you father finds out, you know what that would mean.
You must live, Kathryn.

Ms. Stuart would never forgive her if she turned back.

But could she forgive herself if she didn't?

Kat turned and reached the end of the hall. She leaned against the doorway and panted. No, she would do as Ms. Stuart had instructed. She would leave and find Ms. Stuart's nephew. She would find Stephen Grey.

With that in mind, Kat scurried down the stairs to the kitchen. The shouting grew dim.

She fought the urge to turn back and instead ran through the kitchen, the moonlight streaming in through one of the windows her only source of light.

She reached the door and turned the knob just as a bang rang out across the house. A wave of dizziness rushed across her body. Ms. Stuart!

Kat wrenched the door open and stumbled outside. The air was damp and cold, almost paralyzing her already shaking fingers. She fumbled with the cold metal of the gate latch, glancing back. No one. She couldn't hear the shouts anymore either.

The gate creaked open. She bit back the sob inside her throat and wiped her eyes. Fog filled the alleyway and the gas lamps on the corner created an ominous light.

She reached the corner and paused, her breath coming in hot, wispy pants. She looked right, then left, her mind blank. All she could think about was Ms. Stuart and that shot.

Kat, get a hold of yourself. You need to keep moving. She looked around again. *But where do I go?*

She tried to remember the layout of World City, but nothing came to mind except images of Ms. Stuart back at the house.

Did people know already? Was Ms. Stuart right? Would the police be after her because of the fire? Would her father come after her?

Breathe, Kat, breathe. Right now, you need to get away.

She held the carpetbag close to her chest. Left. Left would lead her to Samford Street. But she would need to take it slow and use the side streets. No proper woman would be out at this time at night, at least not without an escort. And she would need to find a place to change. She couldn't arrive at Stephen's office in her evening gown.

The damp night air seeped into her dress and hair until dark curls formed around her face. Her teeth began to chatter, and she could barely feel her toes inside her shoes. She gripped the carpetbag with numb fingers and pushed onward. She would walk all night if she had to, and she probably would. Samford Street was quite a way away.

A tear trickled down her cheek, leaving her skin cold and wet. Would Stephen Grey help her? What if he found out what she could do?

Why, *why* did she have to be born this way?

She blew her breath out her mouth and straightened her shoulders. This was no time for self-pity. She couldn't change the past, or who she was. She could only change her future. And Ms. Stuart had provided a way. If Stephen Grey couldn't help her, she would continue on her own until she found Dr. Latimer and a cure for whatever this was inside.

Nothing would stop her. Nothing, except death.

14

Dr. Bloodmayne stood beside one of the marble pillars that circled the main room in the Capitol building. A dome of glass let in natural light two stories above. The early rays of dawn painted the white marble floor in a myriad of colors.

Long, narrow windows bordered the octagonal room and opened to a garden full of lush greens and bright flowers outside. Here and there among the pillars, high back chairs and small tables provided semi-private meeting space for the various political lackeys serving in World City's government.

At the moment, the room was empty except for councilman William Sterling, who stood against another marble pillar a couple of feet away, his arms folded. Sterling was a few years older than Bloodmayne and from one of the oldest and richest families in World City.

Sterling's icy stare bore down on him. Dr. Bloodmayne ignored the aristocrat and watched a shadow pass across the floor as an airship traversed the sky overhead.

Both men looked up when a brass-colored automaton came rolling in through the double doors, carrying a tray of teaware between a set of clamp-like fingers. The automaton was made from three different sized brass globes, the bottom globe the largest and by which it moved by rolling. The other two served as the midsection and the head. Two oversized green lenses gazed around the room.

Dr. Bloomayne stiffened and took a step back, his mouth dry. The automaton had a whimsical look to it, similar to the life-like contraptions his wife had invented before . . .

The automaton couldn't possibly be hers, could it?

No, he'd had all of her inventions destroyed except Cricket. He couldn't part with her bird, although he kept it in the dining room back home, one of the rooms he rarely used after Helen died.

The automation rolled toward one of the tables with a series of clicks and whirrs. It gently placed the tray down and started pouring cups of tea.

Dr. Bloodmayne turned away from the automaton and watched the door. Seconds later John Ashdown, head councilman, came in trailed by three men dressed in black. Ashdown stood a head taller than most men and wore a robe the color of amaranthine over his dress clothes. His black hair was pulled back in a tie, revealing long, jagged scars along his jaw, just below his neatly trimmed beard. He gave both Sterling and Bloodmayne a firm nod.

Dr. Bloodmayne crossed his arms and scowled at the men behind Ashdown. They were the ones who had broken into his home last night. He clenched his teeth. Ashdown was a fool. He should have known better than to send those thugs to retrieve Kathryn. Between them they had less tact than an airship sailor on leave. Now Bloodmayne had a dead housekeeper on his hands, and his daughter was missing.

One of the men glanced in his direction and flinched. Good. They should fear him. If he had his way, they would be hauled to the Tower and strapped to a table inside his private laboratory. He would probably get more use out of them that way. Unfortunately, they were not his to use.

"Gentlemen." Ashdown gestured for Bloodmayne and Sterling to sit, which they did, albeit as far from each other as they could manage at the small table. Ashdown continued, "I apologize for the early hour of this meeting, but, as you both know, circumstances have arisen that need to be addressed as soon as possible."

Dr. Bloodmayne let out a quiet cough, though his anger ratcheted up a notch. "Perhaps this little talk should have occurred last night when I informed you of what happened at the gala. *Before* you sent your goons after my daughter."

Ashdown frowned. "I did what I thought was best at the time. Your daughter is a danger to society."

"She was the one link we had to discovering the power of matter. If you hadn't sent those fools to break down my door, I could have reasoned with her." His fists clenched. "Instead, you bumbled into my home, shot my housekeeper, and terrified my daughter, who has now vanished!"

Sterling rounded on him. "And what about my son, Blaylock? Your daughter burned him! Even if he lives, he will be scarred for life!"

Dr. Bloodmayne sniffed and sat back. "Come now, Sterling. Blaylock is not your heir, so don't act so heartbroken over the boy. He was slated to become one of my apprentices. I will still take him. I might even be able to heal some of the burnt tissue. He can live at the Tower, and you never need to bring him out into society again."

Sterling worked his jaw. "He could have been much more if your daughter hadn't lit him on fire."

Dr. Bloodmayne sneered. "We both know your son is a cad and a scoundrel. I know you've hushed things up. The parlor maid on your country estate . . . the third-floor cleaning girl at the Tower . . . You're far better off having him locked away where he can cause no further embarrassment. Leave Blaylock to me, Sterling."

Sterling blanched and glanced at Ashdown. "I will think about it," he muttered. "But that doesn't negate what your daughter did."

Dr. Bloodmayne dismissed him with a wave of his hand. "In the end, it doesn't matter. You underestimate the value of my daughter. Comparatively, she is priceless. She is the embodiment of what we have been trying to do for years: unlock the power of the universe itself. And now"—he looked at Ashdown and the men beside him coldly—"she is gone."

Ashdown folded his arms. "Yes, things should have been handled differently. But what is done is done, and we need to figure out what to do next."

Dr. Bloodmayne breathed in through his nose and let the air out slowly. "You're right. The most important thing now is finding Kathryn."

Ashdown nodded. "I suggest we put the World City investigators on this case."

He shook his head. "Not enough. I want the best looking for her. Men who will do anything to find their quarry. I suggest we put a warrant out for her and let the bounty hunters bring her in."

Sterling jerked up. "You would send bounty hunters after your own daughter?"

"Set the amount high enough with a no-harm stipulation, and she will be found and brought back alive. And I need her alive. I need to find out how she set that fire—and any other abilities she possesses—and if we can replicate them. She is what we've been trying to create for years. She holds the key."

"Then bounty hunters it is." Ashdown rubbed his lower jaw. "We might have to twist a couple of the facts from last night in order to secure a high priced warrant. Murder is the only crime that would allow for such a bounty."

Dr Bloodmayne nodded. "We can compensate the families involved and maybe urge them to send their sons out to the country. Or maybe to the frontlines. Then we spread word that the young men died."

"Yes, that would work. I will have the bounty hunters coordinate with the investigators. Between the two groups we should be able to locate Miss Bloodmayne and bring her back for your examination."

Dr. Bloodmayne bowed his head. "Thank you, head councilman. That is all I want: my daughter back unharmed. Now, if you'll excuse me, I have research to attend to." He straightened, ignoring the brass automaton that sat beside the still steaming teacups. "And if you have no more need for the gentlemen behind you, I will be happy to employ them myself. I need graves dug and fresh corpses brought to my labs."

The three men shifted from foot to foot, and none of them looked toward Dr. Bloodmayne.

Ashdown waved his hand. "They are yours. Do with them as you please."

Dr. Bloodmayne smiled. "I will."

15

With the barest hints of sunlight trickling through the window, Stephen peered into the mirror that hung above the small table inside his bedroom. A haggard man with bloodshot eyes and a stubble-covered jaw and chin stared back. He rubbed his face and turned away.

He could handle late night hunts and information gathering, but not parties. Especially not ones with women who reminded him of Vanessa. Dancing with that young woman from the academy—Miss Bloodmayne—had brought back old nightmares.

Stephen shook his head. Never again.

He crossed the room, bypassing his bed—already made and pulled his clothes from the wardrobe, dressed, and finished his personal hygiene.

Another glance in the mirror minutes later confirmed the broken man from last night was gone, replaced with the cold, hard bounty hunter he had become. This man he liked better. This man could not be hurt.

He pulled on his leather duster and hat, pulling the brim over his forehead, and left his flat.

The narrow streets of World City were already bustling with life as the sun made its way into the sky. Smoke drifted through the alleyways. Women hung laundry from second-story windows, and children ran along the streets. Men left their flats, most of them dressed in the dull gray uniforms of the factories.

A few people glanced at him and nodded. He nodded back, tipping his hat to a couple of the ladies. These were his people, the working class. Those high up in World City cared little for the men and women they used in their industries and sweat factories, and the police took their cue from the men holding the public purse strings. So it fell to men like him to keep them safe.

After twenty minutes, he reached Samford Street and went right. A three-story brick building occupied the length of the block. Long, narrow windows framed in white lined the upper stories, while the first floor offered only a single door halfway down the otherwise unbroken length of red brick.

Stephen approached the door and stepped inside.

Gaslights hummed along the hallway and voices echoed from the offices that lined either side. A faint scent of mildew and smoke hung in the air, and the wooden floor was worn smooth down the middle.

Stephen followed the hallway to the back of the building and up the wide staircase to the second floor. Three doors down to the left was a door with words painted in white: *Stephen Grey, Fugitive Recovery Agent.*

He grinned at the words as he opened the door. Jerod, his assistant and case manager, had insisted on the title. He said 'bounty hunter' conveyed a darker picture, but it came down to the same thing: catching criminals for cash.

Jerod sat behind his desk, a pile of papers already waiting for his attention. His tawny hair hung across his forehead, and his glasses had begun a slow descent down his long nose. His eyes darted back and forth, intent on whatever he was reading.

"Mornin', Jerod."

Jerod looked up and pushed on the bridge of his glasses. "Good morning, Stephen." He rolled up the newspaper and frowned. "Rough evening?"

"You could say that." Stephen fished out a small tin from his coat pocket. "Peppermint?"

Jerod raised one eyebrow. "No, thank you."

Stephen popped off the lid and took out one of the small, round white candies. His eye caught the newspaper at the edge of the desk. "Mind if I look at today's *Herald*?"

Jerod waved at him, then gathered up his documents and began reading again.

Stephen grabbed the newspaper and headed toward his office. All he wanted to do was sit back and read for the rest of the morning. He pushed open the door to his office.

Jerod shouted behind him. "Wait, you have a client!"

Stephen paused inside his doorway.

A woman sat on the edge of the couch against the left wall. He could hardly see her in the dim light seeping in through the window behind his desk.

His heart stopped. Vanessa.

She looked at him, her face veiled in shadows. No, not Vanessa. Still, a bitter taste filled his mouth.

Jerod came to the doorway. "Miss Bloodmayne arrived early this morning. She was waiting at the door when I arrived."

Bloodmayne? He did a double take at the woman on his couch. Kathryn Bloodmayne? The woman from the gala last night?

"She said it was urgent." Jerod lowered his voice. "She appeared frazzled, and kept looking over her shoulder. I couldn't leave her out in the hallway."

Stephen nodded, his brain still frozen.

"Well, then. I'll leave you two be." Jerod backed away and Stephen heard his chair scrape across the wooden floor as he returned to his desk.

He could see her face now: those porcelain features, her rich, dark hair piled on her head, though on closer inspection, a bit disheveled. And deep, beautiful eyes.

A feeling stirred inside his chest.

Stephen clamped down on the sentiment and scowled. He walked past Kathryn without looking at her. He didn't want her drama. He just wanted to read his newspaper and hide in his office. He dropped the paper on his desk. "Why are you here?"

Her chin rose a fraction. "I was told you could help me. But perhaps I was mistaken." She reached for the carpetbag that sat beside the couch.

Blazes! Why'd he do that? "Wait, Miss Bloodmayne—"

She paused, her hand on the carpetbag. "What, Mr. Grey?"

He rubbed the back of his neck. "I apologize."

"You seem to do a lot of that."

Not before last night. He stared out the window beyond his desk, at the thickening clouds and the cityscape of brick buildings, smokestacks, and airships traveling through the hazy morning air.

This was not how he wanted to spend today, with a woman who reminded him of Vanessa.

His gut clenched, almost taking his breath away. He closed his eyes. *She's not Vanessa; she's just another client. The sooner you do business with her, the sooner she will leave and you can go on with your life.* He took a deep breath and nodded. *I can do this.*

"I'm sorry about that." He faced her and straightened his jacket. "I had a tough job this week, and it's left me out of sorts." That was partially true. Bringing Victor in hadn't been easy.

She tilted her head. "A job?"

He paused. "You do know what I do, right?"

"You find people."

Stephen smirked. "Something like that. So, Miss Bloodmayne, what brings you to my office? Hard night after the gala? Have a beau you need me to chase down?"

"No. Nothing like that."

He studied her face and abruptly regretted his flippancy. There were dark circles under her eyes, and her hands shook across her lap. She quickly folded them.

"Does your father know you're here?"

She looked up and her face went cold. "No. And it must stay that way."

Interesting.

Stephen walked across the room and shut the door. "Don't worry, I keep all my private cases confidential." He went back to his desk and sat down in a wooden chair near the window. He placed the newspaper beside a stack of paperwork awaiting his review and signature. At least Miss Bloodmayne was keeping him from that odious job.

He folded his hands and laid them across the desk. "My work generally involves finding criminals. I'm guessing the person you seek is no felon, so who am I finding for you? A relative? A tenant delinquent on his rent?

"No. A doctor."

Stephen sat back, forcing down a laugh. "A doctor? I'm sorry, Miss Bloodmayne, but I'm not a private investigator. You would be better off taking your case to one of them. In fact, I can recommend a good one."

"Your aunt said I could trust you."

That shut him down. Stephen carefully refolded his fingers. "My aunt?"

"Millicent Stuart. She is our housekeeper."

Stephen narrowed his eyes and tugged at the bit of hair beneath his lips. There was more. His aunt would not send her charge to him just to find a doctor. Unless . . .

Miss Bloodmayne fidgeted on the couch. "So will you help me?"

He sat rigid in his chair. "Like I said, I catch criminals. So unless your doctor is a wanted man, I'm afraid you've come to the wrong office."

Miss Bloodmayne opened her handbag. "If it's an issue of money, I can pay. In fact, I'll pay up front."

"It's not about money."

She looked up, her eyes wide. "Please, Inspector Grey—"

"Mr. Grey."

"Mr. Grey." She took a deep breath. "I have no one else I can turn to, no one else I can trust."

"Why can't you go to your father?"

Her gaze darted toward the other side of the room. "Let's just say I don't think my father would want me to find this doctor."

Stephen gritted his teeth. "Is this doctor some secret lover?"

Her head swung back and color blossomed across her cheeks. "What? No! I—that is—I need help. And only he can help me."

"And you don't know where he is?"

"No, I only have a name."

Stephen tugged at the bit of hair again. "What is so special about this doctor?"

She dropped her gaze. "I have a . . . condition. One that he might be able to help me with."

"And your scientist father can't help you?"

"No." The word came out firm and hard, leaving no room for questions, although it raised many in his mind.

"But my aunt knows about this condition?" Wait, was Miss Bloodmayne with child? Stephen went cold.

"Yes, she knows. That is why she sent me to you. She said if anyone could help me, you could."

Stephen shook his head and stood. "I'm sorry, but I'm not in the business of helping young women with 'conditions.'" Why would Aunt Milly send Miss Bloodmayne to him if that were her problem? Aunt Milly would have sent her to the country.

"What?" Then Miss Bloodmayne's mouth dropped open as realization dawned across her face. "Wait, Mr. Grey. It's . . . it's not that." Her face turned so red he could see it in the shadows.

"Then what is it? I don't have time for games, Miss Bloodmayne."

"Fine." She stood. "It seems Ms. Stuart—your aunt—was wrong. I don't think you can help me." She grabbed her carpetbag and headed for the door.

"Wait!"

"No. I can see myself out."

Stephen raced across the room and reached the door the same moment Miss Bloodmayne did. Their hands touched as they both reached for the doorknob. She looked up and his heart stopped. This young woman wasn't anything like Vanessa. Petite, young, innocent. And scared. He could see it in her eyes.

She didn't deserve his rancor.

"I'll do it." The words flew from his mouth before he could stop them.

Her eyes narrowed. "You'll do what?"

"I'll help you."

"I don't thin—"

He pulled her hand back from the doorknob. He was between jobs at the moment. The payment from Victor's capture would see him through for a month. "I owe my aunt a lot. I can do this one thing for her. As long as . . ."

"As long as what?"

Stephen swallowed. Was he being a fool? Where was the hard, cold bounty hunter he hid behind? "As long as you're not with child."

"It is highly improper to talk to a man about—"

"I left propriety behind when I became a bounty hunter. If we're going to work together, I need you to be honest with me."

She swallowed. "No, I'm not with child. But I need to find this doctor soon."

"I will get onto it today. His name?"

Miss Bloodmayne drew her hand back. "Dr. Joshua Latimer. He was part of the Tower ten years ago, but has since disappeared."

Stephen shook his head. "Never heard of him. Do you have a rough idea where he might be?"

"I don't. I've read some of his articles. That's how I found out about him."

"I have some contacts I can start with. How do I reach you when I know more?"

Miss Bloodmayne turned back toward the door. "You don't. I will contact you in three days. Will that be enough?"

"I should have something by then."

Her face softened and she let out a long sigh. "Thank you, Mr. Grey."

"Stephen."

She gave him a quizzical look.

"Call me by my first name."

"That is highly improper."

He raised one eyebrow.

"Very well, Mr. . . . er . . . Stephen. And if this is how we are going to work, then call me Kat."

Before he could say anything, Kat pulled the door open and strode across the reception area, leaving a hint of lavender in her wake.

Jerod held the office door open for her, smiling like an idiot.

Stephen went back to his desk. *This is business, strictly business.* But Kat had woken something inside him, something he had closed off for a very long time.

And it scared him.

16

Stephen pulled the collar of his duster up against his throat and barreled into the rain outside. The water whipped across his face and knuckles, seeking ways inside his coat and hat. Between the rain and the biting wind, it felt more like March than May.

He hurried down the block and turned left. No one was out this morning, not even the street peddlers. He rarely saw the streets this empty, like a ghost town he once read about in a penny novel. With the wisps of fog drifting from the river nearby and the rain, he could almost imagine a ghost floating around the corner.

He shuddered and pushed those morbid thoughts aside.

Jimmy had been a dead end. And Miss Bloodmayne—Kat—would be here in two days. There were a couple more men he could contact, but Harvey was way down south, almost near the coast. And Captain Grim might be in port here, or in Covenshire, which was a half-day's train ride away. Harvey specialized in the comings and goings across the Narrow Strait, especially those who didn't want to be followed. Grim knew everything else.

However, Dr. Latimer did not strike him as a shady kind of

man. Then again, if his line of work had taught him anything, it was that everyone had a core of darkness inside him. Perhaps Dr. Latimer was a felon after all.

Stephen reached his office twenty minutes later, soaked through. He sloshed across the hallway and up the stairs. Jerod frowned when he walked in dripping wet, but Stephen ignored him and crossed the reception area to his own office in the back.

He tossed his duster up on a hook and his hat on top. Water pooled beneath the sodden garments. On his desk sat a copy of the *Herald*, still folded. He grabbed the paper and sat down.

Time for a breather. He opened the paper—

Murder in World City

Dr. Alexander Bloodmayne's housekeeper was found murdered inside the Bloodmayne residence. No clues yet as to who the perpetrator is or why the famous Tower scientist's home was targeted. More on Page 3.

He turned to page 3 and gripped the paper tight, hardly able to read the words as he scanned the article.

It couldn't be. Not Aunt Milly.

He read the article twice, then sat back. The paper slipped from his fingers to his desk. Why hadn't he been informed?

There was a knock at his door.

Stephen tilted his head and stared at the door. He couldn't think. Everything inside his mind was a blur.

"Stephen?" Jerod's voice came muffled through the wood.

He opened his mouth, but couldn't form the words.

"Stephen?"

The door opened and Jerod stood in the doorway. Behind him stood two more men, police officers from the look of their olive uniforms.

"Stephen? There are some officers here for you."

He nodded and finally found his voice. "Thank you, Jerod. Come in, gentlemen."

Both men removed their hats and came to stand before his desk.

"I know why you're here." Stephen refolded the newspaper and tossed it into the rubbish bin beside his desk.

"Stephen."

"Patrick."

Patrick stood beside his desk inside the precinct and ran a hand through his hair, leaving it standing on end. "You know I can't give you any details about the investigation of your aunt's death."

"I know."

"Then why are you here?"

Stephen stuffed his hands into the pockets of his duster. "I wanted to look you in the eye and have you tell me you are doing everything you can."

Patrick looked up. "You know I am. But we are overflowing with cases right now. In fact, I wanted to run one by you . . ."

"Not interested. I will be checking my own sources regarding my aunt's death. Until I find out who killed her, I'm not taking any other cases." Except Miss Bloodmayne's. But, then, perhaps the two were connected.

Patrick closed his mouth and seemed to struggle with himself. "But this one makes no sense," he burst out after a moment. "And the accusations . . . A fire was lit inside the building where the gala was held last week. It looks like arson. One of the Sterling family's sons was badly burned—he'll probably be disfigured for the rest of his life."

Stephen held up a hand. "Sorry to hear that, but I'm not interested. If you find out anything about my aunt, you know where to find me."

"But—"

"My aunt is dead, Patrick. The only family I had. Do you really think I care that some spoiled little aristocrat lost his looks?"

Patrick drew back, shock and disappointment furrowing his forehead. "Very well. I'll be in touch when we know something about Ms. Stuart."

Stephen nodded then shoved his hat onto his head.

He'd only gone a couple of steps when Patrick called, "Hey, Stephen?"

He paused with his hand on the doorknob.

"I'm sorry about your aunt."

"I am too." *Now I'm alone.*

Stephen stood beside the grave, his hat in hand. The last two days had been a blur of sound and detached movement. Aunt Milly's minister came and spoke over her body, and the undertaker took care of everything until—at last—she was buried beside his parents, grandparents, and extended family in the local graveyard.

Dr. Bloodmayne had insisted on paying for everything, but Stephen had refused. Aunt Milly had been his only family. It was his duty to take care of her now in death.

A soft drizzle fell across his head and shoulders and the smell of fresh turned soil filled his nostrils. A lump filled his throat. He hadn't seen Aunt Milly in over two years, but she always wrote each month. It was his fault. He should have made time for her. Instead, he had buried himself in work.

Stephen gripped his hat and turned away. He should have done more, spent more time with her. After all, where would he be now if she hadn't taken him in after his parents died? She had done everything for him. And how had he repaid her?

He looked down at the fresh mound, darkened by the rain. A tombstone had been placed at the head, etched with her name and a short epitaph.

"I'm sorry, Aunt Milly." There was only one thing he could do: find her killer.

The World City police were already on the case, but he had what they did not: connections to the underworld. He still couldn't piece together why someone would kill his aunt. The only thing he could think of was that the murderer was after someone else and his aunt had simply gotten in the way. It had to be. Aunt Milly wouldn't have been involved in anything sinister.

However, he could well imagine Dr. Bloodmayne had enemies. No one in power stayed that long without acquiring enemies. And the Tower especially had enemies.

Or maybe—Stephen tugged at his mustache—maybe Kat was the one in danger. He had seen many innocent family members get caught up in street wars in his line of work. Did his aunt die to protect her from some enemy of the Bloodmaynes?

It would explain why her father had looked so concerned at the funeral and why Kat hadn't made an appearance.

However, it had seemed like Kat and her father were not on good terms. Or at least she didn't want him to know about her search for Dr. Latimer. What was that about? And was there a connection between their strained relationship and Aunt Milly's murder?

Stephen pinched the bridge of his nose. He had been on this merry-go-round of thoughts for two days and come up with nothing concrete. And now his head hurt.

He let out a long breath and readjusted his hold on his hat. The minister had already prayed over the grave, but it didn't seem like enough.

It was time he prayed as well.

He tightened his hold on the brim. *God.* He mentally recoiled. He hadn't talked to God ever since that day he found out about Vanessa's indiscretion. Before then, he had faithfully gone to church, prayed, even read the small black Bible his parents left for him.

But his heart had died that day, and he had left faith behind.

Just . . . just watch over Aunt Milly for me.

Stephen crushed his hat onto his head. That was it. That was all he could muster for now.

Something moved among the oak trees near the edge of the cemetery.

Stephen paused, his hand still near his face. There. Next to one of the oaks. The figure was dressed in a dark blue skirt and coat, her hood pulled over her head.

Stephen dropped his hand and made it appear as if he were leaving the graveyard. He followed the path between the graves and green grass toward the iron gate near the church. From the corner of his eye, he watched the trees.

The figure moved again.

He reached the gate and exited, followed the side of the church where he couldn't be seen from the cemetery, and made his way to the tree line where the figure had been moments before.

She was no longer among the trees. Rather, she was now making her way to the gravesite he had just left.

Kathryn Bloodmayne.

Kat looked around, then pulled her hood back. She stood for a moment beside the mound, then fell to her knees in the grass and bowed her head.

A white hot ball formed inside Stephen's middle. Why was Kat here now? If she were still in danger, she would be hiding. To come here meant she was free to come and go. And if that was the case, why didn't she come this morning when everyone else was here?

Was she responsible for his aunt's death?

Stephen emerged silently from the trees and headed for the grave. Kat didn't notice him. A sob escaped her and she bent down to the ground and grabbed a handful of dirt. That only intensified the white ball inside him.

He reached the mound just as she looked up.

Her eyes were puffy and red, and wet trails glistened across her cheeks. She scrambled to her feet and wiped her face, leaving dirt streaks behind. "Mr. Grey?"

"What are you doing here?"

"I—I . . ." She trailed off, looking dazed.

He pointed at the mound "Who did this?"

"I don't know!"

"You know more than you're letting on!"

Her gaze darted to the mound, then back to Stephen. Her lip quivered. "I don't know who k—k—" She looked away.

"Killed Millicent Stuart?"

She looked over her shoulder at him. Her face was tight and pale.

"What are you not telling me, Kat?"

Kat shook her head and took a step back. "I don't know anything. But Ms. Stuart, she suspected something that night. . ."

"What night?"

Kat didn't seem to hear him. "I never should have left her." She pressed her hands to her face. "It's all my fault." A long moan escaped between her fingers.

The ball inside his middle dissipated. Either Kat was a good liar, or she'd had nothing to do with his aunt's death. Stephen rubbed the back of his neck. "Listen, Kat. I want to help you, but you need to tell me what you know. You have to be honest with me."

She drew her hands away from her face. Mud smudged her forehead as well as her cheeks now, and the rain had saturated her hair. "I don't know who" she swallowed "who killed Ms. Stuart." Her voice went quiet. "The night before I came to you, there were people at my home. I don't know who, but Ms. Stuart told me to run."

"Run? Why?"

Kat sucked in her lips and shook her head. "I don't know, other than that Ms. Stuart believed I was in danger. I don't think she thought they would hurt her. She told me to run, so I went out the back and past the yard. All night I made my way through World City to your office. The last thing she told me was to find you and get your help."

"What help? You mean finding that Dr. Latimer?"

"Yes."

"But what does that have to do with her death? Who would want to kill her?"

Kat looked down at her fingers. "Mr. Grey—"

"Stephen."

She let out her breath. "There are things you don't know about my father, things he has done in the name of science."

Stephen's eyes widened. "You think your *father* had something to do with my aunt's murder?" His mind tried to wrap around that fact and failed. Why would Dr. Bloodmayne kill his own housekeeper? Unless . . .

It was to silence her.

He clenched his hands and his nostrils flared. *Slow down, Grey. You're jumping to conclusions without the facts.*

Kat shrugged and gripped her arms in front of her. "I don't know anything right now. Other than I'm not safe."

There were so many dots, but none of them formed a picture. Kat's search for a doctor, her mysterious condition, his aunt's death and her connection with Kat. And now Kat's cryptic words about her father, Dr. Bloodmayne.

His head gave another hard throb. Blazes! It made no sense. And his grief was making it hard for him to think clearly.

Something moved beyond the fence. His hand went to his gun and he scanned the trees.

They were not alone.

Two men stood just beyond the shadows.

At the same moment, the minister came walking around the church corner.

Kat caught sight of the minister and grabbed her skirt as if to run. "I need to go." She started in the opposite direction from the church, toward the gate at the other end of the cemetery. A couple of ravens cawed and fluttered up into the trees.

"Wait, Kat."

She ignored him.

Stephen caught up to her while keeping an eye to the left where the men stood beneath the trees. "None of this makes sense. However, if you're in danger, I will help you." *Especially if my aunt thought you were and gave her life to save you.* "And I want to find my aunt's killer. I think the two are connected."

Kat didn't say anything. She kept right on walking, following the path between the gravestones. Apparently she hadn't noticed the men.

"Where are you going?"

She glanced at him. "I've been staying at an inn down in Banther. But I can't linger long. I need to keep moving." She looked back. "The sooner I find Dr. Latimer, the better."

"And you won't tell me what's wrong with you?" Stephen was certain it was a vital piece to this whole mystery. "Or who might be after you?"

"It is better if you don't know."

"Why?"

She pressed her lips into a firm line and kept on walking.

"So you won't tell me?"

Kat looked over at him. "Please don't make me. The one person who knew is now dead." Her chin trembled. "I don't want you to die as well."

Stephen slowed and Kat pulled ahead. The look on her face—if he pressed her, it would be akin to torture.

But what if she had vital information? He hurried forward. No, she *did* have vital information, information she was withholding. Information that might explain why his aunt had died.

The bounty hunter inside him wanted to press Kat and get answers, no matter the cost. However, the shadow of the man he had once been stopped him. He would not torment an already grieving woman. He would just have to wait for her to open up.

They reached the fence.

Kat spun around. "So will you still help me?"

Stephen stopped and stared into her face. Could he help Kat without having all the facts? Was he comfortable with that?

Did his aunt really die to save this young woman?

If so, then he knew what he needed to do. It was the least he could do for Aunt Milly.

"Yes, I'll help you. But I'm not going to let you return to that inn down in Banther."

"Why?"

He nodded toward the trees. "Because you're being followed.'"

17

Kat felt numb all over. This couldn't be real—none of it. Only a week ago she was taking her finals and chatting with Marianne.

Now she was on the run and Ms. Stuart was dead.

She glanced back as Stephen stopped beside the street beyond the cemetery and motioned for an empty cab clattering by. Where were the men Stephen had seen? The trees were empty. So was the cemetery. Kat shivered and turned back.

The carriage was small, barely large enough to fit two passengers. The driver stopped and Stephen opened the door.

As Kat lifted her skirt and stepped in, she overheard Stephen tell the driver to head toward Samford Street. She took a seat to the far right and Stephen climbed in behind her.

Stephen shut the door and sat back into the seat. The cab started with a lurch, then settled into a comfortable bounce. There was hardly any space between them and twice his knee knocked into hers.

The wind and rain intensified outside the windows, and Kat held her hands together on her lap to keep them warm.

After ten minutes, they turned onto Samford Street.

Stephen glanced at Kat. "Stay here. I'm going to get a few things from my office, and then we'll be on our way."

Kat nodded. She doubted she could say anything, even if she wanted to.

Stephen left the cab and hurried inside the three-story brick building.

The horse neighed and shook its head.

Minutes ticked by before Stephen emerged again and got back into the cab.

"To the rail station," he told the cab driver.

Rail station?

The cab lurched forward and Kat grabbed the window sill to steady herself. "Where are we going?"

"South, to the coast. I had two more contacts I wanted to connect with before I learned of my aunt's death." He handed her a handkerchief. "Here. You have dirt on your face. I thought you might want to clean up a bit."

Kat flushed but took the damp cloth. "Shouldn't I get my things from the inn?"

"No. We can't take the chance that someone is watching the inn."

She wiped her face a couple of times, then placed the cloth down. "Do you think we lost whoever was following us?"

"I'm not sure." Stephen didn't say anything more. Instead, he looked out the window.

She sat back. She was a hunted woman now. Maybe she should just turn herself in. After all, it was her fault Ms. Stuart had died. Ms. Stuart had kept her safe and then paid with her life.

I should have died in her place. I was the one who set the fire. The look on Marianne's face that night flashed across her mind, and her stomach twisted inside her.

I am a monster. And I must never forget that.

Never.

The cab came to a stop beside the local rail station, a small brick building beside a double set of tracks. People bustled along the platform between the building and tracks.

Stephen helped Kat exit the cab as, far off, a train whistle blew and the crowd on the platform grew excited. Stephen let go of her hand and pulled a small wad of bills from his trouser pocket to pay the driver.

Kat reached for the small pouch deep in the pocket of her skirt. She should give him something for the fare. Before she could pull it out, Stephen was heading toward the ticket window.

"Two tickets to Covenshire."

"You're just in time, son," said the man behind the window. He pulled on the ticket wheel and tore off two tickets, then filled in the spaces with slow, careful handwriting. The whistle sounded again. "That's the train for Covenshire now." He took the bills from Stephen and counted them twice before handing Stephen the tickets.

A train came rolling in with puffs of steam and a couple of whistles. Kat raised her hands to cover her ears when the wheels squealed under the brakes as the train came to a stop in front of the platform.

"This way." Stephen grabbed her hand and weaved through the crowd, his fingers strong and warm against hers.

Kat caught the glances from the people around her and blushed. She tugged, but Stephen did not let go. Instead, he gripped even tighter.

There were shouts and greetings around them as people embraced and chatted loudly. Trunks and carpetbags were placed on the platform, and men in navy blue uniforms scurried to make the exchange of passengers.

Stephen led her to the first car, all the while glancing around. Were they being followed again?

Kat looked around as well, then almost fell when he pulled her into the car. Up the stairs she went and to the left. Rows of red velvet seats lined either side of the narrow walkway and hint of pipe smoke hung in the air.

Stephen dropped her hand. "Kat, I want you next to the window on the right, away from the platform."

She nodded and scooted into the first available row. From where she sat, she could hear but no longer see the people bustling around outside on the platform.

Stephen sat down next to her and removed his hat. His wheat blonde hair was swept back and fell across his collar. He patted the lumps on either side of his hips and looked satisfied. It took her a moment to realize they were probably his guns.

She leaned toward him. "Are we safe here?"

He turned and looked at her, his face inches from hers. There were specks of yellow inside his hazel-green eyes and a few gray hairs in his mustache. His eyes dilated, then contracted. "We are safe enough."

Kat backed away, her heart thudding oddly inside her chest. "All right." Her cheeks were still warm from minutes ago. She pressed a cold hand against her face and looked out the window.

People filed into the car and filled the rows. She watched an older couple sit down in front of them, the man gently fussing over his wife until she shooed him away in loving exasperation. Kat smiled, brief and wistful.

She glanced at the man beside her. Though Stephen barely moved his head, she could tell he kept tabs on everyone who boarded, weighing each as a possible threat.

How different her situation, how desperate.

The numbness returned like a hole opening inside her chest, sucking away emotion and thought. As the train pulled from the station, buildings slid by and the feeling intensified. She had never left this part of World City before. All of her life she had spent here, on the northern side of the river, traveling between her home, a few shops, and the Tower.

Now she was leaving it all behind, and with a man she hardly knew.

You can trust my nephew. Some of Ms. Stuart's last words to her. But she'd also told Kat not to reveal her secret, and for good reason. Kat was sure it was what had gotten Ms. Stuart killed.

Too many people knew she had set the fire at the gala. She wanted to believe Marianne wouldn't have told, but that still left Blaylock and the other young men. Kat swallowed. They must have talked. But to whom? Who was after her? And willing to kill to get to her?

Kat watched the scenery outside as the train passed buildings and factories, everything sodden and gray.

They zipped by a church. She kept her gaze on the whitewashed building until it drew out of sight, then sat back. She knew very little about God, other than that he lived in churches or something. And he was powerful.

She needed someone powerful right now. But how did one talk to God?

God?

She glanced around, half expecting people to hear her thoughts. But no one looked her way, and Stephen seemed focused on something at the front of the train.

God, if you're real, please help me. Kat twisted her fingers together and looked out the window. *Please.*

Nothing happened. No lightning, no flashes of light.

Kat sat back and swallowed. Maybe she was alone. After all, why would God help a monster?

An hour into the train ride, Stephen looked over to find Kat had fallen asleep. The telltale streaks across her face revealed she had been crying quietly next to him without him ever knowing. Perhaps that was for the best. He had no idea how to comfort people.

Stephen, it's all right to cry.

Stephen remembered looking at Aunt Milly and shaking his head. They stood beside the dual graves of his parents on a warm spring morning. He remembered the crocuses had just started to pop up from the ground and that was all he could focus on while the minister spoke.

How could he explain to his aunt that he couldn't cry? That everything was bottled up inside, topped off with a cork? And that the pressure hurt? But no matter how much he tried, he couldn't cry.

He felt that same way now, ten years later. He couldn't cry for Aunt Milly. He could feel the pressure building up inside like steam in pipes, but there was no release valve. Instead, the only thing he could do was to keep moving until the pressure finally dimmed.

At least Kat had found a way to release the pressure.

She gave a small whimper and curled up toward the window.

A different kind of ache burgeoned in his chest. He shifted in his seat and turned away from Kat. Blazes! After two years, he thought he would never fall for another woman and here he was, his heart slowly attaching to the one next to him. Why now? And why her?

I don't have time for this. He narrowed his eyes. *Just get the job done. Find that doctor, pass her on to him, and you'll be free.*

But something told him it wouldn't be that easy. There was more to this job than he could see, and he didn't like that.

The train whistle blew just as the sun began to sink across the windows to the right. Kat sat up and blinked. She brushed her hair back and looked around. "Are we there?"

"No, not for a couple more hours."

Kat nodded and turned her attention back to the window. They were now at the edge of World City. Bits of the country poked through dingy and worn down buildings. Tall oaks. Lush green fields. The way the world used to look before civilization took over and converted everything to machinery and steam.

"I've never been outside World City." Kat turned and looked at him, her eyes dark and wide in the dim light.

Stephen swallowed, but found his mouth dry. "It's different," he finally said.

Kat turned back to the window.

The train pulled up to a small station. A couple disembarked from their car and two men took their place. They sat down a couple of rows ahead, their faces shadowed by their hats.

Suddenly uncomfortable, Stephen watched them closely. Though they never looked back, he got the feeling they were monitoring him and Kat. He felt the revolver again beneath his jacket. The men were unlikely to make a move on the train, but he would be ready anyway.

With a shrill whistle, the train lurched from the station. The last sliver of the sun sank beneath the western horizon.

Stephen settled back into his seat and let his mind wander. When they reached Covenshire, he would need to talk to Kat and get her to open up. There were pieces he was missing. Who was after whom? He doubted anyone was after his aunt. She had been caught in the crossfire. The more he thought about it, the more he was sure of that.

So were they after Dr. Bloodmayne? That made the most sense. Jealousy. Passion. Greed. There could be any number of reasons why someone would want Dr. Bloodmayne dead. He had seen them all on the job. Or perhaps it was an assassin from Austrium sent here to kill the lead scientist creating the weapons against their country. It had happened before, during other wars.

But . . .

Stephen looked over at the young woman beside him. None of that explained the mysteries around Kat. Why was she looking for this particular doctor? And what did she mean there were things about her father?

Stephen sighed and pinched the bridge of his nose. Whatever the case, his aunt had sent Kat to him to keep her safe. He would do that, and help her in any way he could.

Starting with the two men in front of them.

18

The train came rumbling into Covenshire a little after eight o'clock that evening. Buildings stood like black silhouettes against the brilliant red sunset. The air held a hint of salt and far off, the ebb and flow of the ocean sounded across the sleepy fishing city.

As the train came into the station, Stephen leaned over to Kat. "Don't look around, just remain focused on the seat in front of you."

Her brows scrunched up, but she kept her gaze forward.

"We are being followed."

She took a quick breath.

"Once we get off, I'm going to try and throw them off our trail. Follow my lead even if it seems odd. All right?"

Her gaze came up to meet his, clear and resolved, then she gave him a small nod.

He let out the breath he had been holding. Good.

Stephen stood the moment the train came to a stop. The two men never looked back, but he had guessed who they were during the last hour. Black bowler hats. Black trench coats. Carefully trimmed hair and mustaches. And an eye embroidered across the right sleeve, which he had caught sight of in the window.

World City investigators.

Stephen grasped Kat's elbow and helped her to her feet. He leaned in, blocking the front of the train from her view. "Stay close to me."

He stepped into the aisle and let Kat out, then followed her to the back of the train. Using the windows, he glanced behind them. The two men had stood and were following about a car length behind.

Kat headed down the stairs and onto the platform outside. Heavy fog hung over the dark seaport city. A smile touched Stephen's lips. The fog would prove useful.

He looped his arm through Kat's.

She shot him a look. "What are you doing?" she whispered.

He leaned in as if to give her a kiss on the cheek. "Act like a couple," he whispered back.

She narrowed her eyes and worked her jaw.

His gaze followed a tendril of hair that had escaped her chignon and now lay near her mouth. Maybe he should close the distance and really kiss her. He was half tempted. It would help with the charade.

Until she slapped him.

Stephen backed away. Of course she would slap him. And where did that thought come from anyway?

"All right," she whispered back, and gave his arm a small tug.

Stephen blinked, his mind still muddled from the desire of moments ago.

"Stephen?"

"Yes. This way."

They walked as a couple across the platform and toward the stairs to the left. The train station stood at the end of Main

Street. Gas lamps stood like fireflies frozen inside the fog. The scent of sewage and fish filled the damp air.

Kat held a hand to her mouth and coughed.

Stephen smirked. "Welcome to Covenshire. Purveyor of fine fish from the Narrow Strait."

"Ugh. I can tell."

He led her down the first block, then took a left. Another block, and a sharp right. Still, the men stayed a block behind them, casual enough that a regular person never would have realized they were being shadowed. But he had trailed enough people to know when he was being followed himself. He would have to step up his game.

He went around the next block, two more, crossed the street, and headed for the dance hall nearby. It was a two-story structure with multiple paned windows. Wide stairs led to the double doors and a sign hung across the top, the name of the establishment written in curly letters that promised a good time.

Kat caught sight of the hall and pulled back. "I agreed to hold your arm. But I am not going in there!"

"We're not going to stay."

"But . . ." Her face darkened in the dim light.

"Trust me."

She looked over at him, deciding. "And you're sure we're being followed?"

"Yes, although I don't know who exactly or why." All he knew was they were investigators, but Kat didn't need to know that.

She visibly swallowed. "All right."

Stephen patted her hand and led her up the stairs. He opened the door and motioned for Kat to go first. Music drifted through the air: a high feminine voice accompanied by a piano. Hazy blue smoke hung in the dark foyer, drifting in from the double doors flanking a short counter. Gaslights sputtered next to the doors.

Kat held a hand to her chest, her eyes wide. He could only imagine the kind of stories she had heard about dance halls. Yes, some were rowdy and uncouth. But the dark interior and loud music could provide the cover they needed to throw the investigators off their trail.

Stephen followed her inside, glancing back as the door shut. The investigators were already crossing the street. They would have to move fast. "This way, to the right."

Kat gave him a quick nod, her bearing stiff.

He led her through the doors. The room opened up into one large auditorium. A dark wood counter ran along the left side, and small, round tables dotted the main floor. The hall was full tonight. At least a hundred customers.

A stage stood in front, where a woman dressed in a tight blue corset and a short, ruffled skirt stood with her hands clasped, belting out some kind of love song with the tinny piano pounding away in the back. The black feather tucked inside the upsweep of her chestnut hair fluttered side to side.

Kat stared at the woman, then turned away, cheeks deep red beneath the chandeliers.

Most of the audience was men, with a few women waiting the tables, their attire similar to that of the woman on the stage. Stephen had a pretty good idea they were here to sell more than just liquor. He tightened his grip on Kat's hand and searched the room. Somewhere dark, somewhere near an exit—

There. Near right side of the stage was the back door. He glanced behind him. The investigators had not entered the hall. Perhaps their sensibilities would not let them. After all, the dance hall was not a place for gentlemen.

But if they were good investigators, they would follow.

The men from the nearest table looked over, their eyes roving across Kat. One whistled and gave her a wink. Stephen sent the man a scathing look and let his duster fall open just enough to reveal the smooth handles of his revolvers.

The man's eyes went wide and he turned back toward the stage. The other men followed suit.

Stephen guided Kat along the aisle, staying close to the dark drapes that hung along the walls. Others glanced up and away as quickly as the first group. He rubbed the back of his neck. Maybe coming here had been a bad idea.

Halfway across the room, the woman ended her song with a high note and the audience clapped and hooted. The investigators appeared in the back.

Stephen sat Kat down in an empty chair and took a seat between her and the door. "Watch the stage," he hissed.

She nodded, her eyes as wide as two saucers.

Stephen kept his hand on her elbow, his other hand near his gun. Out of the corner of his eye, he watched the investigators. They stood in the rear, moving their heads back and forth.

Just blend in, he reminded himself. *Act like you belong here.*

One glance at Kat and it was obvious she didn't belong here. She looked neither like a mistress nor a workingwoman. Her waist shirt was modest, covered by a simple blue corset and jacket. Her hair was pulled back in a chignon, with that one small curl that clung to her neck.

He could almost picture her in a classroom with chalk in hand, writing across a blackboard. A schoolteacher. Not a fugitive here in Covenshire, in a dance hall.

The subtle scent of smoke filled his nose. Stephen blinked and sniffed again. Fire. He glanced around, searching for the orange flames. A glimmer of light caught his eye—

Stephen looked down at the table. A small flame flickered on the tablecloth right near the candle in the center.

He frowned and put out the flame with his thumb. A black spot remained where the flame had been, and a whisper of smoke drifted toward the ceiling.

Kat stared at the spot, mesmerized by it.

"Just wax," he whispered and went back to surveying the room.

Kat remained focused on the burn spot. Her hand flew upward and she clutched her neck. "I can't stay here."

"*What?*" His head whipped back toward her.

"I need to get out of here," she whispered, her eyes wide.

"We can't, not yet. Sit tight, we will leave just as soon as . . ." He spotted the men again. They had moved toward the opposite corner from where he and Kat sat, their forms just a shade darker than the shadows. They were still searching the crowd.

He glanced back at Kat, whose eyes were still fixed on the spot. Was she afraid of fire? "Don't worry, the place won't catch on fire."

She didn't appear to hear him. *Was* she afraid of fire?

Band music suddenly blasted across the hall, and a row of women clad in tight red corsets and ruffled skirts came through the curtains to the right.

The women caught Kat's attention. Her head swung up and her eyes went wide again, moving back and forth along with the women on the stage. "What are they *doing?*" The dancers started kicking in unison to the beat of the music, showing almost every inch of leg.

Kat gasped.

Stephen ran a hand across his face. *Good job, Grey. You just exposed a lady to saloon dancing.*

He peered between his fingers. One of the investigators was focused on the dancing women, giving Stephen an idea. He motioned for one of the house ladies. Kat wasn't going to like this. He'd apologize later.

The barmaid approached his table, an empty platter held against her hip. She sized him up and gave him a bold smile. "Can I get you something?"

"See those men in the corner. The well-dressed ones?" He pointed toward the investigators. The first one was scowling at his partner.

"You mean the gents?"

"Yes." He pulled out a couple of bills. "I need you to distract them."

She took the bills and gave him a wink. "Sure you don't need the distraction yourself?"

"Already here with a lady."

The barmaid looked past his shoulder then shrugged. She tucked the bills into her cleavage and headed toward the investigators.

Stephen turned around.

Kat's gaze bounced between him and the retreating barmaid. "Why did you . . ." She held up a hand and cocked her head down, eyes closed. "Wait, I don't want to know. The sooner we leave, the better."

"Hopefully this will provide just that opportunity."

A minute later, Stephen peeked behind. Sure enough, the first inspector seemed to be railing at his partner, whose attention was divided between him and the barmaid playing with his collar. The first man grabbed her arm and pulled her away.

Stephen shook his head and grinned. Bad move.

Bouncers appeared in the doorway seconds later and beelined for the investigators. Even some of the other patrons were turning to watch the conflict rather than the dancers on stage.

Stephen gripped Kat's elbow. "Time to go."

"I agree," she said under her breath.

They rose, and he ushered her toward the exit to the right as the sounds of a scuffle broke out behind them. Stephen chanced one more look back. A bouncer had one investigator in a prisoner hold while the other waved a badge in his face and shouted. Stephen bit back a chuckle. Given the impassive look on the bouncer's face, the investigators wouldn't be pursing him or Kat anytime soon.

"Are you *laughing*?" Kat hissed, sounding scandalized.

Stephen shook his head, then quickly closed the door behind them to hide his grin. As the latch clicked, the last bit of light vanished from the hallway.

"Stephen?" Kat whispered, and this time there was a tinge of fear in her voice.

He sobered. "Here."

A hand found his arm and clamped down. Using his other hand, Stephen felt along the wall. An exit should be just down the hall. His fingertips brushed over curls of wallpaper and old glue. Cigar smoke and perfume filled his nose. Kat breathed next to him, her hand tight across his forearm.

Seconds later his hand met with a doorframe. He trailed his fingers along the wood until they met the knob.

He swung the door open. Fog and pale light from a gas lamp at the end of the alley filled the doorway. "This way," he said, leading Kat into the cold, dark night.

19

A half an hour of back streets and seedy alleys later, Stephen and Kat reached the pier. Turning, they walked along the waterside street, listening to the seawater ebb and flow unseen below them. Ahead—drawing nearer with each step—the warm glow of gaslights beckoned. As they reached the end of the street, the fog rolled back to reveal an inn at the edge of the docks.

Rows of windows graced the first and second story, a single door stood to the left, with a large sign above. In faded green paint it said *The Screaming Siren*. Stephen had no idea what a siren had to do with the inn, or why it was screaming. His only guess was the name came up during a very intoxicated evening and had stuck ever since.

Kat pointed at the building. "Are we staying there?"

"Yes. An old friend owns the establishment."

Stephen opened the door and ushered her in. A low ceiling hung over a large room filled with wooden tables and chairs. Booths lined the outer edges, each one sporting a fishing net or ocean knick-knack on the wall above it. Despite its name and outer appearance, the Siren was warm and smelled like fresh bread.

As Stephen breathed in the air deeply and sighed, he sensed Kat relax a degree beside him. His stomach grumbled.

A couple of old sailors sat in the corner, already stuffing large chunks of bread dipped in the daily stew into their mouths. One looked up, grunted, and went back to eating.

Marty ran a clean establishment. Kat would be safe here while he made his inquiries.

Toward the back of the room stood a long counter with a mirror behind it. The man behind the counter turned as they approached. Long strands of dark hair were pulled across his bald head, and a second chin wobbled beneath the first. His shirt barely fit over a girth that had expanded since the last time Stephen had been here over a year ago.

The man looked up with watery eyes. He blinked and grinned. "Stephen Grey."

Stephen gave him nod and a smile. "Marty."

"What brings you to Covenshire?"

"Business. Always business. I need one of your private rooms for a couple of days."

Marty's eyes wandered toward Kat and gave her a glance over. "Mistress?"

Kat stiffened again, but Stephen spoke up quickly. "No. I'm working a case. And she's part of it. I'll take the suite if it's available."

Marty came around the counter, his shirt rolling up to reveal the flab beneath. He pulled the shirt down and tucked it into his sagging pants. "How long will you need the room?"

Stephen paused. "Five nights." That would give him time check on Harvey, a retired policeman a day southwest of here, and to see if his old friend Captain Robert Grim was in town.

If anyone knew anything, especially if it concerned Austrium, Grim would.

"I'll give you the yellow suite."

Stephen nodded. "All right."

Marty headed across the room. Stephen followed with Kat close behind. Marty puffed his way up the stairs, pausing at the top to open a door. Instead of a room on the other side, there was a long hallway. A single gas lamp lit the corridor.

"Can't thank you enough for what you did last year." Marty pulled a set of keys from somewhere inside his pants as he lumbered down the hallway. "Collier about wiped me out. If you hadn't arrested him when you did, I would have lost the inn."

"Just doing my job."

Marty stopped at the third door and worked the lock. "Still, it was mighty helpful. Tell you what"—he pushed the door open and turned—"the rooms are on me, as a thank you for last year."

Stephen tipped his head toward the innkeeper. "That is very generous. Thank you, Marty."

The room was about the size of Stephen's living room back home and covered in mustard-colored wallpaper. A large, round table and four chairs took up most of the space, with a green lamp that hung low over the table, casting the rest of the room in shadows. Cigar smoke clung to the space like perfume to a woman's body. A door stood on either side of the room, leading to two private bedrooms. Perfect.

Marty stepped back. "Need anything else?"

Stephen turned back. "Not at the moment."

Marty tipped his head. "Stephen. Miss." He headed down the hall, whistling some rowdy tune.

Kat watched him, her mouth slightly open, then turned back to Stephen.

He shrugged. "I meet a lot of interesting people in my profession."

She raised one eyebrow. "You certainly do." She looked back into the room. "So . . . What is this place used for?"

Stephen walked in. "Card games."

Kat wrinkled her nose.

He pulled out a chair. "Please, take a seat."

She walked over and sat down.

Stephen shut the door and joined her. As he sat down, he took off his hat and placed it on the table. Kat clasped her hands in her lap and looked around at everything but him.

"How are you doing?"

She blinked and looked back. "I . . . uh . . ." Her mouth opened and closed a couple of times. "Not so well," she finally admitted and looked down at her hands.

Stephen leaned back into his chair and folded his arms across his chest. "Everyone grieves in their own way."

"I wish I could have been there. At the end."

"And why weren't you?"

Kat looked up.

"Your father was there. At the funeral."

Her face tightened. "You asked me to be honest when we first met. Then let me tell you this. My father and I are not on good terms. In fact, we haven't spoken to each other in years."

That confirmed his suspicions about Kat's relationship with her father. "So you stayed away because of him?"

She paused. "Yes. I thought it would be better if I kept away from the funeral."

Stephen pulled on the bit of hair beneath his lip. "You said earlier that there were things about your father, things I would never imagine. Do you think he murdered my aunt?"

Kat met his eyes. "No." She turned her gaze to the table. "At least not first hand. Science is my father's life. He is always pushing the boundaries, eager to explore the unknown. Sometimes that has meant choosing to use more . . . unconventional methods in his research."

"Such as?"

Kat rubbed her arm and said nothing for a long time. Just when he thought she wouldn't answer, she began. "I've seen his laboratories in the Tower. Not the ones available for the public to observe. His private ones. When I was twelve"—she rubbed her arm harder—"I stumbled into one of the back rooms. I thought I had heard something . . ."

The color in her face washed away to a pallor. Silence filled the space.

Stephen leaned forward. "And?"

"I found . . . humans."

She spoke so quietly that at first Stephen didn't catch the word. But the look on her face, and the way she said it sent a shiver down his spine. "Humans? Are you sure?"

"Yes."

"Alive?"

She stopped rubbing her arm and instead clutched it. "I—I don't think so. Except one. It moved." When she finally looked at Stephen, her eyes were large and dark, and her lip trembled.

Humans? Could they possible be . . .? Stephen worked his dry mouth. Were they the missing people? He grasped for any other explanation. "Perhaps your father was treating them." Yes, that made sense. His shoulders relaxed. Kat was young;

maybe she didn't understand what she had seen. But the look on her face . . .

She shook her head. "The bodies were laid out on metal tables with metal contraptions attached to them: to their heads, to their chests, to their arms. Naked. A strange green light filled the laboratory from miner's lamps set around the room." She went trancelike, as if reliving the memories. "I knew my father would experiment on rats and guinea pigs. I always felt awful for the little creatures. But this . . . this was very different."

Stephen licked his lips, the hair along his arms rising. The room seemed darker. "Did your father catch you in there?"

"No." The word came out in one breath, her eyes still focused on something beyond. "I ran back to the other laboratories. Ms. Stuart took me home and . . ." She went still.

"Kat?"

Muffled singing came through the floor from the tavern below.

Stephen raised his hand and waved. "Kat?"

She blinked and jerked up.

"What happened when my aunt took you home?"

"I—I told Ms. Stuart about the lab I had found."

"So my aunt knew something."

"Yes."

Stephen narrowed his eyes. The hesitation in Kat's voice indicated she was holding something back. "Anything else?"

"No." She went eerily calm. "That is all for now."

"Are you sure?"

She looked him straight in the eye, and a shiver went down his spine. Something had changed in Kat's demeanor. The terror had vanished. She seemed calm, composed. Completely different than the fearful, grief-stricken woman from moments ago. And the story she had just told . . .

The lights brightened, then dimmed. Stephen glanced up at the lamp. What the—

He ran a hand through his hair and stood. "Listen, I'm going to get us something to eat. Will you be all right?"

Her eyes flickered. She shook her head as if to clear it.

"Kat?"

"Yes, yes." She rubbed her forehead and her body lost that calm rigidity. "Actually, food would be good. I haven't eaten since this morning."

"Maybe I can even round up some tea."

She looked up and gave him a small smile. "Tea would be wonderful."

Stephen doubted Marty had tea, but he would do anything to keep this Kat talking, and not the other one, the scary one he had glimpsed a minute ago.

He stepped outside the room and quietly shut the door behind him. He leaned against the door and let out a shaky breath. He was spooked, that's all. But he couldn't shake that look on Kat's face, or the images she had spoken about. Her words continued to play inside his mind.

Humans. Alive. Bodies laid out in green light.

There were rumors that the Tower might be conducting illegal experiments. Was it possible the institution was also responsible for those people who went missing two years ago? Those taken by the reapers? Like Mr. Hensley?

Stephen looked back at the door. Could Kat be right? Had she really seen humans in Dr. Bloodmayne's laboratory? And were those experiments still happening?

Was Kat one of them?

Right after the door shut, Kat held her head in her hands. She had tried to repress that memory, bury it deep inside her mind. But the moment Stephen had asked, it had shot up like air bubbles in water. She never went back to her father's laboratory after that day. For years she wondered if she had been mistaken in what she had seen. But the sight of that hand, rising from the table, followed by a long moan . . .

She put her fists to her temples and pushed against her skull. The little girl inside her still longed for her father. Even now. But the woman demanded that she give up these dreams and accept who her father really was: a cold-hearted scientist. A man who would do *anything* to achieve his goals.

A monster.

"Ms. Stuart, I wish . . ." Tears prickled her eyes. "I wish you were here. I wish we could talk one last time. I wish I knew why you died." The last words escaped her lips with a sob. "I don't think I was worth it."

Kat rocked back and forth in her chair, letting her heart flow over until she heard footsteps in the hall outside. She wiped her face and pushed her hair back as Stephen stepped into the room with a tray in his hands.

He spotted her, but didn't react to what he saw on her face. Instead he placed the tray on the table. "Surprisingly, Marty did have tea." He poured the dark, steaming liquid into a cup and passed it to Kat.

She took the cup without looking up and cradled the warm ceramic. Two bowls filled with chunks of beef, carrots, and potatoes in thick brown sauce sent tendrils of steam into the air. Between them, elevated on a stack of something, sat a dinner plate with a loaf of sliced bread.

Stephen waved his hand toward the tray. "It's not much, but it should help the hunger pangs."

"Thank you," she said in a small voice. She set a bowl and a spoon in front of him, then took the other for herself. For several moments, neither of them spoke, the only sound the clinking of spoons against their bowls.

When they had finished eating, Stephen sat back, and crossed his arms. Silence filled the room, no longer the companionable quiet of a shared meal. Kat took a sip of her tea, her gaze on the tips of his boots. His duster hung over either side of his chair. Beneath his coat he wore dark pants, a dark vest, and white shirt. His revolvers sat snug against his hips. She tried to remember what Stephen had looked like years ago in his police uniform when she first met him, but all she could picture was the man before her now.

The bounty hunter.

She took another slice of bread and blew across the top of her tea, though it didn't need it. Why had he left the police force? Marianne never said.

Her heart clenched. *Marianne.* What did Marianne think of her now? Had Marianne tried to hide the truth to protect her? A memory from that night tore through her mind. Marianne saying her name, and the look on her face.

"I need to leave in five minutes."

"What?" Torn from her reverie, she found Stephen staring at her with unblinking eyes. "Where are you going?"

"I want to get a head start on my inquiries."

"Inquiries?"

"Into your Dr. Joshua Latimer."

Oh. With everything else, she had forgotten about the doctor. "You're still going to look for him for me?"

He rubbed his face, and the hard look disappeared, replaced by fatigue. "Yes, we made a deal. And I always honor my deals."

Kat tightened her grip around the cup. Had she done the right thing, telling him about her father? Until now, she had told no one except Ms. Stuart. Why now? Why him?

Because I trust him.

Kat sat back, the truth of that thought ricocheting through her body. It hadn't taken much to transfer her trust of Ms. Stuart to her nephew. But then, she had no one else.

Stephen looked up and quirked one eyebrow.

For some strange reason, Kat laughed.

He blinked and his brows furrowed.

"I'm sorry." She laughed again, that kind of nervous belly laugh. "I'm sorry, it's been a long day and . . ." She laughed again, because if she stopped, she would cry instead.

Stephen hesitated, then reached over and grabbed her hand. His skin was warm and his grip strong.

Kat hiccupped and blushed.

He looked into her eyes. "I understand. It has been a long day."

He held her hand a moment longer, then let go. He stood and grabbed his hat, pausing with it still in his hands. "You're sure you won't tell my why this doctor is so important?"

Kat shook her head. Ms. Stuart had known about her condition and now she was dead. Maybe there was a connection, maybe there wasn't. But she wasn't about to put another person's life in danger. And she might trust Stephen, but not enough to risk that he might run if he found what she really could do. This was her secret to bear and if she had to, she would carry it to her grave.

Stephen sighed and placed his hat on. "All right, then. You're safe here. Marty is a bit dimwitted, but he knows how to keep his mouth shut. Don't leave the inn. If you need anything, Marty will provide it for you, and I'll settle up with him later. I should be back sometime tomorrow evening."

He moved the bread plate to reveal a small stack of books. "And here. I thought these might help. " He held them out to her and she took them, turning them over in her hands. Not the type she usually read. Just penny novels. But, faced with hours alone in a small room, she was grateful for anything to occupy her mind.

"Thank you, Stephen."

His face softened. "It's not much at the moment. But you should be safe. Hopefully I will find out more about this Dr Latimer."

Before Kat could say anything, he turned and walked out, shutting the door behind him.

Instead of moving to the bedroom on the right, Kat lay her head down on the table and closed her eyes. For the first time in a long time, she felt safe.

20

You always did like brunettes.

Patrick's words from years ago whispered through his mind, words spoken shortly after he'd met and fallen hard for Vanessa. Apparently things hadn't changed.

Get your mind back in the game, Grey.

Stephen stepped off the train platform and out onto the street, his hat pulled low, his collar tucked high around his neck. Harvey had been a dead end, which meant an entire day wasted. However, word had reached Stephen that his old friend Captain Grim had just docked in Covenshire. It was the sort of timing he might once have thanked God for—Grim could have been in World City or halfway to Austrium. As it was, Stephen would stop and see his friend, find out what he knew, then be back to Kat right on time.

A quick glance around revealed no one in the shadows. Covenshire was a large city, not as big as World City, but big enough that unless the men who had been following them knew where to go, it would be a while before he and Kat were found. And by then they would be gone.

He followed the pier, passing by crates of imported goods and piles of rubbish washed up by the sea. Here and there a rat scurried between the circles of light cast by the gas lamps on every block. Out in the harbor, ships bobbed along the black water, a few with twinkling lights within.

He turned his gaze upward. The ship he sought wasn't the kind that took to water.

Near the end of the pier stood a circular wooden tower with platforms set in a spiraling height progression around its circumference. A sky tower for airships. Stephen paused to examine the structure. He could only see the two lowest platforms; the rest were hidden in fog and darkness. One held a small blimp, probably an inland cargo ship, and the other was empty.

Of course, Grim wouldn't dock on one of the lower platforms. Unlike many of the vessels that traversed the skies suspended below a balloon filled with gas, the *Lancelot* rode the wind on solar-powered rotor blades. The force of air created by those whirling blades on landing and take off caused havoc among the other airships' more fickle rigging, which meant the dockmaster would have assigned Grim the highest spot.

Not that Grim complained. He was always planning for an easy escape, should he need it.

Stephen sighed. That meant a long trek up the tower.

He headed toward the wooden door on the side of the tower. Water lapped quietly in the nearby darkness and rigging creaked in the wind. The door that led inside the tower was thick and dark and groaned as he opened it.

A musty smell greeted his nose and Stephen sneezed. The sound echoed up and around the inside of the tower. There were no lights, only small squares of gray where traces of light from the outside trickled in.

He could barely make out the steps that wound around the inside of the tower, but he didn't feel like taking the time to find a lamp. He gripped the banister and gave it a tug. At least it didn't wobble. With his hand sliding along the railing, Stephen began the climb up and around. A minute later, he reached the first platform, where a doorway led out onto a narrow wooden walkway. The small cargo ship tugged against the rope restraints that held it to the platform.

Stephen bypassed the entrance and continued up. Around and around he went, most of the time the railing his only compass. The air grew colder and the fog thicker the higher he went. He passed two more platforms, both empty.

He paused and looked up again, his breath coming out in hot puffs. A trickle of sweat followed the side of his face and fell beneath his collar. Perhaps Grim wasn't here after all.

A lamp twinkled high above.

Stephen pursed his lip into a half grin. Looked like it was his lucky night.

As he neared the top of the tower, two men came to stand in the doorway at the top of the stairs. One held a lamp, the other a rifle.

"Halt! Who goes there?" said the one with the lamp.

Stephen stopped ten steps beneath them and held onto the rail. "I come seeking Captain Robert Grim. Is that his ship docked up above?"

The man with the rifle stepped forward. "What is your name and what is your business with Captain Grim?"

"Tell him Stephen Grey is here to see him, and I seek information."

The two men conversed, then the man with the lamp handed it to the one with the gun and disappeared out onto the platform.

The other man, now armed with light and gun, stood in the doorway, blocking it from Stephen's view.

Stephen took the opportunity to quietly check his own revolvers. Not that he was expecting a fight, and he certainly didn't want to start a shootout with Grim's crew, but a person could never be too careful.

"So. . ." the man said above him.

Stephen looked up.

"Grey, huh. You're not that bounty hunter from World City, are you?"

Stephen pressed the revolver back into his holster. "I am."

The man stepped onto the top step inside the tower. "I've heard a lot about you."

Stephen gave a grunt and folded his arms. He could well imagine what the man had heard. In two years, he never lost one bounty: not to a runaway, and not to death. Hence the reason the World City council usually hired him. It had also given him a name in the underworld. The criminal sector knew if their name came up, there was no place they could run from him.

Before the man with the rifle could say more, his partner returned. "Captain Grim said to bring you to his quarters.

The smile came back.

Stephen followed Grim's men outside onto a narrow platform about fifteen feet long. The light from the lamp illuminated the walkway and fell off into darkness on either side. Only a fragile railing separated the three men from access to the airship and a long, long fall.

Good thing he wasn't afraid of heights.

The men led the way across the walkway, the light soon brushing over the hull of Grim's famous airship, the *Lancelot*.

Apart from the flying apparatuses, the *Lancelot* looked like a water vessel, though much more luxurious than any found in a shipyard. The ship itself was as large as one of the dual story flats back in his neighborhood. Dark wood made up most of the hull, with intricate carvings inlaid in gold along the railings and edges.

The deck held the usual platforms, ropes, and pulleys, but instead of masts, there were six rotor blade towers: two smaller ones on either side of the bow and stern, and two taller ones amidships. In the air, the blades moved and directed the airship. But here in port, they were still, only moving when a breeze came along, and the vessel was held in the air by an inflatable balloon that would be retracted when the time came for the *Lancelot* to take flight.

Below the main deck were two more levels. Small glass windows surrounded the middle floor, darkened now in the absence of the crew. A wall of glass held in place by steel rods made up the bow, and soft light shone through the panes.

As he neared the ship, Stephen could see rich tapestries and furniture inside the wall of glass: Grim's private quarters. He could well imagine the view those windows offered in flight and for one moment wondered what it would be like to sail high above the land, gazing down on towns and counties, even World City itself.

The men led Stephen across the gangplank—another precarious affair—onto the top deck. The moment he stepped onto the wooden planks, a door opened to the right and a man emerged. He was of medium height and wore a black leather duster similar in fashion to Stephen's own. The rest of his clothing was dark as well, with the exception of a gleaming cutlass that hung on his right side and a revolver tucked away on his left.

He wore a leather patch across his right eye, with the leather strap cutting across his cheekbone. Dark stubble covered his chin and jaw, and his black hair hung in strands around his face. The light from the sailor's lantern twinkled in his one eye. "Stephen Grey."

"Robert, it's good to see you."

Robert smirked and walked across the deck. "You presumptuous scoundrel. What brings you to the *Lancelot*?"

Stephen grinned back. "Information, my friend."

"And who are you chasing this time? Not anyone I know, I hope." He clasped arms with Stephen and gave him a good shake.

Stephen shook his head and stepped back. "Actually, for once I'm not searching for a criminal."

"Oh?" Robert eyed him curiously. "Well, let's not stand out here in the wet. Come, follow me back to my cabin. I have a nice brandy waiting for us." He turned and headed back toward the door he had exited through a minute ago. "Harding, Reid, let me know when the crew gets back. I want to sail at first light."

"Aye, captain," said both men and they walked back to the railing.

"So you're here by yourself tonight?" Stephen asked as Robert held the door open for him.

"Sometimes I need a night off. And so do the men. Although my version usually involves silence and watching the city from my cabin."

Stephen stepped inside the narrow hallway. "I'm sorry to interrupt, then."

Robert laughed. "I always have time for an old friend. Just follow the passage to the last door."

Stephen did as directed. The passage only ran about fifteen feet, with a door on either side in the middle. He could barely see the door at the end as he reached for the handle and gave it a turn.

The door opened into a room as large as his living room, kitchen, and study combined back home. To the left stood a double canopy bed built into the side of the ship and covered in a deep red bedspread. Ahead was the wall of glass he had seen from the outside. A polished metal table stood in front of the windows with matching chairs around it, the style more industrial than classic. Maps, papers, and navigation tools were spread across the top of the table—including what looked like a brass globe with a revolving spherical framework of rings around it—and a decanter half filled with an amber liquid and two round glass tumblers.

On the right side was a bench built into the wall, covered with a plump scarlet cushion. Next to it was a wardrobe and a desk, both made from the same polished metal as the table and chairs. Various swords and long tapestries from around the world hung on the wood-paneled walls. A simple chandelier hung above the table, lighting the cabin.

The subtle scent of pipe smoke hung in the air. One of the windows was open and a cool breeze blew through the cabin.

Robert shut the door behind him and walked toward the table. "Welcome to my cabin. I don't think you've been in here before."

"No, I haven't." Stephen looked around the room in appreciation. He placed his hat down on the bench. "Interesting choice in furniture."

"Aluminum. Helps keep the weight down on the ship."

That made sense. "I take it the, um, 'privateer' business is doing well."

Robert poured a small glass of brandy and held it out to Stephen. "I prefer the term 'blockade runner.'"

Stephen snorted as he reached for the glass. "And I'm a fugitive recovery agent."

Robert laughed and poured himself a glass. "Is that what you're calling yourself these days?"

"My assistant thought the term would be more palatable to polite society."

Robert smiled and held up his glass. "To labels that have nothing to do with us."

"And to friends who always live just inside the law." Stephen clinked his glass with Robert's then sniffed the amber liquid. A fruity, spicy smell filled his nostrils. He was tempted to take a sip, but placed the glass down instead.

Robert lowered his own glass. "Still don't drink?"

"No." Stephen ran a finger around the rim. "Still sticking to that promise I made myself a couple of years ago."

"I understand."

"I'm sure it's a good brandy."

Robert winked at him. "Only the best, my friend." He took a sip, then rotated the glass between his fingers. "So you're here for information, correct?"

Stephen nodded. "I'm working a case."

"Yet this one doesn't involve finding a criminal?"

"No, it's unique. And it involves a young woman."

"Interesting." Robert took another sip.

Stephen waved his hand. "Nothing romantic. She was the charge of my aunt."

"Is this the aunt who works for Dr. Bloodmayne?"

"Yes."

"Go on."

Stephen walked toward the table. "Long story short, my aunt was murdered a week ago." Robert didn't respond, so Stephen went on. "The next morning, Kathryn Bloodmayne showed up at my door in search of a certain doctor. She won't tell me why." He tapped a finger along the table. "My aunt was very fond of Miss Bloodmayne, and I feel an obligation to help her. But not only that, I think she's in danger and the men who are hunting her are somehow connected to my aunt's murder."

Robert cleared his throat. "Stephen, I'm sorry about your loss. What are the police doing about it?"

"Patrick—an old colleague of mine—is working the case, but it's against regulations to bring me in because I'm family."

"Odd." Robert rubbed his chin. "You would think they would make an exception for a man with your skills."

Stephen shrugged. "Sometimes it's best to keep family members out of a case." He paused, mulling over Robert's words. His friend had a point. It may be regulation to exclude family from cases in process, but he was ex-police, a proven bounty hunter with a case record better than anyone on the force. It made no sense. Too many things made no sense.

"You know, you're right, Robert. The deeper in I get with Kat's case and my aunt's, the more I see that they are connected. And from what I gather"—he shuddered, remembering her story and the icy calm that followed—"the Bloodmaynes have secrets. And maybe not just them. I think something more is going on. I think the World City council is behind the secrecy."

Robert snorted. "You know how I feel about the World City council. A bunch of snakes dressed in robes."

Stephen couldn't help the smile that slipped across his lips. Robert might run the Austrium blockade for World City, but it was only for gold, not for a love for city and country. If Austrium paid him more, Robert would probably change sides. Regardless of the title he had chosen for himself, he was a pirate through and through, like the seafaring ones of old.

Not that he could blame Robert. The council did what was good for them and their privileged benefactors, not for World City or its people.

"So who's this doctor you're looking for?"

Stephen looked up. "His name is Dr. Joshua Latimer."

Robert shook his head. "I've never heard of him. What makes him special?"

"I'm not sure."

Robert looked at him over the rim of his glass. "You know, Stephen, it's not like you to take a case without all the facts."

"I know." He rubbed the back of his neck and looked out the windows. The city of Covenshire twinkled below like a thousand fireflies on a dark summer night.

"Do you like her?"

Stephen dropped his hand and jerked his head back toward Robert.

"Do you like this Miss Bloodmayne? Kat, is it?"

Did he? Yes, he was attracted to her. Very attracted to her. But he also felt a connection with her via his aunt. Because of that he wanted to protect her.

Or was there more?

Robert nodded knowingly. "Good for you. It's about time you stepped outside Vanessa's shadow."

Stephen didn't flinch at the name of his former fiancée. He paused at that. Was it possible he was finally moving on?

"So what can you tell me about this Dr. Latimer?"

Stephen tore his mind away and back to the present. What was it Kat said about the doctor? "He used to work at the Tower. Ten years ago, I think."

"The Tower? You mean that scientific nut house?"

"Well, I wouldn't call it that, but, yes."

"Probably best the man moved on. Ten years ago, you say? That's a bit of time to cover."

"I know."

"Anything else?"

"Kat read some articles by Dr. Latimer. That is how she found him."

"Recent articles?"

"I'm not sure."

Robert sighed. "Well, it's not much to go on, but I'll do my best. I'm heading to Austrium in the morning, via World City. I'll check for him while I'm over there. Who knows, maybe he decided to find another academy to work for."

"Thanks, Robert." Stephen walked over to the bench and picked up his hat. "Send what you find to my office in World City."

"Will do."

"I'll have Jerod wire you your usual finder's fee." Stephen put his hat on, pulling the brim down across his forehead. "And thanks for the drink."

Robert grinned. "Anytime. Take care, Stephen."

"Same to you."

Stephen crossed the cabin and headed out the door. What people didn't know was that he was a good tracker because he had good connections. If Dr. Latimer was outside World City,

Grim would find him. And if Dr. Latimer was somewhere inside World City, it was only a matter of time before he himself tracked the good doctor down.

21

Kat slipped further and further into the sleepy recesses of her mind until she leaned forward and laid her head across the table, the penny novels in a neat pile next to her. Her damp hair—now clean and sweet smelling—was tied back in a loose chignon. It was past the usual time she went to bed, but Stephen had said he would be back tonight. And she would be waiting to hear any news he brought.

She closed her eyes. So tired. She wrapped her arms beneath her head like a pillow. Her breath evened out and the darkness beckoned her. Just a few minutes of rest. That's all. As her body relaxed, the memories began.

"I don't want to go!"

Ms. Stuart stared at fifteen-year-old Kat with that no-nonsense look, her hands planted on her hips. "You do not have a choice. Your father said—"

"My father?" Kat laughed. "My father has had *nothing* to do with my life. Why should I bend to his whims now?"

"Kathryn," Ms. Stuart said warningly.

"No!" She slashed the air in front of her with her hand. "Not this time!"

Ms. Stuart lowered her hands from her hips, her gaze darting to Kat's fingers. "Kathryn, please."

Kat laughed again and flashes of color erupted across her vision. The sunlight streaming in from the large window across the library seemed brighter. Air whooshed across her face and around her body. Something burned deep inside her, something dark, something alive.

Ms. Stuart looked around the library and took a step back. "Kathryn, control yourself!"

"I'm always controlling myself!" Her voice took on a feverish pitch. "*Kathryn, behave. Kathryn, watch yourself. Kathryn, you're such a disappointment—*" She raised her hands. "Well, not this time!"

The air stopped moving and silence filled the library, as if the room were holding its breath. Then Kat flung her fingers wide.

The books that lined the oak shelves shook and wobbled. First one, then another flew off the shelves. The chintz chair in the corner scooted across the wooden floor as if being pulled by a rope toward Kat.

The fire inside her took over, burning every part of her. It felt good to finally release the pressure. More books flew off the shelves, flying toward her, joining the tornado of pages revolving around her. The chair came to a stop between her and Ms. Stuart. The small table and lamp joined the chair.

Ms. Stuart took another step back and threw her hands into the air as a book came whizzing by. "Kathryn! Stop!"

The bookshelves rumbled. One by one, they left the wall and raced across the floor.

Ms. Stuart ran toward the door.

Kat laughed.

The shelves came to a stop beside the chintz chair, blocking Ms. Stuart from Kat's sight, except for a small square of space. Books flew around Kat, dancing in the air.

This isn't you.

Kat paused and the books slowed.

This isn't you, the voice whispered again.

Ms. Stuart held her hand out, her face deathly pale. "Kat, please, stop!"

The voice and her nickname broke through the fiery haze.

She gasped and stumbled back. The books fell to the ground with a thousand loud bangs and thumps. The shelves gave one last wobble and stopped.

Silence filled the library once again.

Kat stared in horror, first at the books, then at the barrier of bookshelves, chair and table. She raised her hands, half-expecting her palms to be on fire, but found only faintly pink skin.

Slowly, fearfully, she looked through the tiny square space at Ms. Stuart.

"Ms. Stuart. I—I don't know what happened!" She was going to retch or faint. Or both. The black spot inside her vision expanded and she was falling . . .

Kat jerked up from the table and looked around. She was in a small sitting area with a round table and four chairs. A door stood beyond the table. The walls were covered in hideous yellow wallpaper and a hint of cigar smoke hung in the air.

Covenshire. The inn. Waiting for Stephen to come back.

Kat let out her breath and rubbed her face, her heart returning to its normal beat. That was the third nightmare in two days. No, not nightmare. Memory.

She held her head between her hands. Ever since sharing about her father's secret laboratories, the memories had started coming back, rushing to the forefront of her mind as if something had slipped open the door and let everything out.

"I don't want to remember," she said between her fingers. The room remained quiet. The silence pressed down on her. The lamp's light wavered.

Kat sat back and swallowed. She had been stuck in this room, waiting for Stephen, long enough.

Don't leave the inn.

Forget the inn, she hadn't even left the room except to use the privy. Marty brought food, tea, and hot water so she could wash. She lingered over her ablutions, over her meals, over the books Stephen had left her. But when her eyelids grew too heavy, the silence came, dredging up old thoughts best left forgotten, twisting into nightmares when she fell asleep.

"I don't want to be alone." She shook her head and brought her hands down on the table. She looked at the door. "And I won't be. Not tonight."

Before she could change her mind, Kat hurtled from the chair and through the door that led out into the hallway. Already another memory was bearing down on her, but she focused on the faint voices drifting along the narrow corridor.

Didn't Stephen say he was coming back tonight? She pressed two fingers to her temple. She couldn't remember. Hopefully he'd understand. After all, she was only going downstairs.

She dropped her hand and followed the hall light to the door at the end and opened it. The voices from the dining room below grew louder.

Kat carefully made her way down the stairs and stopped at the bottom. Most of the tables in the dining room were empty, as were the booths that lined the outer walls. A couple of men sat at the bar, talking and downing pints of ale.

Marty stood behind the counter, laughing with one of the men. He looked up and smiled at her. Without another word to the men, Marty made his way past the counter and headed across the dining room.

"Stephen said you'd be staying in your room until he returned. Decided to come down, eh?"

Kat rubbed her hands together and glanced away. "Yes. It was a bit too quiet."

The smile slipped from Marty's face. "Everything all right? Do you need something?"

Kat let out her breath but didn't answer.

Marty placed a hand on her elbow and led her toward one of the booths. "Why don't you sit down?"

Kat nodded. The memories still clawed at her mind, but it was easier to keep them at bay in the presence of another person.

Marty guided her into the booth. She slipped across the leather cushion and sat near the candle that burned at the end of the table.

"How about something to drink?"

Kat looked up. "A drink?"

"You look like you could use something."

Kat touched her cheek. Was she really that pale? Before she could answer, Marty waddled back across the dining room. One of the men turned around on his stool and looked at Kat.

Kat ignored him and glanced out the window. A gas lamp stood on the corner with a pool of light beneath it. The rest of the street was dark.

Where had Stephen gone? He said he wanted to meet with a couple of his contacts, people who might know where Dr. Latimer was.

She pressed the side of her head against the window and closed her eyes. The coolness seeped into her skin and a chill went down her spine. She shivered and wrapped her arms around her body. She wanted to curl her legs up beneath her skirt, but that wouldn't be ladylike.

God. The word came unbidden to her mind, but she pressed on. *Please let Stephen find Dr. Latimer. Please let him cure me. I don't want to live like this anymore! No more memories. No more incidents.*

Like the other night at the dance hall.

Kat cracked one eye open and glanced down at her fingers. She had seen the surprised look on Stephen's face when he saw the small flame. He thought it was from the candle. But she knew.

The power inside her was growing. And it wouldn't be long before she couldn't contain it.

"Here you go."

Kat sat up as Marty placed a glass and a bottle of something on the table. Wait, wasn't he bringing her tea?

He opened the bottle and poured a dark red liquid into the glass. "I don't usually keep wine—the men usually prefer a different kind of spirit, but a lady like yourself shouldn't drink such stuff."

Kat eyed the glass suspiciously. Father didn't believe in imbibing spirits of any kind. He said they clouded the mind and a true scientist should have control of all his faculties at all times.

Well, Father wasn't here. A rebellious will filled her chest. Maybe the wine would help her forget, at least for one night.

She took the glass and gulped the drink. The wine flowed down her throat and warmed her belly.

Marty's eyes shot open. "Well, I must admit I've never seen a lady drink quite like that."

Her cheeks burned, whether from embarrassment or the wine or a combination of both, she didn't know. "I—that is—" She looked away. "A friend of mine died last week."

Another partial truth. Her cheeks burned even hotter. Yes, she still grieved Ms. Stuart, but that wasn't what was ailing her tonight.

Marty gave her a knowing nod and poured another half-glass of wine.

She shouldn't, but the memory of the gala started dancing across her mind and she took up the glass. *I don't want to remember the fire, or Blaylock or . . . or Marianne.*

It didn't take long for the alcohol to hit her bloodstream. Marty stayed and chatted while she nodded and sipped, her mind slipping away from the sharp-edged memories into a more comfortable lull until—finally— the memories slipped away altogether.

Kat wasn't sure how long she sat there in the booth. After a time, Marty came and went, talking quietly and kindly, but she never heard the words, just the tone. It felt nice to have someone talk to her that way. It made her feel warm inside.

The men from the bar soon left, and it was just her and Marty. He started watching the door as if waiting for someone. But who? She looked that way as well.

A man's face swam before her eyes. Dark blond hair, hazel-green eyes. A carefully trimmed mustache. He drew back from her, dressed in the dark olive uniform of the World City police.

No. Now he was dressed in a long leather duster, white shirt and dark pants beneath, and a revolver strapped to each hip.

Stephen.

Kat sat up and her eyes went wide. Stephen would be here. Or was that tomorrow? And she was supposed to be up in the room, right?

She stood and the tavern began to spin. Whoa. She pressed her hands down on the table and waited for the room to stop.

From the corner of her eye she saw Marty jog toward her just as the door opened from the outside.

Kat blinked and looked again.

Stephen walked in.

"Stephen," she whispered, and something shifted inside her heart. The strange feeling swelled. It felt like the world had been off kilter, but the moment Stephen walked in, it righted itself.

Stephen paused inside the doorway and scanned the dining room. His gaze stopped on Kat.

She went to leave the booth, but her legs wobbled beneath her. Marty arrived at that moment and reached for her, blocking her view of Stephen.

Marty caught her and held her up. She glanced at his broad face and smiled. "Stephen's here."

"I noticed."

She tried to push the bartender away, to right herself, but didn't seem to be able to make her body do what it was supposed to.

"Marty, what the *blazes* happened here?"

Marty finished helping her out of the booth, then looked over his shoulder. "The lady said she was lonely. Wanted to come down."

Kat pushed away from Marty and straightened her skirt. At least she tried. But she couldn't make her skirt stop moving. And why was the ground coming toward her?

Someone rushed in front of her, blocking the floor from her vision. She fell against a body and looked up. "Stephen . . ." Oh, thank God he was here.

His nostrils flared and he looked over her head. "So you got her drunk?"

Somewhere inside her mind, she heard Marty answer, but the words were jumbled.

Stephen answered back sharply, then turned her and led her toward the stairs at the end of the dining room.

She patted his arm. "It's all right, Stephen. I didn't want to be alone. Marty kept me company."

His jaw tightened. "Like blazes he did!"

Kat swayed, a frown across her lips. Stephen didn't seem happy.

He helped her into the stairway and followed a step behind her, a hand on her elbow.

Halfway up the stairs, Kat turned around. Stephen almost crashed into her, stopping a step below her, right where she could look directly into his eyes. The light from the dining room below left most of his face in shadow, but she could still see the curvature of his cheek and lips, and his neatly trimmed mustache.

There seemed to be two Kats inside her at that moment: the proper Kat and the Kat who had no inhibitions. The latter Kat reached over and cupped his cheek.

His eyes widened, but she kept her hand there.

She had never felt a man's face before. It was different, rough and smooth at the same time.

He visibly swallowed. "Kat, we should keep going."

Her fingers brushed his lips.

"Kat," he said hoarsely.

"Stephen, I didn't want to be alone. The memories, they kept coming. And—and I missed you." Somewhere inside, she knew she shouldn't be touching him like this, shouldn't be saying these things. But she didn't seem able to control her fingers or her tongue. Whatever came to mind rushed out of her mouth.

Stephen's face changed. Ever so slowly, he moved his head closer until she could feel his breath. Before she could figure out what he was doing, he touched her lips with his.

22

"*I don't want to be alone.*"

In that moment, Stephen knew exactly how Kat felt. He didn't want to be alone, either. For too long he had shut off his heart, sealed it so deep inside that no woman could ever touch him again.

But as they stood there on the stairs, her dark eyes looking into his, her hand against his cheek, the seals broke and it felt like his heart beat for the first time since that day Vanessa broke it.

His gaze was drawn to her lips, slightly open. He closed the distance between them, the rush of his heart directing him until his lips brushed hers.

She was soft and gentle and smelled like sweet berries.

No, I shouldn't do this. "Kat," he said again and pulled back, but she moved forward and kissed him again.

She doesn't know what she's doing! Marty had given her wine and it was messing with her. But another part of him could only feel her lips and his own desire.

So he kissed her back.

Kat wasn't like Vanessa. Vanessa had been possessive and hot. Kat was strong and cool and eager, which fed his blood even more. He ran his hand through her hair, pulling her chignon loose, and cupped her head, deepening the kiss. He spread his other hand between her shoulders, fingering the top of her corset.

Warning.

I need . . . to stop . . .

Kat went slack in his arms, her knees buckling beneath her.

Stephen sucked in a breath and tightened his arms to support her, his mind and body racing with heat. What the—

Her head sagged to the side, her eyes closed.

A chill replaced the heat.

"Kat!" He gave her a small shake. "Come on!" He gave her another shake. A small snore escaped her lips.

Nothing was wrong with her. She had only passed out.

Kat gave another snore and her lips turned upward in a contented smile.

His heart twisted at the sight. He brushed back a loose curl, then dropped his hand and scowled. He had completely taken advantage of her! *Grey, you fool!*

Disgusted, Stephen maneuvered himself around and tried to pull Kat up the stairs, but her limbs kept hitting the wall or catching on the steps. Finally, he just picked up her and carried her the rest of the way.

She was small and light, hardly anything to her. And her smell . . .

Stephen clamped his lips shut and hurried down the hall to their rooms. He shifted Kat to one arm and managed to open the door.

Inside, he took a left at the card table and entered the dark bedroom. A simple double bed stood against the far wall with a nightstand on either side.

He didn't bother turning on the lamp. Instead, he placed Kat down on the coverlet, debated whether to make her more comfortable, then decided he had done enough damage without removing any of her attire.

She gave a small whimper and shifted to her side, curling her legs up beneath her skirt and tucking a hand beneath her head. Her dark hair splayed across the pillow.

Stephen sighed and rubbed his eyes with one hand. Would she remember their kiss in the morning? He hoped not. It had been a moment of weakness, one that he would not repeat. Even now, he could feel his heart sinking back to that deep place where it could not be touched. But it beat now, and that was something he could not stop.

But did he want it to?

Stephen turned away from the room. He didn't feel like sleeping. He didn't feel like doing anything. So he grabbed one of the chairs by the card table and pulled it over to the window that overlooked the street below.

The street was dark, with only the light from a nearby gas lamp. He laid his head against the glass and watched the darkness.

He could hear Kat breathing in the other room, a comforting sound. It moved him. How long had it been since he let another human being into his life? Jerod didn't count, the man simply worked for him. And he had kept Patrick at bay since he had left the force.

Stephen sat back in the chair and spread his legs out in front of him, crossing them at the ankles. He folded his arms and rested his chin on his chest, and listened to Kat's breathing.

In . . . Out . . . In . . . Out . . .

Faint light streamed across Stephen's vision. He woke up with a jolt and sat up in the chair. The street outside was lit pale yellow as the early morning sun dawned over Covenshire. The blue sky above promised a beautiful day.

He ran a hand across his face and took another long breath. He couldn't remember his dream, but it had left him feeling nostalgic and wistful. Something about a family—his family— with a wife and kids. And a big white house in the country.

Stephen settled back into the chair and looked out the window, the feelings draining away, leaving him cold inside. That kind of life wasn't for men in his profession. Best to put those thoughts away.

Kat!

Stephen jerked around and stared at her bedroom. He could barely see inside, only a lump on the bed. He held his breath. He couldn't hear her.

He came to his feet and took a step toward the room when the lump groaned and moved. He dropped his shoulders and shook his head. She was not going to feel good once she woke up. He should probably go get something for the headache she would undoubtedly have, and maybe a bucket too.

Just as he turned for the door, something outside caught his eye.

Stephen turned back. Three men. No, four men, were making their way along the street toward the inn. Another one joined them from the alley to the right. From the purposeful way they walked, he was pretty sure they weren't coming for breakfast.

He checked his revolvers and shoved them back into his holsters. He glanced one more time at Kat, then headed for the door. They had company, and he would be sure to give them a warm welcome.

"We are looking for a man and a young lady. We received a report that they stayed here last night."

Marty splayed his hands on the bar and stared at the men in front of him. "Look, I don't make a habit of giving out private information. Good way to drive paying customers away."

"But did you provide lodging for them last night?" The investigator fished his badge from an inside pocket. "You should know, the penalty for abetting a fugitive is quite high. Think carefully before you answer."

Stephen leaned against the wall at the bottom of the stairs and crossed his arms. His revolvers sat snuggly against either side of his hips, within easy reach. He cleared his throat and looked at the counter. "Last I checked, harassing a barkeeper usually makes him tight lipped."

The two men turned, but before they could speak, another voice broke in.

"Well, well, if it isn't Stephen Grey."

Stephen went rigid and slowly scanned the room. He didn't know the two investigators personally, but he knew that voice: Jake Ryder, fellow World City bounty hunter, though that was where the similarities ended. He stood to the right, just beyond the bar counter, his flaxen mustache curled perfectly on either side of his face. His cap was pulled low over his eyes, the sleeves of his white shirt rolled up, revealing the colorful tattoos scattered across his arms. His hand rested on top of the revolver that hung at his side.

Piers Mahon leaned against the counter next to Jake. More gentleman than bounty hunter, he sported a small, dark mustache and bit of hair beneath his lower lip. His cream colored top hat matched perfectly with his coat, which, in turn, complemented his gray vest and matching silk ascot. The monocle he sported over his right eye seemed to complete the image, but it was not for aesthetic value. Rather, a specialized scope for sniping. The cane at his side concealed his unusual rifle.

Rodger Glennan, also known as "the Judge," stood in the corner—all muscle, no mercy. He had lost an arm during a scuffle a few years back and now had a weaponized prosthetic attached to his shoulder that could put a fist-sized hole in a man from a hundred feet away. Buckles and belts crisscrossed his body, with holds for daggers, small guns, and instruments of pain. Lots of pain. Not that anyone ever lived long enough to remember. Rodger always brought his bounties in dead.

"I should have known you would be here, Grey." Jake fingered his revolver. "With a bounty this big, everyone will be after the woman."

What bounty?

Piers smiled and straightened. "He'll have to catch her before I do."

"Before *we all* do." Jake shot a look at Piers. The other man shrugged and adjusted his monocle. Rodger just grunted from the corner. "Remember, we are in this together."

Stephen's eyes went wide. Jake, Piers, and the Judge were all working together on a bounty? Hell must have frozen over during the night.

Stephen pulled his duster back, making sure his revolvers were visible, and leaned against the doorway. "Since when did you three start working together?"

All three men shot each other dirty looks. "Since none of us wants to die on this bounty," Jake said, turning back toward Grey. "We figured it was better if we split the money instead of killing each other over it."

Stephen sifted through every bounty he knew of, but couldn't pinpoint one where the cash was high enough to involve any of these three, let alone all of them together. Especially one that involved a woman. *What woman? They couldn't mean Kat, could they?* But then he would have heard about the bounty. Jerod would have telegraphed him.

Piers tapped a finger along his cane. "You know, you're not a bad hunter yourself, Grey. Perhaps we could let you in on it."

Rodger growled in the corner and brought his prosthetic arm up to point at Piers. "I'm already losing enough money on you two," he said in a gruff voice. "I won't lose any more."

Piers smiled, his black facial hair making him look devilish. "And we both know Grey would have a bullet in your head before you finished firing that ridiculous arm cannon."

"Men, men." Jake raised his hands.

Piers laughed, and Rodger scowled.

Jake pulled his revolver out and inspected some invisible speck. "Don't bait Rodger, Piers. Grey might be faster, but you're not. And you would hate to get blood all over that dandy suit of yours."

Piers nodded, a smile still tugging at his lips. "True, true." He smoothed the front of his vest.

Judging from the tension between them, Stephen wasn't sure if these men could actually work together without one of them ending up dead. Best to find out what this bounty was all about before the shooting began. He cleared his throat, and all three men looked his direction. From the corner of his eye, he kept tabs on the two other men, who thus far had made no further move. "Tell me more about this bounty."

Silence filled the room.

Piers moved his monocle again as if trying to get a better glimpse of Stephen. "Wait, you don't know about the bounty on that woman from the Tower? The bounty set up by the World City council itself?"

The Tower? And the World City council? His stomach dropped.

Rodger looked at him wide-eyed, his prosthetic arm drooping slightly.

Jake lowered his revolver. "You can't be serious, Grey."

Stephen shrugged, but the hairs rose along his neck. "I've been out of town on another mission."

Jake laughed. "Stephen Grey, famous World City bounty hunter, doesn't know about the bounty of the century?"

Stephen crossed his arms and raised one eyebrow.

"Then why are you here, unless . . ." Jake glanced at Piers, and Piers gave him a small nod.

The wheels were spinning inside Stephen's mind. Bounty. Woman. From the Tower. His mouth went dry and the blood rushed from his face. There was one woman here who fit that description perfectly.

But it couldn't be! There had to be some mistake.

Piers narrowed his one eye, his gaze fixed on Stephen. "Our men reported that a gentlemen was seen escorting the woman, and that he was good at shaking off anyone on his trail."

The two men near Marty nodded.

This couldn't be happening! Kat couldn't possibly have a bounty on her. What in the world could she have done to warrant such a high reward? She would have had to murder someone high up, and even then?

It's ludicrous! Kat couldn't have killed anyone.

But she's been keeping information from me.

But murder?

Stephen's head began to pound. There was something going on. Either Jake, Piers, and Rodger had the wrong woman—which they were too professional to do—or something deep and dark was happening back home, and somehow Kat had ended up right in the middle of it. And the World City council now wanted her arrested.

Well, not today. Not until he had the whole truth from Kat herself. Then he would decide.

Stephen slowly moved his hand toward his revolver.

"You have a choice now, Grey." Jake checked the chamber of his revolver. "Turn her over to us and we'll give you a ten percent cut. Or . . ." He snapped the chamber shut.

Stephen grabbed his gun and dove for the nearest table.

23

Shots ricocheted across the wall behind Stephen the moment his knees hit the floor. He used his momentum to roll to the table and, with a hard shove with his shoulder, lifted it up and onto its side. The wood was thick enough to stop the bullets, but he wouldn't last long under this barrage.

The slugs hit the side of the table with loud thunks. Bits of wood shot into the air, and one bullet left a trail across the wooden floor to his right.

He glanced at the stairs behind him. He couldn't let the men get to Kat. He had to defend the stairs. Even if it cost—

"Not right now," he muttered and drew out his other gun.

One, two, three.

Stephen lifted his head above the table and sent two shots toward Jake and Piers. Both men ducked behind the bar.

A whine filled the dark corner where Rodger stood and lightning arced around his prosthetic arm-cannon.

What the—

Stephen ducked just as a white beam sailed over his head, singeing the ends of his hair, and hit the wall behind him.

Boom!

The floor shook. Stephen maintained his balance on his knees and hands. Acrid smoke filled his nostrils, along with the smell of burnt hair. He looked back and found a gaping hole in the wall with smoke spewing from the edges. That was close. A couple more inches and his head would have disintegrated.

He crawled back to the table, his revolvers still in his hands. A mug lay nearby where it had rolled off during the fight. Setting one of his guns down, he grabbed the mug and flung it into the air. Gunshots went off and ceramic pieces rained down on his head. Something moved over to the left, past the table.

Stephen brought his other revolver up and shot.

A man yelped and dove out of sight.

"Stay out of the way," Jake yelled over the din.

Stephen pressed his lips into a grim line. He must have hit one of the two investigators.

A couple more shots ricocheted off the top of the table and another whine filled the room.

Another beam.

Stephen curled up into a ball near the left side of the table. How accurate was that cannon of Rodger's?

The beam slammed into the right side of the table, shoving it a couple of inches and leaving behind a burned half-moon hole along the right edge.

Gunshots hit the left side. A bullet grazed Stephen's shoulder, leaving a stinging wound. He grunted and gritted his teeth, moving the table back in place with his right shoulder. If he didn't take Rodger out soon, the man was going to blow the whole place up.

He took a deep breath and picked up his other revolver. One . . . two . . . three . . .

He leaned to the right and shot twice at the corner.

Rodger had moved.

Stephen swung back into the protection of the table, both guns now in his hands.

"Stephen, what the blazes are you doing? The woman is not worth dying over," Jake yelled.

Stephen snorted.

"This is your last chance to hand her over."

Stephen adjusted his grip on his revolvers. He didn't know why there was a bounty on Kat's head, but he needed to find out for himself. "I don't think so."

There was a pause.

"Then so be it."

A volley of shots hit the table, blasting away the wood.

Sweat poured down his face and tension squeezed his shoulders. He leaned against the table and stared at the stairway. If it were any other men, he might have a chance at making it out of this fight alive. But Jake, Piers, and Rodger weren't ordinary men. And they would kill him to get to their bounty.

Stephen closed his eyes. *God.* He let his breath out. He hadn't prayed in years, not since Vanessa . . . except at his aunt's grave. At the time, he'd thought that had been only for Aunt Milly's sake, but the truth was, he still believed in God. And would soon meet Him.

I just don't want to meet you this way. I'm . . . I'm sorry.

A shot ripped through the table near his left ear. Stephen swung around, crouched by the table, guns in hand.

I don't deserve it, but help me save Kat. And if I live, then we can talk.

Stephen snorted. Actually, if he died, they would be talking as well.

Just give me one chance to make things right. Then you can take me.

Stephen took a quick breath and blew it out through his lips. He gripped the revolvers. He would have one chance to take one, maybe two of the men out before they blasted him. He visualized Piers, that spot just below his ascot tie. And Jake's heart.

One. Two. Three.

"Stephen!"

What the—

Stephen swung around.

Kat stood near the middle of the stairway.

His face flushed and his hands shook. "Kat! What the *blazes* are you doing?"

Bullets flew overhead, sending Stephen to the ground. He panted and clenched his teeth. Could things get any worse?

24

Kat gasped and flattened herself against the side wall. The room spun for a moment and bile filled her mouth. *I shouldn't have come down. I'm in no condition to help.*

No. She clenched her hand and swallowed. *I won't let Stephen fight alone.*

Across the room, beyond the haze, stood three men next to the counter: one in a white suit with matching hat, one in what looked like a brawler's outfit, and one with . . .

Did he have a cannon for an arm?

"There she is!" The tattooed brawler pointed toward Kat. "Don't shoot! Don't shoot!"

There was a loud whine and arcs of light appeared around the big man's strange prosthetic.

"Rodger, don't—"

A white beam shot from the cannon, sizzled across the room, and hit the left side of stairs. The stairway exploded into a shower of wooden planks and splinters.

Kat fell to the ground and threw her arms up over her head. Wood rained down on her, slicing across her arms and cheek.

Someone leaned over her and pushed her down even further. Hot breath blew against her cheek. "Kat, what are you doing here?"

Kat looked up at Stephen. "I heard shots and—"

"So you came downstairs?" Stephen grabbed her arm and pulled her toward the table nearby, propped on its side. A shot followed them, barely missing Stephen.

She scowled. "It's not like that! If you're in trouble because of me, I won't wait up in my room while you're shot at! I've already lost one person I care about, I won't lose—"

Her eyes went wide, and her gaze collided with Stephen's. Had she almost admitted she cared about him?

He crouched lower, his eyes growing wild. "Listen, you need to run. You need to get out of here."

"Not without you!"

"You can't help me!"

Kat stared back, her face hard. Yes, she could. The moment she heard gunshots from her room upstairs, she'd chosen to come down here and do whatever she could to save Stephen. Even use her power if need be.

Another volley of shots hit the top of the table.

They both ducked.

Sweat streamed down Stephen's face, and his breath was ragged. Kat read their fate in his body language. There was only one way they were both getting out of here alive.

Her stomach coiled tightly inside her middle. Could she do it? Could she unleash her power and control it?

Stephen raised his revolvers. "There is a back door to the right. I'll cover you."

Movement caught her eye.

The man with tattoos sidled to the right of the table and raised his revolver.

Kat threw her hands out. "Stephen, watch out!"

Stephen turned, but she knew it would be too late.

It was now or never.

The man pulled the trigger.

Kat closed her eyes and let the dark heat fill her. It responded, exploding across her body with such force that it lifted her to her feet and blew her hair and skirt back. Laughter bubbled up her throat, but she held it back. She was in control this time, not the power.

She opened her eyes.

Time had stopped.

Everything stood still. Stephen in a half-turn. The tattooed man, his arm extended, his finger on the trigger. A glint of silver in the air. The bullet. Even the air had stopped. Smoke, drifting a second ago, now stood frozen in mid-air.

She could see every particle inside the room and felt each particle's connection with the power inside her, like a web.

She could control matter.

Insane laughter filled her throat, but Kat clamped her lips shut. No, she would not lose control.

She focused on the tiny bullet hanging in the air. Its trajectory would take it directly toward Stephen's head.

Move away.

The bullet wobbled.

Now.

The bullet whizzed across the room and embedded itself in the wall to the right.

Flashes of red filled her vision.

No, fight it! I can't lose control.

The men, she needed to take care of the men.

Kat raised her arms. *Burn them, burn them! Just like last time!*

"Noooo!" She tapered off with a scream and waved her hands. Like a puppet, the man with the tattoos rose into the air. Kat threw her arms toward the wall where the bullet had disappeared moments before. The man hit the wall without blinking and fell to the ground, silent.

A chuckle left her throat.

All of them. Do it to all of them!

The rest of the frozen figures rose at her command: the one in the white suit, the one with the strange cannon-arm, Marty, and two others she spotted to the left. They hung in the air, their legs dangling beneath them. No one blinked, no one said a word.

With another yell, Kat waved her arms. The men zipped across the room toward the wall where the first one lay on the ground. They each hit with a loud thud and tumbled to the ground on top of each other.

Sweat trickled down the side of her face, but Kat hardly noticed. The power burned inside her. She could do anything. Just a squeeze of her fingers and she could close the distance between matter. Or ignite it. Yes, she liked igniting things.

Laughter gurgled inside her throat, and the air around her began to churn, whipping her skirt around her ankles and pulling her hair back.

The tables around the room vibrated and chairs skidded across the floor. One bottle, then two crashed to the floor behind the bar.

Kat raised her hands even higher and laughed.

Something caught her eye.

She paused and glanced down. Stephen knelt at her feet, still in a half-turn.

Stephen.

I need to stop.

The fire roared inside her, threatening to drown her in flames. Darkness spread across her eyes, and she heard laughter—high-pitched and eerie. It was her but not her. As if she had split in two and the other Kat was in control.

No, this isn't me! She struggled toward the surface of her consciousness, pushing against the dark waves dragging her down. *No! Don't let me drown! Don't let it take me over.*

Kat raised one hand toward the ceiling. "God, help me!"

25

Stephen couldn't move, couldn't blink, could barely breathe.

She was a demon. Or a monster. Like a witch out of those old fairytales his mother read to him when he was young.

But how? There was no such thing as magic.

Kat's terrifying laughter turned to a gurgle and a gasp. She dropped one hand, but held the other up toward the ceiling. "God, help me!"

Was she crying out to God? Would a monster do that?

His body unfroze and Stephen collapsed onto the ground. Kat fell behind him into a sobbing heap.

The pile of men began to groan.

What do I do? Stephen glanced at Kat. A part of him recoiled from her. She was not like him, not like anyone else in this room, or perhaps in this world. She had just moved a bullet and thrown six grown men against the wall with only her mind.

I don't even want to touch her!

Kat sobbed and pressed both fists to her eyes.

His heart slowed and an ache filled his throat. This woman lying on the ground, she was not the monster from moments ago. That had been the other Kat, the one he'd glimpsed in their room two days ago. This Kat was human. Broken, scared, and in danger if she stayed here much longer.

He couldn't leave her here.

Stephen grabbed his guns, struggled to his feet, and stumbled over to Kat. He bent down and turned her around. "Let's go." Before she could answer, he gathered her up in his arms.

She gasped, then clutched the front of his shirt. "Please, Stephen. Hel—help me." Her face was pale and her eyes dilated.

Stephen worked his mouth, part of him moved, the other part still horrified by what he had witnessed.

Her eyes fluttered, then shut. Her body went limp.

"Kat?" He gave her a shake.

The men groaned again behind him.

Stephen held her loosely, almost afraid the other Kat would awaken. But he wouldn't leave her here, not in the clutches of Jake, Piers, and Rodger.

Stephen carried Kat to the back door and outside. He would make his way through the alleys and side streets until he found a ride back to World City. He would also find a way to send a message to Jerod to find out the details on Kat's bounty.

In any case, he wasn't going to keep her for long, only long enough for her to tell him the truth. She owed him that much.

Twenty minutes later, at the edge of Covenshire, he signaled a coach at the crossings. His arms ached and sweat poured down his face. Kat never moved. The only evidence of life was the slow but steady rise and fall of her chest and the intake of breath every few seconds.

The coach pulled to a stop beside the dirt road and the horses snorted and whinnied. Birds chirped in nearby trees, enjoying the rare glimpse of sunshine.

"Something wrong with your wife?" the driver asked as he opened the door along the side of the carriage.

Stephen ignored the marital reference. "She's sick. I need to get her back to World City as soon as possible."

"What about a doctor here?"

"She needs a special doctor." *Was that why she was looking for Dr. Latimer? Did she hope he could cure whatever it was she did back there?*

The driver took a step back. "Not contagious, I hope."

Stephen shook his head. "No. But it is dire that we make it back by sundown."

The driver nodded and kept his distance, leaving Stephen to maneuver Kat inside the cabin. The leather seats squeaked as he settled her in the far corner. He joined her a couple of seconds later and the driver closed the door behind him.

Kat was still out cold, but some color had returned to her lips and cheeks. Her head lay wedged in the corner, and her breath came out in shallow puffs. Her hair flowed around her shoulders like liquid chocolate.

Stephen settled in the other corner, his arms folded, and stared at her face. The coach gave a lurch and started forward.

Slowly the morning caught up to him. And as it did, he began to burn inside. At the very beginning, when Kat had first walked into his office, he had asked her to be honest with him. That's all. Just be upfront. He knew she had kept some things from him. But this went beyond small details. She should have told him about the warrant! Or about this—this power she possessed!

He clenched his hands and breathed through his nose. Instead, Kat had lied to him!

He turned away from her and stared out the window, his body tense. Once again he had been lied to by a woman. He had fallen for a pretty face and then, wham! The truth had knocked him upside the head.

But she didn't really lie.

She didn't exactly tell me the truth.

Perhaps there is a misunderstanding.

Her bounty is high enough to send three of the top bounty hunters after her!

Stephen glanced at Kat from the corner of his eye. What could she have done to warrant such a large bounty? Was it . . . was it that power of hers?

He turned and stared out the window again. Gnarled black oaks and fields of green grass flew by the glass pane.

He snorted. All of it made some sort of sense now: the bounty from the Tower and Kat's search for that doctor. He could well imagine the Tower would want to study someone like her. And the doctor—Dr. Latimer—did she hope he could cure her?

What exactly had she done back there? And . . .

Was he safe?

Was anyone safe around her?

There was a small sigh, then something heavy fell against his shoulder. Stephen looked over to find Kat had shifted in the seat and now lay against his side, pinning him to the corner.

His pulse quickened, then he frowned. How could someone so small do what Kat had done back at the inn? He lifted his hand, paused, then pushed her hair back from her face. Her lashes were dark against her skin, which now had full color. A sigh escaped her lips and he felt that same tug inside from hours ago.

"Kat, what are you?" he whispered. "What happened to you?"

Would she tell him?

A half hour later they reached Stonefield. Stephen took a couple of minutes and sent a telegram to Jerod inquiring after any high priced bounties on women, and told Jerod to send his reply to Lyndown where they would stop for lunch.

Kat continued to sleep inside the coach. Whatever had happened that morning, it had tuckered her out.

After obtaining fresh horses at Stonefield, the coach continued along the country road at a good clip. Morning passed and noon approached. His stomach rumbled in hunger.

Lyndown was a small farming community with an inn, telegraph office, and local sheriff. The coach rode past the few storefronts and stopped in front of the telegraph office, where a new team of horses waited.

Kat stirred. She sat up and blinked her eyes. "Where are we?"

Stephen reached for the door. "Halfway to World City, in a small town called Lyndown."

She rubbed her eyes. "Halfway to World City?"

Stephen didn't answer. They would grab a bite to eat before he went to see if Jerod had telegraphed back about Kat's bounty. He wanted to give Kat a chance to explain herself first before he found out what the council had on her.

The air felt warm and promised a hot day, one of the first of summer. The sky above was a bright blue, and the trees were already green and lush with foliage. Whitewashed buildings lined the single street through town, each with a sign posted from a pole above the front door.

Stephen turned back toward the carriage and held a hand out to Kat. She wore a guarded look now as she reached for him. Her fingers were cold, like icicles.

He frowned and helped her out of the carriage. Why was she so cold?

He led her across the muddy street to a small inn. Inside there were a few tables and chairs, about five in all. Not where he wanted to have his conversation with Kat.

"Wait here." Before Kat could say anything he went in search of the proprietor in the back rooms. He paid for a loaf of bread and a wedge of cheese, then rejoined Kat.

She stood where he had left her, right beside the door, her hand curled in a fist and pressed to her chest, watching him with wide eyes. She had found something to tie her hair back, and now only a small strand followed the curve of her chin.

"This way. I thought we could eat outside." They had passed a small patch of wild grass at the edge of town. Seemed like a good place to eat and talk in private.

Kat nodded, her lips unusually tight.

She followed him to the end of the street, where an old black oak stood with tall grass fanned out beneath. He pulled out the bread and cheese, wrapped in paper, and handed the package to Kat. He went to take off his duster and paused, his hand near his revolver.

He still had a couple of shots left.

Stephen looked over his shoulder. Kat stood with the food near the tree, her gaze downward, her shoulders slumped as if she were carrying the world. She didn't look like she would go all-powerful right there on the edge of the street. But then again . . .

Stephen closed his eyes and let his breath out. "Don't make me shoot you, Kat," he whispered. He took off his duster and laid it across the grass. "Come, sit down."

She looked up and hesitated. The tension in the air was almost visible.

"You need to eat."

Kat licked her lips. "Stephen, listen—"

"We'll get to that once we've eaten."

Stephen took the food from her and sat down on one corner of the coat. Kat sat down on the other side, careful to tuck her skirt around her legs and ankles.

He opened the brown paper and offered her a chunk of bread.

She took it and held it between her fingers.

"Would you like some cheese?"

Kat stared at the cheese as if she had never seen cheese before. Then she shook her head and looked away.

Stephen shrugged and broke off the corner of the wedge and stuffed it inside the soft part of the bread. They ate in silence for a couple of minutes. Kat picked at her food while Stephen finished off his bread and the rest of the cheese.

Finally, Kat laid her half-eaten chunk of bread back on the paper. "Can we talk now?"

Stephen brushed his hands and dumped the crumbs in the grass. He wanted to know everything. And at the same time he didn't. That . . . thing . . . she had become back in Covenshire was like nothing he had ever seen.

He looked up. "Start talking."

26

Even with the sun's rays beating down on her back, Kat felt as cold as a winter's night. The area around her heart had been numb since the moment she woke up inside the carriage. Just like the night after the gala. In the shop she had pressed her fist against her chest until her corset cut through her shirt and into her skin. Nothing.

Only now did she feel a prickling sensation spreading across the area, as if her heart were thawing out from a deep chill.

Kat sucked in her lips and looked away. Just another reminder that she was different. That something cold and dangerous dwelt inside her.

And Stephen had seen it, all of it. Since that morning, every time he looked at her she could see it on his face: his fear, his revulsion, his reluctance. If he wondered in his innermost thoughts if she was a monster, he would be right. She *was* a monster. And the monster part of her was growing stronger by the day.

He was waiting now for her to speak, but the bravado from minutes ago had vanished like a vapor in the wind. Her heart pounded inside, compounding the frigid ache. She wanted to rub the area, or press a heating pack to it, but she didn't want to show any discomfort. She needed to be strong, confident, if she was going to convince Stephen she had this under control.

Just another lie from the pit of hell.

Stephen sat back, one hand behind, bracing him. "Tell me one thing."

Kat tried to swallow, but there was no moisture in her mouth. So she nodded instead.

"Did you kill my aunt?"

Kat blinked. *What?* She shook her head, more vigorously each second. "No, no. I had nothing to do with Ms. Stuart's death." Then she sucked in her lips. That wasn't true. Ms. Stuart had gotten in the way of those hunting her just like Stephen had this morning.

Stephen's face grew hard. "You're not telling the truth."

Kat flushed and gripped her fingers. "I am! That is, I never touched her."

Stephen continued to glare.

"Please, I would've never hurt Ms. Stuart!" But that wasn't true either. That one time, when she pulled everything in the room, she had almost hurt Ms. Stuart. She closed her eyes. *Oh God.*

"Then what happened that night?"

She let her breath out through her nose. "I don't know." She opened her eyes and stared back at Stephen. "People were pounding on the door. Ms. Stuart told me to run and to find you. I swear, Stephen, that is all I know!"

"You don't know who was at the door?"

She shook her head. "No."

Stephen stroked his beard, his cold stare focused on her.

She wanted to turn away and hide, but she held still.

"Did my aunt know about . . . about you?"

The time for the truth had come. Her hands began to shake, but she held them tight. Her insides felt like they were going to spill out. "Yes." The word barely came out.

He sat up. "She knew what you could do?"

"Yes."

Stephen's eyes widened. "Does anyone else?"

Kat licked her lips. "I don't know." However, chances were yes, after the night of the gala when she set Blaylock on fire. The night Ms. Stuart told her to run.

Did her father know? Was he the one hunting her down? Or the World City police? Did they know she set the hall on fire, and those men?

Kat gripped her throat and looked at Stephen. He stared back, unreadable. What would Stephen do with her now?

"What did you do back there?" His voice was cold and hard.

"I—I don't know."

He arched one eyebrow.

Kat dropped her hand and looked down at her lap. She worked her sweaty fingers, her face flushing under his gaze. Her heart beat so fast it felt like it would burst from her chest. Her middle clenched hard and her throat dried out. How did she explain the monster inside her?

She raised her chin slightly and glanced at Stephen. "When I am angry, or afraid, or feel something strongly, something happens inside here." She made a fist and held it against her heart. "And then I make things happen. It's been like that all my life. And each time it happens, it feels like something is dying inside me."

She looked away, unable to watch Stephen's reactions, or lack thereof. "For years Ms. Stuart helped me keep my feelings under control. Most of the time I succeeded, or was at least able to bring my emotions back before . . ." She took a deep breath. "I only lost control twice in Ms. Stuart's care. But lately . . ."

She heard Stephen shift across the coat. "So every time you feel some strong emotion, you can throw men against the wall? With your mind? How is that even possible?"

She shrugged. "I don't know. Neither did your aunt. During my time at the academy, I spent a lot of weekends in the library, researching, trying to figure out what was wrong with me. I found nothing."

"What about this doctor you're looking for? Does he know what's wrong with you?"

She shrugged again and stared down at the coat. "I don't know."

"Then why find him?"

Kat shot around. "Because he's the only one who might have an idea!" The cold lump inside her chest started thumping. *Oh no. No, no, no!* She held her hand against the top of her corset and turned away. *Breathe, Kat, breathe.*

"Is it happening now?"

She licked her lips and nodded. It didn't seem to matter how much she kept herself under control. The monster wanted out, and it was finding more opportunities to do so.

A coach came riding by. Neither she nor Stephen spoke. The coach continued through the small town and disappeared in the distance. Silence descended between them.

"Have you ever hurt someone?"

Her cheeks burned at his question, but she didn't answer. She could only imagine what he was thinking.

"Have you ever killed someone?"

She didn't answer that one either. She didn't know. Ms. Stuart said she didn't kill anyone that night, but some of the young men had been burned, one badly. Did he survive?

"Are you even human?"

Kat watched a couple of wild daisies wave nearby in the warm breeze and brought her hand down. "I believe so." But no living human could do what she could do. She felt more like a lab mistake than a human being. Her throat tightened at the thought. Maybe she was one. But how?

Could her father have possibly . . .?

No. Not even he would have stooped to such low depths. Would he?

Kat drew her legs up beneath her skirt and wrapped her arms around her body. Her father was cold and calculating, and never had anything to do with her. If she had really been an experiment of his, he would have been a part of her life. At least to study her. He wouldn't have just let her live her life.

Bile filled her mouth. That much she knew about her father. His obsession with his work. He would have been obsessed with her too. Unless . . . unless he never knew about her. She looked up. That was entirely possible. It would explain why he left her to Ms. Stuart to raise while he went about his "great work" for World City. He really didn't know.

"So you believe this Dr. Latimer can make you better?"

Kat twisted the edge of her skirt between her fingers, bringing her mind back. "I hope so. He's the only option I have left."

"But what about your father? The Tower? Couldn't they help you?"

Before Kat could answer, there was a whistle from the town square. Both of them looked back toward the town. Stephen glanced at the coach they had arrived in, then toward the buildings that lined the main street. He stood and brushed his pants. "We need to go."

Kat unwrapped her arms and slowly stood. She felt like she was going to retch.

Stephen never looked at her. Instead, he gathered up his coat, gave it a good shake, then hung it over one arm.

She pulled at her fingers, her chest tight. *Go on, ask him. The worst he can do is say no.* "So will you still help me?"

Stephen shrugged, his back still to her. "I'm not sure yet."

Kat dropped her hand and pressed it against her abdomen. She should leave. Now. Before things got worse. She could catch the train and head west to Cathage—

Tears welled up in her eyes. *I don't want to be alone. God, if you can hear me, please help me!* She looked up at the bright blue sky and puffy white clouds. Maybe God didn't like monsters. After all, if he was God, he had seen everything she had done. Perhaps she deserved to be discarded—

"Are you coming?"

Kat looked back and found Stephen waiting for her, that same unreadable look on his face.

Her mouth fell open. "You still want me to come?"

"I'm not going to leave you in Lyndown."

Kat blinked. It wasn't quite the answer she was looking for, but she would take anything right now, if it meant not being alone and left here.

She gathered up her skirt and caught up to him. He turned around and headed into town.

Near the coach, Stephen stopped and spun around. "I need to check on a telegram. Wait here."

Kat nodded, almost afraid Stephen would leave and disappear forever. He crossed the dirt street and headed into the tiny, whitewashed telegraph office.

She stood beside the carriage, the sun's rays warming her back and head. Maybe God *did* care about her. Stephen was still here, even after what he had witnessed her do back in Covenshire, and heard her story.

It was a small comfort, but she clung to it. It was all she had.

27

Stephen stepped into the small telegraph office. Sunlight streamed through the window that overlooked the street outside, highlighting the dust motes in the air. A small man sat behind the counter, his white hair carefully combed to the side. His wire rim spectacles sat low on his nose, but he made no effort to push them up as he continued to tap his fingers across an apparatus covered in ivory keys. The bronze plated machine was connected to the wall by a dozen wires. Next to it sat an additional machine on which a paper tape continuously rolled as a set of typebars printed incoming messages.

"Is there a telegram for Stephen Grey from Jerod Martinson?"

The clerk looked up, studied Stephen, then bent over his desk and ruffled through a small stack of notes to his left. "Ah, yes." He pulled a note out and looked at Stephen again. "From World City, correct?"

"Yes."

The clerk stood and handed the note over the counter. Beneath the heading were four sentences:

Substantial live bounty on Kathryn Bloodmayne set by World City council.

*Suspect wanted for murder of two sons of lesser noble
houses and the burning of Blaylock Sterling.
Patrick said you turned down the case.
Is she with you now?*

Stephen stared at the middle sentence, a chill racing through
his core. Murder. Kat had murdered two young men. And
burned Blaylock Sterling.

He reread the sentence twice more before it finally sank in.
There was no reason for Jerod to send him a false note. And
he remembered Patrick saying something about that case—
something about Blaylock Sterling and the fire at the gala—the
day he walked in to the precinct to inquire about his aunt's
murder. At the time he hadn't been interested in taking on a
case.

He held the paper tight. If only he'd known then what he
knew now.

"Everything all right?"

Stephen looked up and found the clerk staring at him.
"What? Oh, yes." He folded the paper and placed it in the
pocket of his duster, adrenaline still racing through his body.

"Do you want to send an answer back?"

"Give me a minute." Stephen walked over to the window
and looked toward the carriage. Kat stood where he had left
her, her arms around her body, looking like a lost little kitten.

Yesterday he would have scoffed at the telegram. Yesterday
there was no way a young woman like Kat could have done
what the telegram said she did. Murder? Burning?

But after what he had seen that morning, he could well
believe it.

Blazes, how could he have fallen for another dishonest woman? Did every woman lie? Granted, Kat was trying to find a cure for whatever was wrong with her. But she lied! To him!

If only she had just told him the truth.

Would you have believed her?

He snorted. *Probably not.*

But that didn't change anything. His hands began to shake. He didn't care about the bounty's amount. Not this time. Kat had deceived him.

Stephen no longer saw Kat or the coach outside. Instead, he saw Vanessa, sitting there in Harrison's bed, the coverlet pulled up to her neck.

He spun around, his heart beating madly, and headed back to the counter. He had his answer.

You know what they're going to do to her. They're going to lock her up so tight that she will never be seen again.

Stephen clenched his hands. *I don't care. She's dangerous.*

A fire burned inside his chest, replacing the chill from moments ago. He would never let a woman lie to him again. Kat would go back to World City. Besides, perhaps if he took her back, someone could help her with . . . whatever this was. Yes. It was both good for her and society.

He turned around and approached the clerk. "I'm ready to send back my answer."

A few minutes later, he returned to the coach. The sun beat down across his head and shoulders, but the warmth never reached his heart.

Unwilling to alert Kat to his plan, he gave her a curt nod as he approached. "Ready to go?"

She rubbed her elbows. "I think so. But why are we going back to World City? And why were those men after us? Do they have something to do with Ms. Stuart's . . .?" She shivered and looked away. "Won't they follow us back?"

"There is a new lead I need to follow up on."

"You found Dr. Latimer?"

Stephen stuffed his hands into his pockets and averted his gaze from the hope in her face. "Not quite."

The driver came around the other side of the coach, a pocket watch in his hand. He looked up and nodded toward Stephen and Kat. "Just in time. We need to leave now if we want to make it to World City before nightfall."

The driver's gaze moved toward Kat, and he smiled. "Looks like your wife is doing much better. I'm glad to see it."

Before Kat could answer, Stephen had her by the elbow and was guiding her to the door.

The driver chuckled and hauled himself up to his perch at the top of the coach.

When they were safely inside, Kat pinned him with a sharp look. "What did he mean, 'your wife'?"

"The man made an assumption I never bothered to correct."

Pink dotted her cheeks. Yesterday her look would have made his insides do flips, but they did nothing to him now. Everything Kat did, every look she wore only made him think of Vanessa.

Vanessa was never convicted of her offense. But Kat would be. And justice would win out in the end.

The setting sun turned red within the haze of World City as the coach approached from the south. Kat hardly said a word during the rest of the trip, something which Stephen was thankful for. As each hour passed and they drew closer to their final destination, his questions grew until he felt like two ravenous dogs were fighting inside his chest.

Maybe there was still more to Kat's story.

But she murdered someone!

She said she was looking for a cure.

She is a danger to society and needs to be locked u—

"Thank you."

Stephen started and looked over.

Kat leaned against the side of the coach, the buildings of World City taking shape outside the window as they entered the city perimeter. The dying light played across her face. He could see no trace of the other Kat, but he knew she was there, lurking somewhere beneath. "For what?"

She gave him a soft smile, sending his guilt-meter to a ten. "For helping me. You saw what I was and"—she looked down and pulled at her fingers—"you're still willing to help me. I don't know where I would be if it weren't for you."

Stephen turned away from Kat and looked out his own window. "I always fulfill my contracts." Only, he would be turning her in first. Then he would look for Dr. Latimer. No one should have that kind of power.

They reached the station just as the sun set. Stephen pulled out a couple of bills, handed them to the driver, and hailed a smaller cab. "We need to stop at my office first," he explained to Kat as he helped her inside the small cabin. She just nodded, dark circles staining the skin beneath her eyes and her posture drooping. She was probably exhausted. He was too, having barely slept the past week. And considering what he was going to do, he probably wouldn't ever sleep again.

You don't have to turn her in.

He ignored the voice.

Instead, he gave the driver the address to his office and settled down inside the cab next to Kat. She blinked a couple of times and leaned her head back. The cab took off with a lurch and rode through the narrow streets of World City.

Lamplighters were already making their way to the street corners and lighting the street lamps. Couples walked side by side on their nightly stroll. Cats prowled in alleyways looking for their evening meal.

Stephen leaned forward and shrugged off his duster. With all the buildings and paved streets, the day's heat clung to the city well past sunset. Kat breathed quietly next to him, those deep, even breaths of sleep.

He folded the coat across his knees and watched her. The fire inside his chest had cooled. He had not changed his mind, but he no longer burned with bitterness. "I wish things could have been different," he said quietly.

Perhaps he was destined to find the wrong kind of woman, to never marry and raise a family.

He sighed and looked out the other window. It was best just to get this over with and move on.

A half hour later they reached his office. Stephen left Kat sleeping in the coach and hurried inside the three-story building. At the end of the hall, he went up the stairs, taking them two at a time to the second floor. A light shone through the frosted glass door with his name across the top. Good. Jerod was still here.

Stephen held up his coat, pulled out his ring of keys and inserted the right one into the keyhole. The lock gave a small click and he opened the door.

Jerod sat as his desk, his tawny hair even greasier than usual, his glasses halfway down his nose. He looked up and pushed on the bridge of the wire rims. "Stephen. You made it back."

"Yes. Just arrived a half hour ago. Did you get the information I was seeking?"

Jerod pulled out a long piece of paper from beneath a stack of fliers. "I did. But—" He looked up, troubled. "It doesn't make sense."

"What do you mean?" Stephen held out his hand. Jerod placed the piece of paper across his palm.

The familiar World City logo was printed across the top. Kat's full name and the bounty amount came below. Then a couple of paragraphs about her offense. Blaylock and the two young men were listed. Then in bold letters that the fugitive was wanted live. And . . .

Stephen held the paper up closer and shook his head. "They want her brought to the Tower? That doesn't make any sense. A convict is always brought to precinct."

"Yes. And that's not the only thing. How in the world could Miss Bloodmayne have done those things? We have both met her. Kill two men, burn a third? All three from World City families no less." Jerod leaned forward across his desk, causing a couple of pieces of paper to flutter to the floor. "It seems more like a cover up for something else. We both know the Sterlings would do something like this to hide something distasteful done by one of their sons."

Stephen shrugged, his heart cold inside his chest. "Perhaps there is more to Miss Bloodmayne than we know. Or maybe one of Dr. Bloodmayne's enemies is targeting his daughter and the accusation is false."

Jerod leaned back in his wooden chair and wrapped his hands around his knee. "I would have thought so too, except that it was her father, acting with the World City council, that put the bounty out on her."

Stephen looked up, the paper held tight in his hand. "Dr. Bloodmayne placed the bounty?"

"Yes! Doesn't that seem odd to you? Her own father! What kind of man puts out a bounty on his daughter?"

Stephen shrugged, but his insides coiled at the thought. What father, indeed? Given what Kat had said about her father, maybe Dr. Bloodmayne could. Especially if he knew what she could do.

"I don't know, Stephen." Jerod let go of his knee and pulled out a piece of paper with scribbling across it that looked vaguely like his handwriting. "Things are not adding up with this whole situation."

Just when Stephen was going to acquiesce to Jerod's points, the scene from that morning blazed again across his mind: The bounty hunters thrown across the room, the furniture moving, and Kat's high-pitched laugh. No, Jerod was wrong. He just didn't know all the facts. Anyone would think what Jerod did, unless they knew the truth. "I don't think we know Miss Bloodmayne as well as we think we do."

Jerod looked up from his notes. "Wait, are you saying you agree with the bounty? You really think Miss Bloodmayne could have done those things?"

Stephen carefully folded the piece of paper in his hand. "I know from my own past that women are capable of many things, more than we give them credit for."

Jerod stood and leaned across his desk. "Stephen, Miss

Bloodmayne is not your former fiancée. You can't keep placing Vanessa's face across every woman who crosses your pa—"

"That's enough!"

Jerod shut his mouth and his face paled. A drop of sweat dripped off the edge of his nose.

Stephen breathed deeply and looked away. He hadn't meant to snap. "My past is my own. And you will never bring it up. Do you understand?"

Jerod slowly sat down. "I understand. My apologies."

Stephen took another breath and let it out. "Having been with Miss Bloodmayne for the last couple of days, I can assure you that there is more to her than you know."

Jerod steepled his fingers together, the emotions from moments ago erased, leaving behind a neutral face. "Just one more thing. Be careful, Stephen. Something is happening inside this city. More convicts are disappearing from Delmar Penitentiary, Antonio and his gang have pulled out of the southern district, and there are several cases of grave robbery from the St. Lucias Cemetery."

Stephen frowned. "How do you know all this?"

"Rumors on the streets. Even the police are on edge right now. And now this bounty on Miss Bloodmayne, right after the death of your aunt—her housekeeper. It's all just strange."

Stephen stuffed the paper into the pocket of his duster. "I'll keep that in mind."

"So you're still going to turn her in?"

Stephen let his breath out. "Yes. I am."

Jerod pressed his lips together. "I'll be in tomorrow to process the check. Please be sure you're doing this for the right reason."

His face darkened. "I am."

Jerod nodded and stood. He grabbed his hat and coat from the nearby coat rack. "Will there be anything else tonight?"

"No, thank you, Jerod. I'll see you in the morning."

Jerod jammed his hat on, gave Stephen a curt nod, and headed for the door.

A minute later Stephen found himself standing in the middle of his office alone and silent. The dogs were fighting once again inside his chest. To give Kat over or to keep her safe. He ran a hand through his hair. He could still see her face in the shadows on the stairs, her dark eyes, her lips slightly parted. He could hear the loneliness in her voice again. *I don't want to be alone.* And the way she tasted when he kissed her . . .

He spun around and let out a growl. *No. I will not be tied to a woman again. She is a danger to society. I must do this.*

Jerod's warning rang in his ears. *Be sure you're doing this for the right reason.*

Stephen tore the door open and headed out into the hallway. "I am." He shut the door behind him and locked it up. His hand paused by the keyhole.

But was he really?

28

Kat sat up, jolted from the darkness of her mind by the sound of the cab door opening. She stifled a yawn with the back of her hand as Stephen slid into the seat across from her. "Did you get what you needed?"

"I did."

"So you have a new lead?" A pool of warmth sprang up inside her middle.

"Not exactly."

The cab lurched forward and started down the streets of World City with a steady cadence. Lamplights were lit, casting the smog filled city into something more soft and warm.

Kat studied Stephen. His face was turned toward his own window, his chin resting on a closed fist. The light played across his face, accentuating the firm lines, his lips pressed tight, and the small mustache and beard he kept trimmed. His eyes moved back and forth as if searching for something outside the window.

Slowly, the warmth inside her belly turned to something more, like she had missed a step and was falling. Heat spread across her cheeks, and she placed a hand across her middle.

A fuzzy memory played at the back of her mind. Something about last night. Standing in the stairway. Staring into Stephen's eyes. And . . .

Her heart flew up into her throat and for one moment she felt like she was suspended in air.

They had kissed.

Kat pressed a hand to her cheek, her mouth dry.

It all came back now.

Stephen had pulled away, but she had reached for him again.

And then everything had become a jumble of feeling, colors, and fire.

She sat frozen, staring at Stephen, her body fluctuating between hot and cold. She had kissed him. She, who had never even been courted by a man, had kissed him. Against all that was proper and right, she had kissed him.

She couldn't breathe. Even as she tried to draw in a mouthful of air, everything fell into place, like one of those wooden puzzle toys she played with as a child.

Somewhere over the last few days, she had fallen in love with Stephen.

Her hand stole to her neck. How could this happen? And yet . . .

She trusted him. Respected him. Found something in him she wanted to connect with.

But what do I do now?

Stephen turned and looked at her, not speaking.

Kat sat back and hoped the shadows could hide her heated face. Every part of her could feel the distance—or lack thereof—between them.

At that moment everything she knew about propriety and etiquette vanished. In a different time and in a different world, they would never have been in a coach together at night, unescorted. They would have met at a ball. He would have asked her father if he could court her. She would have said yes. And after many supervised meetings, there would have been a chaste kiss followed by a proposal.

But she didn't live in that world. She lived in this one, where evil dwelt inside her, and, with her mind, she could cause the world to stand still, move furniture, or throw men against the wall. Or burn it all with a wave of her hand.

In this world she was a monster.

The coach jostled, throwing Kat forward. Before she could react, Stephen caught her by the forearms. They stared at each other. Her heart pounded inside her ears.

"Kat," he said hoarsely. "I . . ."

He dropped his hands and sat back, shaking his head as if in answer to some unspoken question. "We should be there soon," he said, turning his attention back to his window.

She licked her lips, her whole body tingling. "Where?" The word came out breathless. She blushed and turned her face aside, hoping Stephen hadn't heard the change in her voice.

"You'll see."

She gripped her hands and sat back as well. Was it possible, after all this was over—after they found Dr. Latimer and she was cured—that she could live a normal life, like every other woman in World City?

She glanced at Stephen. She hoped so.

Wait . . .

Kat turned and looked out her own window. She knew this part of town. The classic architecture of the northern part of World City passed by the window. The many-paned windows, the dark brick with white trim. Classic, clean lines. And in the middle of this neighborhood . . .

Her scalp prickled and a shiver went down her back. She gripped the window and leaned closer. There had to be some mistake. Maybe they were just passing through the science district. But something didn't feel right.

When the coach turned right, the Tower stood at the end of the block. Lights flickered in the topmost windows. Additional lights were lit along the ground, leading to the double set of oak doors that led into that ancient place of learning. The coach rumbled along outside the iron fence that surrounded the Tower.

The hairs on her arms and neck rose. Her thoughts raced at such a speed that she could barely put them together. Stephen couldn't possibly be taking her to the Tower, could he?

She shook her head. No, he wouldn't. Not after what she shared, about her life, about her father. He wouldn't do that to her.

Kat worked her mouth, trying to get enough moisture to form words.

They drew closer to the Tower.

"Stephen," she finally said, barely able to push the word past her dry lips.

He didn't say anything, didn't move.

"Stephen," she said again, a bit louder. They were now a block away from the Tower.

Her thoughts buzzed inside her mind like a hive of bees, and adrenaline drowned out every other feeling. Her breath burst in and out. "Stephen! Are you—are you taking me . . ."

The coach slowed to a stop next to the gates.

Stephen never looked at her, never turned around, and never said a word.

Kat's question died on her lips.

He really was taking her back.

A fire rushed through her, thrusting her into action. She reached across the cabin and grabbed his arm. "You can't do this! Please! Anything but this!"

Stephen shrugged her off and opened the door.

"Stephen!" Her foot caught on the bottom edge of her skirt and she fell forward. She hit the floor of the coach, her hands tingling from the impact. The other Kat was awakening inside her, the burn and desire growing. "No, no," she murmured, pressing a fist to her chest.

The burn dimmed. She scrambled across the floor of the coach. Thirty feet away, past the iron fence, three men emerged from the Tower. Stephen waited a couple of feet away.

Kat glanced left, then right. She had to get away, before the men came, or before the monster inside her emerged.

Stephen spun around as if sensing what she was planning. Before she could react, he closed the distance between them and clamped his hands down around both of her wrists.

Kat looked up into his face. He stared back, hard and cold. "It has to be this way, Kat."

Black spots appeared before her eyes. She swayed. "Why are you doing this? I thought you were my friend. I thought I could trust—"

Everything broke inside her. She dropped her head and let out a sob. Tears followed, like a river let loose. "I was wrong. *I was wrong!*"

She tried to raise her hands, but Stephen clamped down even harder.

The monster roared and her vision turned red. Kat sucked in a gurgled breath, her eyes wide. *No! I can't lose control.*

She focused on him. Even now, her heart beat for him. "Stephen, please," she whispered, her face wet. "Don't do this. Don't let them take me."

He hesitated.

The men were ten feet away.

"Help me find Dr. Latimer. He can cure me."

The first man reached them. Medium height, with brown hair combed to the side and a wide mustache. He was dressed in a white lab coat with a piece of paper tucked into the breast pocket. Kat vaguely recognized him as one of the scientists who worked for her father.

Kat looked back at Stephen.

Stephen grimaced. "I'm sorry."

She stared back, her mouth open. He might as well have shot her in the chest with his revolver.

She was falling again, but not in that pleasant way like during her coach ride. This time she was falling into an abyss, an ever-gaping jaw from which she would never return.

"Good job, Grey," the first man said. "The police said you were the best at tracking people down."

She couldn't move. She was too numb inside, too weak. Even the monster had no will to move.

Stephen turned her toward the man, shifting his grip so he now held her wrists behind her back. Two other scientists joined the first.

"This one is dangerous," said the second man, a bit smaller than the first. "Probably the most dangerous person in all of World City. I'm surprised you were able to catch her."

Kat lifted foggy eyes to the man on the right. He held up a needle and syringe. The fog began to clear with the sudden rapid beat of her heart. "No, no!" She backed away, but Stephen's hold gave her nowhere to go.

"You're not going to hurt her, right?" he said behind her.

She arched her neck and screamed. "Please, help me! Somebody! Anybody!"

"No." The man brought the needle toward her neck. She watched with bulging eyes. "This will just put her to sleep."

Kat screamed and reared back, but Stephen held her in place.

"It's for your own good," he whispered in her ear.

He has no idea what he's talking about!

"I promise I will continue my hunt for Dr. Latimer. Until then . . ."

The needle pierced her neck.

Kat's mouth flew open. Cold flooded her neck, rushing through her body. She slumped against Stephen. "You . . . shouldn't have . . . done . . . "

A dark curtain fell across her vision and everything went black.

29

The man stepped back, the syringe empty in his hand. "There. That should keep her asleep until we can get her upstairs."

"Are you sure?" Stephen said, remembering Kat from that morning and the fleeting look across her face a minute ago. If she hadn't kept herself under control . . . He frowned. Why had she?

"Yes. And we will keep her sedated until Dr. Bloodmayne is ready to talk to her."

"You mean her father?"

The man with the mustache looked up. "Yes." He narrowed his eyes.

Stephen glared back. "What does Dr. Bloodmayne plan on doing with her? Why isn't she being taken to the precinct to be processed?"

"That is none of your concern. Your job was to bring her in. We'll take care of the rest."

The third man, a burly sort of fellow with arm muscles twice the size of Stephen's, reached for Kat.

He didn't want to let her go. A cold hurricane raged inside his gut. He shouldn't have done this. He shouldn't have brought her here. But she lied to him! How could he help a woman who wouldn't tell him the truth?

The burly man grabbed Kat and threw her over his shoulder like a sack of flour.

"Careful!" Stephen yelled and raised his hand.

The brute ignored him and headed for the Tower.

A bitter taste filled his mouth and he lowered his hand. He watched Kat's head bounce with each step the man took, her dark hair, loose from the chignon, swaying back and forth.

Kat would be safe here, right? She had to be. After all, the brightest minds in all of World City were here. Perhaps Dr. Latimer wasn't the only one who could help her.

But deep inside he knew it was all a lie. And yet he was letting the lie continue. How was he any different than Vanessa?

"I will have your check delivered to your office in the morning," the man with the mustache said, offering a handshake.

Stephen grunted and turned away. He needed to leave. He told the driver his address and climbed back into the carriage. The cabin felt cold and empty.

The carriage lurched forward and he let out a heavy sigh, scrubbing his hands over his face. When he had first gone into the bounty-hunting business, it had been hard at times. Not the actual hunt part; he enjoyed the thrill of the chase. And most of his bounties he knew without a doubt were guilty. But there were those occasional ones that left him feeling sick after he deposited them at the precinct.

Like he felt now.

Twenty minutes later the carriage reached his street. It was late, the time when decent people were already in bed, but then, Stephen felt anything but decent at the moment.

Upstairs, he pulled off his boots and tossed them into the corner, then fell on his single bed. He pulled his pillow up beneath him and stared at the wall ahead.

Vanessa. He hadn't allowed his mind to dwell on her in almost two years. But ever since Kat had shown up in his life, Vanessa had been there, standing in the shadows of his thoughts.

Yes, they were alike in some ways. Both women had long, dark hair and matching dark eyes. Pale skin, tinted pink when embarrassed or angry.

But that is where the comparison ended.

Stephen shifted to his side and stared out the small window that opened up into the alley. Hardly any light shone through the panes, leaving him in darkness.

Vanessa had been a predator, feigning innocence when in reality she had been a tiger.

But Kat . . .

Stephen sat up and placed his feet on the floor. He gripped his face in his hands. Kat wasn't Vanessa. She had an innocence about her, and a hidden strength. Or was that stubbornness? A small smile crept across his lips. Just when he thought he had her figured out, she would surprise him. Like last night, when she reached for him and kissed him.

He swallowed, his heart thudding inside his chest.

Then she surprised him again this morning. The other Kat.

"God, what do I do?" he whispered, then pressed his lips shut. He had no right to talk to God. He had left God behind a long time ago.

Instead, he rubbed his face and lay down. Eventually he fell into a fitful sleep. Kat's face appeared in his dreams, first smiling, then sad, then . . .

They were standing on the stairway again inside the inn at Covenshire.

"Stephen, I don't want to be alone." She looked into his face, her dark eyes wide, her mouth slightly open.

"Kat." He drew his head down, closer, closer . . .

The scene melted away into darkness. The darkness morphed into a gloomy green. He blinked and found himself in a laboratory. Long, narrow metal tables lined the side walls. The green came from mining lamps set up at the head of each table. At the end of the room, a form lay on the metal table to the left.

Stephen walked between the metal beds. His hair rose along his arms and neck. There was no sound, no smell. Just him and the metal tables, green lights, and . . .

She lay on the long, metal table in the sickly green light, dressed in a simple white gown, her eyes shut.

"Kat?" Stephen approached. There were tubes and long, thin metal cylinders sticking out from her arms, chest, and legs.

Slowly she opened her eyes. They were empty, like all the life had been sucked from them.

"Kat?" he said again, a shiver running through his entire body.

Her mouth opened and she spoke. "I don't want to be alone." Emotionless, automaton-like. "I don't want to be alone. I don't want to be—"

Stephen woke with a gasp and sat up. It was still dark outside, but the faintest light of morning seeped into the alley outside his window. He ran a hand through his damp hair and sucked in another breath of air.

That place in his dream, he knew where it was from: Kat's story about her father's secret laboratory. He had never been in the actual Tower himself, just the bottom floor, but it was exactly how he had pictured it when Kat had described it.

He stared at the window, his eyes wide. "I shouldn't have left her there."

Stephen ran down the hall toward his office, morning light spilling across the wooden floor from the window behind him. His stomach knotted up inside, every time he thought about last night. He should have looked more closely at the warrant. Everything about it was wrong. Murderers, no matter what, were to be taken directly to the precinct. There was no reason Kat should have been delivered to the Tower. None, unless there was more going on. And his instincts were screaming there was more.

But instead of listening to instinct, he had let his past grievances warp his mind. Then he had assuaged his conscience by convincing himself she would find help for her condition. That the Tower wanted her for benevolent reasons.

He ran a hand across his face. Now his only hope was to undo what he had done and free Kat.

He reached for his office door. There was information about the Tower that his assistant Jerod kept in one of the filing cabinets—

Someone was here.

Stephen paused and listened. Yes, there was someone in his office. And it was too early for Jerod to be here. He pulled out his revolver and soundlessly checked the cartridge. Barely breathing, he reached for the doorknob with his other hand and turned it without a sound.

He led with the revolver, his finger near the trigger, but not on it. He slipped between the gap and did a one-eighty of the room. The front room was still dark except for where a bit of light filtered through the shades near Jerod's desk.

Stephen paused.

A form slouched in Jerod's chair.

On second glance, Stephen realized it *was* Jerod. With blood stained across his front.

"Jerod!" Stephen holstered his revolver and rushed into the room.

Jerod looked up and blinked, his glasses missing from his face. "Stephen? What are you doing here?"

"Never mind that, what happened to you?" Stephen went around the desk and pulled the shades up, then back to Jerod's side and yanked open his vest.

Jerod gave a cry of pain and hunched forward.

"Sorry. How bad is it?"

Jerod panted. "I—I think the bullet missed anything vital. But I've lost a lot of blood."

"I can tell." Jerod's face was pale and glistening with sweat. Stephen eased him back and pulled away the vest again, only more gently this time. He found a hole in Jerod's side but no exit wound. "Who shot you?"

"Don't know. I went to investigate the rumors I'd heard about the Tower."

"Because of last night?"

Jerod glanced up. "Yes. I went to St. Lucias to investigate the grave robberies."

Stephen looked around, spotted one of Jerod's handkerchiefs peeking out of the top drawer, and pulled it out. "I take it you found something."

"Yes."

Stephen folded the handkerchief and placed it over the wound. "Hold this."

Jerod lifted his hand and placed it on the spot.

Leaving Jerod to put pressure on the wound, Stephen dashed across the room and grabbed a scarf from the coatrack. "I'm going to wrap your scarf around to hold the handkerchief in place. Then we need to get you to a doctor."

Jerod grabbed his arm. "It's not safe out there. That's why I came here."

"You'll die here." Stephen wrapped the scarf around Jerod's body and pulled it tight.

Jerod groaned. "But—"

"I know a doctor down in Southbrook. I trust him." He helped Jerod out of the chair. "Come on. Let's get you out of here."

"I was right."

"About?" Stephen asked, wrenching the door open and propping it with his foot as he maneuvered Jerod through.

Jerod sucked in a breath through his teeth, his face clenched in pain. "The Tower *is* involved in grave robbery."

The sick feeling in Stephen's gut solidified further. "How do you know it was the Tower you saw last night?" They stepped out into the hallway. Morning light streamed in through the windows on either end of the hallway.

Jerod gasped and hunched over. "I—I followed them. And I saw Dr. Bloodmayne."

Stephen froze. Kat's words came rushing back. *There are things you don't know about my father, things he has done in the name of science.*

Then it was true. The Tower *was* involved, and probably not in just grave robberies, but in the missing people. And more than the Tower. It couldn't accomplish all of this by itself. The World City council had to be involved as well. And if the World City council, then also the police force at the highest level in order to cover up anything that came to light.

He swayed and his vision darkened. But why? What was their ultimate purpose? And what did Kat have to do with all this?

There could only be one answer. Her power. And—he swallowed—he had handed her right to them.

Outside, Jerod gripped his arm, his eyes wide. "You didn't take Miss Bloodmayne there, did you? Please say you didn't take her to the Tower."

Stephen looked away. He hardly ever made mistakes. But this one was by far his worst.

"You need to get her back. Stephen, you need to get her back!"

"I know!" He grabbed Jerod's shoulder and looked down at his sweat-bathed face. "I know."

Stephen hailed a cab at the corner and paid the driver extra for his discretion. He didn't have time to take Jerod down to Southbrook himself, not if he was going to rescue Kat.

He watched the cab pull away, then raced back into the building.

Everything pointed back to Dr. Bloodmayne: Kat's condition, Aunt Milly's death, the bounty. And he had turned Kat over to her father. The cold hurricane inside his chest returned.

What a fool I've been!

He hurried back into his office and went straight for the filing cabinets along the wall to the right. Jerod was a very precise man, one reason he had hired him. He kept information filed on every district in World City just in case Stephen ever needed something for a mission.

His fingers brushed the T tab, and he yanked out the thick folder on the Tower. Flipping through it, he found what he sought: blueprints.

He shuffled past the plans for the auxiliary buildings: the academy classrooms, the libraries, the dorms. There. The main building, an eight-story behemoth that encompassed an entire block. The Tower got its name from the tower that protruded from the eighth floor at the front of the building, a rectangular citadel rising another five stories, with a steep, sharp roof at the top, like the turret of a castle.

He scanned the plans. Getting in wouldn't be too hard. There were multiple entrances besides the main one in the front, which he planned to avoid. Smaller doors around the perimeter allowed scientists working in the other buildings to cross the street and enter instead of having to use the front entrance. He doubted they were guarded, at least he hadn't seen any guards the few times he'd had business at the Tower.

Even then, getting past guards wouldn't be an issue. He would just flash his badge—the one given to him by the police for bounty purposes—and walk inside.

The real question was where would Kat be?

Stephen pulled on the hair beneath his lip, his eyes darting across the schematics. His gaze hovered on the top floors. Kat said her father's private laboratories were at the top, along with his office. Most likely that was where she was being held.

Or worse.

He clamped his jaw shut. Leaving the mess of papers on Jerod's desk, he went to his own, pulled out the drawer to the right, and reached for the wooden box in the back. Hopefully he wouldn't find himself in a gunfight, but he would be ready if it came to that.

After reloading both revolvers and stashing more rounds in his pockets, he placed the box back in the drawer and closed it. He had his way in, but getting out would be harder. By the time he reached Kat, the Tower would know he was there. His mind tore through every contact he had in World City. Who could help him? Who wasn't in any way connected to the council or police force?

Captain Robert Grim. Robert said he would be stopping in World City before taking the *Lancelot* across the strait to Austrium. It was a long shot; Robert might have already left the city. But if he was still here, Robert might just be the man to get him and Kat away from the Tower.

Stephen holstered the weapons, drew his duster closed, and pulled the brim of his hat down across his forehead. Telegraph Grim. Head to the Tower.

And right a wrong.

30

Kat blinked and groaned. She sat up and brushed her hair away from her face. She lay in a single bed inside a small room, with a table nearby and a window in the wall across from her. The walls were painted a dull gray, and the air held a clinical clean smell, the way her classrooms smelled in the morning after a thorough washing by the janitorial staff.

She looked around again. Nothing but walls and the table. A blanket lay across her lower body. She still wore the blouse and skirt she had been wearing all week, but her corset had been removed, along with her boots.

Kat looked over the edge of the bed, then back at the table. Where was her stuff? *And where am I? Wait . . .*

Her heart dropped. She threw back the blanket and staggered across the cold floor toward the window. Down below she could see World City: thousands of smokestacks and rooftops, the Meandre River to the right, and familiar buildings surrounding the one she was in. If she was this high up, it meant that she was in the main building. The Tower itself.

Kat stepped back, her hand against her chest. *Then it wasn't a dream. Stephen really . . . really . . .* She swallowed and stumbled toward the bed and collapsed across the mattress, bile filling her throat. The one person she had trusted after Ms. Stuart's death, the one person she thought would help her.

Instead, he had turned her in.

"What do I do?" she whispered. Her hands shook and a cold sweat spread across her body. The familiar icy tingle spread across her fingers as her blood began to pound through her veins. The air grew still, until she could see each particle of dust hanging in the light from the window.

Kat gasped.

The world lurched back into motion. The dust fluttered around like glitter in a snow globe. With each breath, she forced her body to calm down. *Can't lose control. Never lose control.*

The thought of Ms. Stuart reminding her of this helped calm her.

Now . . .

Kat stood again and walked toward the window. She pressed her hands against the panes and looked out, counting. She was only on the fifth floor, not in the actual tower, so she wasn't in her father's laboratories. Perhaps this was an exam room, or a recovery room.

She let out her breath and pressed a hand to her middle. Thank God. Her eyes widened. Perhaps she still had time to get away.

The door opened behind her.

Kat spun around, her body back in flight mode.

Her father stood in the doorway, dressed in trousers and a white lab coat. His gray hair was combed back, each strand in place. His face always reminded her of a hawk, that long narrow nose, thin lips, and glinting hazel eyes. Those eyes were now on her, studying her. "You're finally awake."

Her mouth went dry and the room spun for a moment.

Father didn't seem to notice. He walked in and shut the door behind him.

"Father," Kat finally said, breathless.

"You gave me quite a scare, running off like that after Ms. Stuart's demise."

"Running . . . off?"

"Yes, I looked everywhere for you." He ran his fingers along the metal bed frame. "I was afraid that whoever broke into our home and murdered Ms. Stuart had taken you, too. Until the police identified you leaving World City by train to Covenshire, apparently under your own volition. Tell me, Kathryn, why did you run?"

Not for as long as she could remember had her father said so many words to her at one time. She searched his face for any trace of sympathy. Was there even a remote possibility he had feared for her well-being? "You were worried about me?"

"Of course I was. You are my only daughter. What would I do if I lost you?"

Kat mentally shook her head. It wasn't possible. She was having some kind of strange hallucination. There was no way her father had just said that.

She pressed a hand to her forehead and crossed the room. She sat down on the bed and stared at her father's pants, at the way each pleat was perfectly ironed, and every scuffmark removed from his shoes. Perfect, always perfect. "Do you know what happened to Ms. Stuart?"

"The police are looking into her case." No tinge to his voice, no wavering.

Kat sucked in her lip, the deep sorrow rushing back.

"I also offered to cover her burial expenses."

Was that supposed to comfort her? She clenched her hands, then loosened them. No, she could not afford to lose control in front of her father. "So why did you bring me here, to the Tower?"

Her father looked down on her, that same impassive look on his face. "I thought you would be safer here."

He said everything right, so why did she feel so defensive? *Because I don't trust him.*

Maybe she couldn't trust anyone. "So you sent a couple of thugs to bring me back?"

"Not thugs. Professional men to bring you back safely."

The three men from the inn flashed across her mind: the tattooed brawler, the dandy, and the brute with the strange prosthetic arm that shot like a cannon. Did her father actually think they would bring her back in one piece? Did he know they shot at her? Or was he lying? She crossed her arms, her thoughts buzzing around inside her head like a hive of angry bees. "So how long do I have to stay here?"

Her father moved for the first time since he had stepped into her room. He came around and stood in front of her. "Until I know you are safe. And I want you checked out. Rumors have reached my ears . . ."

His face changed. A glow entered his eyes, and his entire being seemed to tremble, like an eager dog.

Kat shrank back.

"I have heard you can do things, impossible things. Is that true?"

Your father must never know what you can do. Ms. Stuart's warning rang in her ears.

With a will stronger than she had ever employed before, Kat forced every emotion deep, deep down until she felt nothing. She smoothed her skirt, aware again of her missing corset and how stained her shirt had become. "I was afraid." Her voice sounded so normal, so even. "That is why I ran. I thought whoever was after Ms. Stuart would come after me as well."

Her father paused. He folded his hands together, his face smoothing back into impassivity. "I see. Are you afraid now?"

Yes!

"A little. May I go home?"

Her father slowly shook his head. "No. I don't think so, not until the killer is caught. And I want you checked out. I want to make sure nothing happened to you." That same gleam jumped back into his eyes.

"I'm fine, Father. I just need to rest."

"Then rest here, at the Tower. I insist."

Why had Stephen brought her here? Was he in league with her father as well? The thought made her sick. All she wanted to do was lie down and curl up into a ball. But the longer she stayed here, the greater the chances were that her father would find out what she had done to those men he had sent to retrieve her. Or maybe Stephen had already told him.

Her stomach clenched at the thought. "I'll stay here, for now." At least it would buy her time so she could find a way to escape. And this time she would do it alone. But she needed to rest first. Already she felt dizzy from the array of thoughts and feelings, and the side effects from whatever the men had used last night to put her under.

Her father knelt down in front of her. Kat drew her hands back and stared at him wide-eyed.

"Kathryn, you are precious to me. That is why I insist that you be checked. I want to make sure everything is fine."

What the—? Precious? Since when?

"Now, rest. You are safe here." He patted her knee with that same eager look again on his face.

She sat still, frozen there on the bed.

Her father stood and walked toward the door, straightening his lab coat as he left.

The moment the door shut, Kat collapsed on her side and stared out the window across from her. A hole expanded inside her middle. A gaping, black hole that seemed to suck everything away until she lay there numb.

I wish I could believe him. I wish Father really did care about me.

She grasped the blanket between her cold fingers and pulled it to her chin. And Stephen . . .

Why? Why did you leave me here?

Fatigue weighed down on her, settling across her head, her chest, and her legs. Clouds rolled across the window, obscuring the sun.

The door opened and Kat sat up. Two men walked in, one heavyset with a thick, black mustache, the other tall and thin. They both wore white lab coats over button up shirts and trousers.

The taller one spoke to her. "Miss Bloodmayne, if you would please come with us. Your father has instructed us to escort you upstairs."

Upstairs? "Are you taking me to my father's laboratory?"

"Yes."

The blood drained from her face. She slowly rose, her gaze darting between the men and the door. Could she make it?

"I wouldn't do that if I were you, Miss Bloodmayne. We hope you will come willingly. But if not . . ."

The burly man stepped forward.

Kat dashed for the door. She made it through the doorway and out into the hall, where she skittered to a stop. About a dozen people stood in the lit hallway, all wearing white lab coats. Every face turned in her direction. One very familiar.

"Marianne!"

Marianne stood next to the wall, dressed in the same lab coat as the other scientists in the hall.

Kat started in her direction. "Marianne! Oh, thank God! Please help me! They're trying to take m—"

A hand clamped down on her shoulder.

"So you've chosen the hard way, eh?" a deep voice said behind her.

Kat screamed and tore away from the grip. She stumbled forward, hands out.

Marianne and the other scientists took a couple of steps back. Kat caught herself and shook her head. "Please, Marianne." She sought her friend's gaze, wishing for the familiar green sparkle, but she found only fear and resolve.

Her hand fell. But . . . why?

Without meeting her eyes, Marianne slipped through a door and disappeared. Kat stared after her, frozen.

An ugly chuckle sounded behind her as the tough approached.

The black fire inside her ignited.

Oh no! Kat gripped her throat. She reached for the man closest to her. "Please, you have to help me. I can't stay here!"

He jerked away.

"You don't understand, I can't control—" She gasped and fell to her knees, both arms wrapped across her chest. She squeezed her eyes shut. *Can't lose control. Can't lose control.*

Air began to whip around her and red filled her vision. The monster was awakening.

She curled into a ball and rocked back and forth. *I . . . need . . . to focus—*

Burn them. Burn them all!

"No!" she screamed.

It's the only way you can escape.

No! I won't hurt any more people.

A small sting pierced her neck. Kat stopped rocking and looked up, mouth open. The hallway was empty. "Just . . . let me go," she whispered. The tiled floor met her face: cold, hard, unyielding.

A voice spoke above her, but she barely caught the words as she sped toward the darkness.

"Strip her down and prepare her for Dr. Bloodmayne."

31

"Kathryn, you are a stubborn woman. Just like your mother."

Kat slowly opened her eyes. Dim green light filled her vision. A second later the smell hit her: a combination of rotting meat and incense. She coughed and tried to sit up.

Her wrists would not move.

Breathing fast, she looked to her right, then to her left. Both of her hands were trapped by thick metal bands welded to the table where she lay spread out. Her ankles were bound too. Only a thin white gown covered her body and ended at her knees. A strange, faint whirring noise resonated to her right. The green light came from a miner's lamp that sat just beyond her head.

Cold air seeped through the gown and across her exposed skin, causing her to shiver. She pulled at the bands and coughed as another wave of the foul scent filled her nose.

"Where am I?" Her voice echoed across the room. As her eyes adjusted to the dim light, she could see tables lined up along the middle of the room, each with dark colored lumps scattered across their metallic surfaces. Steel rods and tubes hung from the ceiling above her. A metal cylinder the size of a footstool sat on a workbench nearby with arcs of electricity flashing around it.

The awful smell seemed to be coming from the other tables. Wait . . .

A scream filled her mouth. That smell, those lumps . . . they were body parts. And the dark pools beneath them . . .

God, help me!

She yanked at the metal bands and arched her back, yelling and pulling with all her might. She had to get out of here!

"You're going to damage yourself, Kathryn."

Kat sucked in a breath and glanced up. Her father emerged from the shadows, wiping his hands on a long piece of white cloth. The green light cast by the miner's lamps made his face look sickly. He dropped the cloth on the nearest table beside the remains of a hand and came to stand beside her.

"I had hoped our little chat in the recovery room downstairs would have made things easier for all of us. Instead, you made things difficult." He sighed and brushed her hair back.

Kat flinched and looked away. Another cold breeze blew across her body and she shivered.

"So much like your mother," he murmured.

She glanced at him from the corner of her eye and her mouth fell open. Father never talked about Mother, not once in all the years she could remember.

He took a step back and cocked his head to the side, the soft look from moments before morphing into something stern and cold. "For years I worked on this project, extensively testing every theory I came up with. But nothing came of it. To think that all this time, the answer's been under my very nose." He placed a hand across his middle and tapped his chin with the other. "Maybe if I had spent more time with you, I would have seen the evidence."

"See—seen what?"

"That you are the culmination of my life's work."

His declaration seemed to hang in the air before it rushed through her ears and lodged its way into her mind. *The culmination of his life's work?* Coming from any other father, it would have sounded like high praise to a child. But that wasn't what her father meant, and the words twisted inside her like metal shards, tearing and shredding her heart.

He had made her this way.

And he was proud of it.

"Yes." He stepped to her side and peered down at her. "I want to know how you did it. How did you set that hallway on fire? And throw those men against the wall? The young woman said you did it with your hands, like witchcraft. What else can you do? How long have you had this power?"

The questions came pelting down from her father's lips.

Kat stared up at him and cringed. "What do you mean?"

"I know you are different, Kathryn." Her father stepped back and ran a hand along the top of his head. "But when did it happen? When did you change?" He started walking around the laboratory, seemingly in thought. "And can I replicate it?"

He knew. He knew all of it.

"That fire—" He turned around and pointed at her. "That fire in the nursery years ago. That was you." He shook his head. "Yes, yes, right there in front of me. And Ms. Stuart never told me!" He clenched his hand, then took a deep breath and let it out slowly, his hand relaxing as he did. He smoothed the front of his lab coat and walked back toward Kat.

She couldn't feel her fingers; they were frozen. And her feet were numb too. The hairs along her arms and legs rose with each chilly breeze that moved through the laboratory. She was exposed, spread out on the table like a specimen ready to be dissected.

A wave of dizziness swept over her, leaving her weak and trembling. Wait, her father wasn't going to do that, was he? Would he—she swallowed—would he really dissect her?

Yes, he would.

The laboratory seemed to be closing in on her. She couldn't breathe! Cold sweat drenched her body, and she shook uncontrollably. The lump inside her chest began to beat. Thump, thump.

Do it. Show him what you can do!

Kat twisted her head to the side and squeezed her eyes shut. She pictured the park near the Tower, the same one Ms. Stuart had taken her to after graduation. She watched the couples walking by, hand in hand, and the bright array of flowers that lined the path. Sunlight poured through the trees.

She breathed. In. Out. Until the lump sank back down into her chest.

Cool fingers brushed her cheek.

Kat gasped and opened her eyes.

Her father's face filled her vision, his hazel eyes darting back and forth as he examined her face. Silence filled the laboratory. After a moment he straightened and tapped his chin with his finger. "I owe you an explanation. From one scientist to another. Perhaps it will help you understand how remarkable you are."

Kat gave him a small nod and stared up at him, wide eyed. The scent of decay filled her nostrils. Anything to keep him talking and not experimenting on her.

"For years I studied our physical world, tested everything I could find, and pushed beyond the knowledge we already possessed. But I knew there was more, more than what we could see. So I reached beyond that. I proved that everything is made of matter. And matter is not only the substance of everything, it is power too. Whoever can control matter can control everything."

Kat swallowed. She knew exactly what her father was talking about. Back at the inn in Covenshire, she had not only been able to suspend matter, she had been able to control it. Everything. The air, the chairs, even people. She could see each particle and do whatever she wanted with it. All with just her mind.

But at what price?

". . . we can control matter now, to a certain extent." Her father walked around the table as if giving a lecture to a classroom full of students. "I can create a fire and ignite matter. I can use my hand and throw matter in the form of an object. But what if a person could control all matter, with no physical intermediary?" He stopped and looked at her. "That was my goal: to unlock that power."

He started walking again. "I began experimenting on matter shortly after I married your mother, with no results. After a couple of years I recognized I needed to explore more unorthodox methods. So I started researching, looking into other means than science. I slowly realized that if I wished to unlock the power of the unseen, I needed to look into those areas of study that specialized in the unseen. I hoped that by combining my understanding of science and certain aspects of the mystical, I could finally discover the secret to unlocking the power of the life that binds us all. Still my experiments remained inconclusive. And then I realized something: what is more powerful than death?"

A tear slipped from the corner of Kat's eye and slid down her face, leaving a cold trail behind. She had never heard that kind of passion in her father's voice, at least not directed toward her.

He went on without noticing the tear, that maniacal gleam back in his eye. A couple of hairs had fallen across his forehead, so unlike his usual kempt self. "Death is the ultimate power, even over matter. All things succumb to it and there is no cure. If I could unravel the power of death, I could unlock the mystery of matter and control it. But then your mother died and I—" His voice cracked. The elation from moments ago bled away and he dropped his head.

The electricity pulsating around the strange metal cylinder crackled and an arc jumped before the contraption resumed its normal mode. The green lights flickered within the lanterns set up along the laboratory and the tubes that hung from the ceiling swung as if a hand had brushed past them.

Her father looked up and swept the errant hairs back in place. He straightened his lab coat and turned. "I put away my secret project and concentrated on expanding the Tower." He walked over to the electric cylinder and turned a knob at the bottom, his back toward Kat. "War broke out with Austrium, and I was commissioned to use my expertise to help with the war effort. I went back to studying death, drawing from every bit of research I could find."

And all the while you left me to be raised by Ms. Stuart. Kat stared up at the tubes hanging from the ceiling. Another tear slipped down her cheek.

"I had limited success, but my subjects always succumbed eventually. And the corpses did no better."

What? Kat twisted her head and stared at her father. "You used corpses?"

Dr. Bloodmayne turned around. "The World City council gave me permission to dig up remains from the common lots in St. Lucias. Only those recently dead proved useful. The closer to the time of death, the better. Eventually it seemed a better choice to find those on the brink of death and use them instead."

Kat stared at him. "You—you killed people?"

"Kathryn, Kathryn." He shook his head as if he were scolding her for taking a lollipop without permission. "They were already dying. There wasn't anything I, or any other scientist, could have done to save them. I didn't kill them, I merely used their last moments of life to further science for the benefit of all people."

She recoiled, her hands and feet straining against the metal bands. She was wrong. She wasn't the monster. Her father was.

Dr. Bloodmayne walked over to the table nearest the one she lay on and picked up the disembodied hand as if he were picking up a teacup. "Even then, I could not release the power I knew existed around death, even when employing some of the pagan rituals of old."

Kat pulled at the metal bands until the skin around her wrists was raw and scraped. Was this his plan for her? Was he going to kill her? His own daughter?

"But what if I was wrong?" He spun around and returned to Kat's side, his face alight with eagerness.

Kat shrank beneath his gaze. The monster inside her stirred again.

"I have been thinking about you, and recent events. I believe you can do what I've been trying to accomplish for the last thirty years. You can control matter. And I don't think that came about from death, but from another source of power:

from life. Somehow, during my initial experiments years ago, what I tried to accomplish through my own body I instead inadvertently passed on to you." He shook his head, amazed. "You were born this way."

The fire grew inside her chest. As she stared up into her father's eyes, she wanted to give in, unleash the fire and burn away the laboratory and all the darkness it contained. Even now she could feel the tingle across her fingers and the power pounding through her veins. A smile crept across her face. Oh yes, she would burn it until nothing remained.

But would she be able to stop with the laboratory? Or would she burn everything, the whole Tower— the whole city?

Kat licked her lips. What was this power doing to her? Every time the power erupted, it felt like it was consuming her very soul. Was there a point where it would consume all of her? Would any part of her remain? Or would she become a living husk, void of her being, with power that could destroy the world?

Her father had no idea what he had done to her.

"So what say you, Kathryn?" He bent over her, a smile across his lips. "Will you join me in uncovering the greatest scientific discovery of our time? Together, father and daughter, embarking on the journey of a lifetime."

Kat blinked. "You mean as your apprentice?"

"Yes, yes. And more. Do you understand what we could achieve together? We could stop the war and save lives. Working together to better mankind. The Bloodmayne legacy."

She stared up at her father. Everything she had ever wanted he was handing to her now. A relationship. An opportunity to work side by side. A chance to win his approval. Perhaps even his love.

She pictured them in one of the laboratories downstairs, side by side, comparing notes. Sharing excitement after a particularly difficult experiment. Photographed together in the *Herald* for all of World City to see.

Everything she had dreamed.

Her heart beat faster. And with it the monster surged forward.

Kat clamped down on the feeling and closed her eyes. She breathed through her nose and let her dream shrivel up and die. The dark fire inside her chest burned down to a low glow.

No, she would never help her father create other people like her. There was a reason such power had been locked away. Maybe God himself had locked it away. This power . . . it burned away the soul. It had to die, even if that meant it died with her.

She opened her eyes. "No." The word slipped quietly from her lips.

Her father grew still. His mouth tightened and his face lost all emotion except for the fire that burned in his eyes. "You realize I will not let an opportunity like this slip away. Either we work together, or I work alone. But I will find what I am looking for, no matter the cost."

His threat hung in the air like a guillotine's blade.

Kat breathed through her nose and looked him straight in the eye. "You mustn't do this, Father. It is not what you think. I do not control this power; it controls me. And I'm afraid if it is triggered again, I will not be able to stop it."

His nostrils flared. "Then that is your choice?"

"I won't help you." Beads of sweat formed along her upper lip and forehead. "And I implore you not to pursue this, for the good of all people." Her limbs shook and the dark fire stirred again. *Stay in control, just a little bit longer.*

The vein along his neck pulsed. "Science would never expand if we didn't take risks. Something I had hoped you would have learned during your time at the Tower Academy. Well then, Kathryn, if that's your choice . . ."

She closed her eyes and nodded, her body shivering from exposure and fatigue.

"Then I will leave you here. Some men will arrive shortly to begin the process."

Her eyes shot open. "Th—the process?"

But her father never answered. Instead, he disappeared into the shadows. A moment later, a bright light appeared in the form of a doorway. His silhouette stood inside the doorway, then the door closed, leaving her in the dark with only the strange green lights.

She stared up at the tubes and metal rods, and her teeth began to chatter. By "process" did her father mean experiments? Or would he go right to dissection?

Kat bit down the scream inside her throat and clenched her hands. Black spots converged across her vision.

God. Her mind fumbled for words. *If you are real and could possibly care about a person like me, please rescue me. Please save me from this place!*

32

Stephen stood on the street corner across from the Tower and stared up at the top floors. It was midmorning and World City bustled with life. Carriages rode by, people walked along the street, and scientists made their way between the Tower and the outlying buildings, hurrying to their next experiment or task, or whatever it was they did.

He pulled on the bit of hair below his lip. He was right about one thing: no guards, at least not on the outside. There would probably be some kind of security person inside, but he had his bounty hunter badge ready.

Stephen dropped his hand and headed across the street during a pause in traffic. The air, usually smog-filled, was fairly clear for World City this morning. The sky above was a light blue with feather-like clouds. The air was warm, but not warm enough that his duster looked out of place.

He walked along the iron fence that marked off the grassy area in front of the Tower and headed along the western side toward one of the smaller entrances. The Tower Academy stood to the north of the main building, the place where he caught his first glimpse of Kat over two years ago. So much had happened during those two years. At the time he had pictured a future with Vanessa, more promotions within the World City police, and a couple of children.

Instead he had become a reclusive bounty hunter with feelings for a woman he wasn't quite sure was human. And then he had gone and betrayed her.

He ran a hand across his face. Tainted. That's what he was. Tainted by his wounded past. And now Kat was paying the price. "Not if I can help it," he said under his breath.

Halfway down the main part of the building, a woman dressed in a simple gray skirt, suit coat, and a wide-brimmed hat exited a small door. She glanced his way, lifted her nose, and headed in the opposite direction.

Apparently the lady didn't think too highly of a man dressed more rogue than gentleman. He was used to it. Strange that Kat never seemed to view him that way. Was that because she lived in a world where men and women worked together and were not bound to the hierarchy that held most of the World City? Or was there more?

Stephen pushed the speculative thoughts aside. Time enough for that later. He moved toward the door the woman had left moments before. Besides, if there had been more between him and Kat, it was gone now. He had burned that bridge when he left her at the Tower last night. His belly knotted up at the memory. His only hope now was to get her safely away.

A church bell tolled in the distance, signaling nine o'clock in the morning. He picked up his pace. Robert had telegraphed that he would be in the area with his airship shortly after nine. Where they would meet up, he still wasn't sure. It would all depend on what happened inside the Tower.

Just beyond the door stood a desk in the hallway, blocking entry into the rest of the Tower. A man dressed in navy blue pants and vest stood behind the desk. He gave Stephen a tired look. "Can I help you?"

Stephen pulled his badge from his pocket. "Fugitive Recovery Agent Stephen Grey. I'm here to see about a fugitive brought in last night."

At the name "Stephen Grey" the man straightened and dropped his arms to his side. "Stephen Grey! I—I don't know about any fugitive here at the Tower."

Stephen glanced down the hall. "Do you mind if I check upstairs?"

"I don't know about—"

"I won't take long. And it's a matter of urgency."

The guard seemed to debate the matter, then nodded. "Go ahead, Mr. Grey."

Stephen gave him a curt nod. "I appreciate your consideration in this matter. And please keep my visit secret. You understand, right?"

The guard nodded again.

Stephen headed down the hall, his boots slapping the tile as he went. The entry doors on either end of the long hallway allowed natural light into the corridor. Interior doors lined the hall, all of them shut. As he walked by, he caught snippets of muffled conversations. Near the middle of the hall, two staircases opened up, one on either side, with a window on each level.

Stephen paused and looked at both stairways. They were identical. He went with the right one. If nothing else, it was closer to the direction he was heading, to the actual tower itself.

He went up eight flights of stairs, only passing two scientists on his way, each one ignoring him. On the eighth floor, he headed down the hall toward the tower. He passed by more rooms, these ones with the doors open. One room was lined with shelves of books, two looked like offices, one was filled with workstations covered with glass beakers and burners, and one with just tables. At the end of the hall, there was another staircase beside a large window that overlooked the front of the building. A sign hung by the stairway: "Private Tower labs. No Trespassing."

Now came the hard part.

Stephen started up the stairs. Depending on how many people worked up here, he might not have much time to find Kat, if she actually was in this part of the Tower.

She is. I know she is.

Stephen reached the ninth floor. Another window overlooked the front of the Tower. From this high up he could see the rooftops of World City and the rounded glass dome of the Capitol building, where the World City council resided.

He was about to continue upward when a smell wafted beneath his nose. He gagged and turned around, reaching for his handkerchief. A door stood nearby, one of several down the narrow hall. Taking a step closer, he removed the handkerchief from his nose and mouth and sniffed. *What the blazes is that?* Like a combination of spices and rotting meat. What were they experimenting on up here?

This seemed as good as place as any to start his search for Kat. Just as he reached for the doorknob, a man pulled the door open.

Stephen registered two things: green light in the room beyond and red blotches splattered across the man's lab coat and clean-shaven face. Too late to turn back. He would just have to improvise.

The man stepped away from the door, which clicked shut behind him. He frowned. "I'm sorry, this floor is restricted. I have to ask you to turn around and head back downstairs."

The red blotches across the man's lab coat looked like blood. Bile filled his throat and his stomach clenched. *Stay calm.* Smoothing his features, Stephen pulled his badge from his pocket. "Stephen Grey, Fugitive Recovery Agent, here to see about a fugitive brought in last night."

There was a flicker of recognition in the man's eyes. He spun around and drew a key from his pocket.

Stephen's hand went for his gun—

No. Killing would complicate things.

He closed the gap between them and brought his arm around the man's neck. Nestling the man's throat between his bicep and forearm, Stephen squeezed.

The man reached back, but Stephen already had a grip on the bicep of his free arm and, using his other hand, pressed the man's head into the crook of his elbow.

One . . . two . . . three . . .

The scientist went limp and Stephen loosened his hold, bringing the man to the floor. Pulling the man's arms from the sleeves of his lab coat, Stephen used the sleeves to bind the man inside his garment. He knotted the sleeves twice, then used the ties from the man's shoes to bind his feet together.

The man groaned.

Stephen looked up and around, then at the door. The key was still in the hole. He would just have to haul the man inside the room and dump him in a corner.

Stephen stood and turned the key, then pushed the door open. Dim green light filled the long, narrow room. A row of metal tables occupied the middle, about ten in all, most covered with odd-colored stains. It was the last one that caught his eye. Something—or someone—lay across the top. A metal cylinder sparked with electricity nearby, and strange tubes swung from the ceiling.

He gagged as a wave of rotting meat and spice breached his nose.

The scientist at his feet began to awaken.

Stephen pulled the man into the lab and dumped him against the wall. He shut the door and glanced around. A thin towel with dark splotches on it hung on a hook near the door.

His prisoner's eyes fluttered.

Gritting his teeth, Stephen grabbed the rag and stuffed it in the man's mouth and tied it behind his head. There, that should keep him still for a while.

Stephen stood and wiped his face, then wrinkled his nose. He didn't know a lot about the Tower or labs or science, but this didn't look like the rooms he had passed downstairs. More like a meat locker, minus the carcasses hanging from the ceiling.

Something moved at the end of the room.

Stephen stared at the form on the last table, the dim green light bathing the figure in a sickly color. It looked . . . human.

Kat's story came screaming back into his mind: about her father's private laboratories and the humans laid out on metal tables. Most of them dead.

And Jerod had said the Tower was involved in grave robberies, a secret they were so desperate to keep that they shot him.

This had to be one of those labs. And that body at the end of the room . . .

Stephen stepped back and grabbed the wall behind him, a wave of dizziness washing over his body. Cold sweat trickled down his back, and two black spots appeared across his eyes.

He almost turned and went for the door. In all his time in the bounty hunting business, never had he encountered such a dark and evil place. Even the mob bosses of World City had a certain civility about them compared with this.

The body moved.

Stephen sucked in his breath and slowly pushed away from the wall. No, it couldn't be.

But deep down, he knew it was.

33

Stephen started across the room. Maybe he was mistaken. *God, please. Don't let that be . . .*

He swallowed. Minutes. He only had minutes. With each step, his vision cleared. Though he breathed through his mouth, he could still taste the smell of blood and decay in the room.

Pools of dark liquid lay on some of the metal tables. He passed them by without a second glance. The metal cylinder let off another electrical current. Electricity sparked around the surface, then the contraption settled back into its dark, pulsating state.

Halfway across the room he identified the figure on the last table as female, dressed in a short, white gown that looked more like a nightdress. With dark hair across her face.

Stephen ran the rest of the way and stopped beside the table. The gown was almost sheer, showing each curve of the woman beneath. Only the slight rise and fall of her chest revealed life within the corpse-like body.

"Kat?" he whispered, the same wave of dizziness from earlier threatening to crash over him again.

The figure didn't answer.

He reached over and brushed the dark hair aside.

Kat lay there with eyes closed, her face so pale it looked white with a tint of green in dim light.

He wanted to yell, but bit back the words inside his mouth. They needed to leave, now!

He tried to scoop her up, but found thin tubes inserted into her wrists. Stephen withdrew his hands and stepped back. On closer inspection, he also found metal rods attached to her ribs, right below her breasts, barely visible beneath the translucent material of her gown.

Tearing his gaze away, he snatched his hat off and raked his fingers through his hair. *What do I do? God, what do I do?* He glanced at her again, careful to keep his eyes on where the metal rods were attached and not on her barely concealed breasts. Even lying here on the metal table, Kat was still a lady, and he would treat her as such.

With a deep breath, he shoved his hat back on. He approached the table again and placed a hand on her middle. Carefully, he tugged at the metal rods along her ribs. They gave with a small amount of pressure. One by one he pulled the rods out. Blood seeped out of the wounds, staining her white garment, but nothing gushed. He let out his breath and pulled the tubes out of her wrists.

He checked around her body for any other attachments. Nothing. She was free.

The scientist he had bound started shouting, but the cloth in his mouth stifled his yells.

Stephen scooped Kat up. She barely weighed anything in his arms. As he readjusted his hold on her, she neither moved nor woke.

"Kat . . ." He bowed his head. She smelled like the room,

like incense and decay. The blood from her side seeped onto the front of his shirt.

He clutched her tighter and moaned. How could they have done this? How could *he* have done this? His stomach clenched. He leaned down until he was inches from her face. "I am sorry," he whispered. "So very, very sorry."

Could she hear him? He didn't know.

The man behind him continued to shout.

Stephen straightened up, then turned and made his way across the laboratory with Kat. As he neared the man on the floor, the prisoner began to wriggle and shout even more.

A fire filled his chest as the red blotches across the man's lab coat caught his eye. Was that Kat's blood?

Without pausing, he delivered a swift kick to the head.

Crack!

The man slumped back to the floor, his eyes rolling up into his head, and a trickle of blood appearing beneath his right nostril.

Stephen wanted to kick the man again, but pulled back and continued out the door. Kat needed him more.

He hurried toward the staircase, the light from the large window at the end of the corridor illuminating his way. At the stairs, he paused and readjusted his hold on Kat. She was still cold. And pale. Death-like.

His stomach lurched. *Would she ever wake up?*

He shook his head. *No time to think about that now. We need to get out of here.*

He glanced out the window. The sky was bright blue with only a couple of clouds in sight. He twisted his neck right and left. Where was Grim with his airship? He should be here by now.

Footsteps echoed up the stairway.

Stephen stepped back and pressed his body against the wall. While holding Kat with one hand, he reached for his right revolver and pulled the weapon out.

A woman stepped out from the stairway, her carrot-colored hair pulled back in a chignon and a white lab coat over her dress.

He held the gun up. "Stop right there."

The woman stopped and her pale face grew even whiter. Her gaze bounced between the gun and Stephen's face, and finally landed on Kat.

Stephen clutched Kat tighter to his chest as if to shield her from the young woman. "I'm leaving with her, and if you try to stop me, I will shoot you."

She shook her head, her eyes wide. "I—I had no idea they would do that to Kat."

He frowned but kept his revolver leveled at the woman scientist. "What do you mean? Do you know Kathryn Bloodmayne?"

The woman gave him a jerky nod. "He said he knew what was wrong with her. He said he would help her." Her voice rose with each word.

Stephen kept his hand steady. "Who?"

"Dr.—Dr. Bloodmayne."

"Well, he lied to you." He glanced out the window behind the woman. The *Lancelot* appeared on the horizon, expanding as it skimmed over rooftops toward the Tower. *About time, Grim.* He turned back toward the woman. He only had minutes to get to a roof.

"Are you helping her escape?"

He narrowed his eyes. "I am," he said slowly, ready to shoot the woman if she screamed or ran.

A shout filled the stairway nearby. The woman looked behind her, and Stephen inched his finger near the trigger. His time was up. They knew he was here.

Just as his finger looped through the trigger guard, she twisted back around. "Maybe I can help."

Stephen blinked. Did she really just say—?

"What do you need?"

The woman could still be stalling, but she was right, he didn't have time to debate it. Either she was lying or she wasn't.

"I need to get to the roof."

"You will never get past Dr. Bloodmayne's office upstairs. Instead, head back down the hall and open the door at the end. You can access the main roof from a window inside. And tell"—she sucked in her lips—"and tell Kat I'm sorry."

Stephen nodded and ran, his gun still out. The redhead seemed familiar. Perhaps he had met her before. He reached the door and glanced back. The young woman was gone. No time to look for her now. Hopefully his trust had not been misplaced.

He shoved the door open with his shoulder and stumbled into what looked like a storage area. Wooden crates and shelving racks were set up in long rows inside the room, with narrow aisles in between. Dust and cobwebs covered the shelves. A large, multi-paned window stood in the far back.

Stephen turned sideways and started down the closest aisle. His lungs burned and his arms were on fire. Kat's blood seeped into his shirt, causing the fabric to stick to his skin.

Voices filled the hall behind him.

He glanced back as he continued down the row. No one in the doorway yet.

He'd reached the end of the aisle when someone burst into the room behind him. Stephen twisted around the stack of crates and placed Kat down below the window and out of sight. He pressed his back against the crates and held his revolver up.

Movement outside the window caught his eye. The bow of the *Lancelot* cut through the air just above the roof of the main Tower building, twenty feet away.

It was now or never. But first he would need to take care of whoever just came in.

Stephen spun around, revolver ready—

And froze.

The man standing in the doorway barely looked like a man. Half of his face appeared as if it had melted off, along with his hair. What hair he had left was blond and wild. He spotted Stephen and started down the aisle in a halting gait.

Stephen shook off his stupor, aimed right above the man's head, and shot.

The man slowed, but continued like a shambling monstrosity.

Stephen twisted back toward the window and kicked at the bottom panes, his heart thrashing inside his ears. What kind of sick experiment had Dr. Bloodmayne performed on that man?

Both panes shattered and the wooden lattice cracked. He kicked again, breaking the wood and the two panes above the first. Glass showered across the floor and the roof outside.

Sailors across the top deck of the *Lancelot* waved. A moment later, a rope ladder dropped over the side, ending a couple of feet above the roof.

Stephen looked back.

The monster-man was halfway down the aisle. His light blue eyes held a crazed glint. "Give her back," he rasped.

Stephen answered with another shot above the head, almost grazing the man. The man dropped to the floor, and a hoarse yell filled the room.

Stephen turned and kicked out the jagged pieces of glass left along the bottom pane. He leaned over the sill and looked outside. The roof was made of slate squares and was steep, much too steep to carry Kat to the rope ladder.

He looked up at the ship and pointed at the roof, then shook his head. The men at the top nodded. A moment later, the *Lancelot* moved away. Hopefully that meant Captain Grim was bringing her back around for a closer retrieval.

A roar sent Stephen spinning back.

More men appeared in the doorway across the room. The monster-man stumbled to his feet with a snarl. "You will not take her!"

Stephen gritted his teeth and aimed for the man's left shoulder. "Too bad," he muttered. The man didn't need another wound, but he was getting one anyway.

The revolver went off with a blast and the man reeled back, hitting the shelving behind him. It started a chain reaction, each shelf and rack hitting the next one over. The room echoed with loud crashes and booms. Dust filled the air in a cloud.

Stephen holstered the weapon and picked Kat up with a grunt. He swung around and hoisted a leg over the windowpane, careful to place his foot on the ridge of the roof. Behind him men coughed, and one let out a long string of curses.

The wind from the *Lancelot's* rotors hit the roof and sent a couple of leaves flying across the city. The whirring sound grew as Grim brought his ship close to the Tower. The rope ladder swung only a few feet away.

Stephen cringed. He was going to have to jump for it.

He took a deep breath and held Kat tight. He leaned out the window, testing the ridge that ran across the roof. It held. "All right, here we go. One. Two. Three—"

Forcing himself not to look down, he stepped out onto the ridge and dashed for the ladder. His foot slipped just as he reached the rope. With a gasp, he hurled himself forward and caught one of the rungs. Kat's head sagged back and her hair flew freely in the wind.

As soon as he got his feet back under him, Stephen wove his arm through the rope and held fast to the ladder. He stepped onto the lowest rung and looped his foot around the rope. He looked up, then down. There was no way he could carry her up the ladder. The sailors would just have to pull them aboar—

A hand grabbed his other foot and pulled him back hard.

Stephen caught himself just in time, his heart flying up into his throat. "Blazes!" he yelled and looked around.

The monster-man lay across the ridge, his fingers wrapped around Stephen's ankle.

How in the—how did the man get out here? He was just shot!

At this range, he could see the mottled red skin that covered half the man's face. The skin beneath his right eye sagged, exposing the socket. His few strands of hair whipped around his light blue eyes.

Stephen kicked out, but the man held on. Kat began to slip from his arms. Adrenaline raced down his spine and his limbs began to shake. *No, it can't end like this!*

He drew deep within for every ounce of remaining strength. Then with a shout, Stephen twisted and jerked his foot back. The man's fingers slipped away. Stephen placed his foot on the ladder and looked up. "Now!" he yelled. "Take us up now!"

The *Lancelot* pulled away from the Tower. Kat slipped a little farther. "No, no," he whispered. He caught her beneath her arms and wrapped his own around her, trapping her between his body and the ladder. "I won't let you go, Kat, do you hear me? I won't let you go! Never again!"

There was a hard pull on the rope, and they slowly rose into the air. Stephen held onto Kat with all he had left. Her hair whipped across his face. Sweat coated his entire body. His limbs slowly went numb, but still he held on.

They passed the hull, up, up, until he could see across the deck. Hands reached down and grabbed Kat. He wanted to shout at them to be careful, but he couldn't form the words. She rose into the air and disappeared over the edge.

Stephen sagged against the ladder. He couldn't make his body move. He couldn't even uncurl his fingers. The rope began to move again, pulling him up to the deck.

At the top, he collapsed across the wooden planks. Men moved around him, shouting orders and waving their hands.

All he cared about was Kat.

"Kat," he said with a groan and turned over. She lay a couple of feet away. He got up on his elbows and crawled over to her. The wind rippled through her sheer gown.

Stephen grimaced and sat up. She shouldn't be out here, exposed in front of all these men. He tugged at his duster, but couldn't seem to get his fingers to work.

Robert appeared to his right, hunching down and gently placing his own dark duster across Kat's body. He turned toward Stephen and rubbed his chin. "Too bad the *Herald* wasn't here to see you in action. That rescue would have made the front page."

Stephen bowed his head and ran a hand through his sweaty hair. Then he laughed.

34

The airship rose into the sky, high above the roofs and smoke-stacks of World City. Behind them stood the Tower, growing smaller by the second.

"Didn't expect to see you again so soon, Grey." Robert tapped his fingers across the wooden planks.

Stephen caught his breath, the tension across his shoulders melting away. "I hope you're not disappointed."

Robert cast a glance at Kat, then back at Stephen. "Sounds like it was a good thing I had an errand to attend to here before sailing off to Austrium."

Stephen sat up. "Indeed."

Robert motioned toward Kat. "Would you like one of my men to take the lady?"

"No." He moved to Kat's side. "I will take her myself. Just show me where to go." He could almost imagine she was simply sleeping, instead of on the verge of—He swallowed and gathered her up into his arms. Maybe he was wrong.

Robert straightened up and snapped his fingers. One of his men moved forward. Stephen recognized him from that night in Covenshire.

"Reid."

The man tipped his head. "Captain."

"Show Stephen to my quarters."

Stephen shook his head and stood. "Robert, we can stay in one of your other cabins."

"It's for the lady. Let it never be said that Captain Robert Grim was not a gentleman. She'll be more comfortable in my cabin."

Stephen nodded before following Reid across the deck, bypassing Grim's crew. None of them showed emotion, standing there rigid, with arms at their sides and the bright blue sky behind them. He hoped they could keep a secret. Then again, Robert would never let a man on board he couldn't trust.

Still, he wouldn't let Kat out of his sight. And if something happened . . .

He focused on the weight that sat on either side of his hips, each gun loaded.

He would be ready.

Reid led him inside the ship and down the passage. At the end of the short corridor, he opened the door and stood back.

Stephen stepped inside Grim's private quarters. Once again he was struck with the opulence and functionality of the room: red velvet cushions, polished metal furniture, and the canopy bed that could easily fit two people, draped in scarlet silk.

He lay Kat down on top of the bedspread, making sure that translucent gown of hers was well covered by Robert's coat. He brushed her hair back from her pale face and sighed.

"I bet there is quite a story here."

Stephen looked up. Robert stood in the doorway where Reid had been moments before. How much should he tell his friend? Could he trust Robert?

The captain shut the door and walked over to the large table. He unhooked one of the chairs from the floor and turned it around, sat down, and meshed his fingers together. The one eye not hidden behind his patch stared back, an icy blue.

Stephen unhooked one of the other chairs and pulled it up next to the bed. He sat down and stared at Kat's face. "I messed up. Big time."

"Stephen Grey made a mistake?" There was a hint of sarcasm and surprise in Robert's voice.

Stephen bowed his head. He rarely messed up. Logic always dictated his decisions. Except where women were concerned. The only other mistake he had ever made was not realizing that Vanessa was a conniving woman with a wandering heart.

He had made the same mistake again. Not realizing what Kat was. Except this time he had been wrong the other way. She wasn't the monster he had assumed. Yes, she had unexplainable power, power she could not control. But that wasn't who she was. The real Kat, apart from whatever was wrong with her, was innocent.

He pressed his face into his hand. He had failed her.

The silence extended inside the cabin. A chair scraped across the floor behind him. Robert must have realized he wasn't ready to talk. Not yet.

Robert cleared his throat. "Well, the crew will need me on deck to set the course. We have one more stop before we head across the Narrow Strait to Austrium."

Stephen looked over his shoulder. "Thanks, Robert, for bringing us on board."

Robert continued to watch him with that one eye. "Of course, Stephen. And if it makes life more difficult for the World

City council or that pet Tower of theirs"—he grinned—"all the better. I'll have dinner brought to this room. Feel free to use the bench over there if you need to rest. Or you can use one of my other cabins."

"I'll stay here with Kat."

Robert paused, then nodded. "You know we can't bring a doctor on board at the moment, but I would be happy to let my cook take a look at her. He knows more than just cooking."

Stephen shrugged, but he doubted the cook would know what to do with Kat. No, the only one who could possibly help her was that doctor she had been looking for. At least that's what Kat believed. He was their only hope.

Well, maybe not their only hope. There was always God.

Stephen pressed his fingers into his temple. Would God actually help them? A heathen woman scientist and a broken man who had walked away a long time ago?

Possibly. At least that was the God his aunt—and his parents—had believed in.

Robert stood. "Feel free to join me later. I'll be at the wheel tonight. We can talk then."

Stephen nodded. There were no words left inside him.

The door shut softly behind him. Stephen stared down at Kat. Slowly, quietly, he pulled her hand out from beneath the duster. Her fingers were frigid. If it wasn't for the hint of breath that blew across her lips, he would have thought she was dead.

He swallowed and wrapped her fingers inside both of his hands. Would she ever wake from this? He leaned toward her until he was only inches from her face. "Kat, I'm sorry. I thought I was doing the right thing. You should have told me about—" He shook his head. They were just excuses. If he had really taken a good, hard look at Kat, he would have known that she could never have done those awful things, at least not under her own volition.

And now she was in some kind of coma and might never wake u—

Her eyes shifted beneath their lids.

Stephen sat back, her hand still wrapped between his own. "Kat?"

She stirred again. A moment later, she opened her eyes. She blinked a couple of times. Her pupils were dilated, causing her eyes to look even larger than usual.

She shifted and focused on him. Her brow furrowed. "Stephen?"

"Yes."

She stared at him as if she could see inside his soul. Then she visibly swallowed and stared up at the ceiling.

The look on her face at that moment—his heart twisted violently inside his chest—like a puppy that had been kicked over and over again.

His lip trembled and he slowly dropped her hand. She didn't seem to notice. It would have been easier if she had been angry with him and yelled. Or cried. He could have handled her tears. But this?

She closed her eyes and turned her face away from his. Moments later, her breathing evened out.

Stephen sat back and held his face. He shut his eyes, and a small moan escaped his lips.

"Oh God, what have I done?"

35

Dr. Bloodmayne stared down at the empty metal table where his daughter had lain. Drops of blood clung to the metal rods that lay across the top, and the thin rubber tubes he had attached to Kat were now on the floor, barely visible in the dim green light.

The cylinder nearby crackled as an arc of electricity bounced around the metal, then it settled back into a steady hum.

He ignored the device and picked up one of the rods. Kat couldn't have escaped on her own. He had made sure she had enough chloroform to keep her unconscious without killing her. And even if she had somehow woken up, she certainly did not have the strength to tie up Dr. Emerson and kick him hard enough to leave him out cold. No, someone came here for her, and he would find out who.

The body near the door began to move. Dr. Bloodmayne turned and bypassed the rest of the metal tables. He would send in his apprentice, Miss Nicola, to clean up the lab. She had already proven herself to have the cold logic and discretion needed to work here in his private laboratories.

Dr. Emerson twisted and turned on the floor until he righted himself against the wall. He was still bound inside his lab coat, and the thin cloth wrapped around his head muffled his words. There was a trickle of dried blood just below his nose, which appeared to be broken.

Dr. Bloodmayne bent down and removed the cloth from Dr. Emerson's mouth.

"Dr. Bloodmayne!" Dr. Emerson panted and straightened himself. "Thank you. I could hardly breathe!"

Dr. Bloodmayne stared coldly down at his assistant. "What happened here? I thought I told you no one was allowed in here."

"The man took me by surprise! I was leaving the lab when he came up behind me and choked me. I woke up and found myself tied up. He walked out with the specimen—"

Dr. Bloodmayne's eyes narrowed. "Who?"

A drop of sweat trickled down the side of Dr. Emerson's face. "I, uh, don't know. He was dressed in a dark leather duster and hat. He didn't look like a gentleman; more like a scoundrel from Southbrook. I'm not sure how he got past security."

Dr. Bloodmayne pinched the bridge of his nose and sighed. It was clear Dr. Emerson knew nothing. He straightened up and headed for the door.

"Wait!" Dr. Emerson yelled behind him. "Dr. Bloodmayne! Aren't you going to untie me?"

Dr. Bloodmayne ignored him. He had no time to help incompetent subordinates. Let Dr. Emerson find his own way out of his predicament.

"Dr. Bloodmayne." A voice rasped behind him.

Dr. Bloodmayne looked back. Blaylock Sterling stood in the hallway, blood seeping from a new wound in his shoulder, a scowl across the left side of his face. The rest of his face drooped and his facial skin appeared even more red than usual. The healing serum had done wonders for the young man in a short amount of time, but it would never fully heal him. He would forever be an aberration to society.

"Did you find her?"

"She escaped. But I saw the name of the airship she left on. The *Lancelot.*"

"Very good, Mr. Sterling. Head up to the laboratory and have someone check on that wound."

Blaylock nodded and turned around.

It wasn't much, but it meant that not all was lost. He would send the bounty hunters after the airship. His boots clapped across the steps as he headed down, the sound echoing through the stairway.

Still, he would rather have Kathryn here now. He should have stayed with her until his experiment had been completed instead of leaving her with Dr. Emerson. The incompetent buffoon!

He clenched his hand and let his breath out through his nose. So close. So close to discovering the mystery and power of matter. If only he had been able to witness it with his own eyes instead of hearing accounts of Kat's power from others. To think, his daughter could lift things with her mind, set fires, and who knows what else. Who wouldn't want that kind of power?

He breathed faster. He had almost held that power in his hands, controlled it—

What would Helen think of all of this?

Dr. Bloodmayne stopped on the second floor and leaned against the wall. "Helen," he murmured. Beautiful, loving Helen. He had married above his station when he married her.

And Kat was so much like her mother: that same dark hair and chocolate eyes. That same small nose, that same stubbornness.

He straightened and headed down the last staircase. It didn't matter. Helen took his heart when she died on the birthing table. That thing that beat now inside his chest was only an organic instrument that kept life flowing through his body. Kat might look like her mother, but she could never replace Helen.

However, Kat could make up for killing her mother by giving him the keys he so desired. The keys to the unseen power that moved and flowed around them. With those keys, he might even be able to bring the dead back to life.

Maybe.

Awakened

The Soul Chronicles:

Book Two

Coming Spring 2017

About the Author

Morgan L. Busse is the wife of a pastor, mother of four children, and the author of the Follower of the Word series.

From the moment she first read The Hobbit, she fell in love with the fantasy genre. Both J.R.R. Tolkien and Terry Brooks are the inspirations behind her writing. Her debut novel *Daughter of Light* was both a Christy Award and a Carol Award finalist.

Morgan lives on the west coast with her family.

Website: www.MorganlBusse.com

FOLLOWER OF THE WORD
SERIES

BY

MORGAN L. BUSSE

| *Daughter of Light* | *Son of Truth* | *Heir of Hope* |
| Book One | Book Two | Book Three |

ENCLAVE PUBLISHING
WWW.ENCLAVEPUBLISHING.COM